Entangling

D1519193

Book One of the Kirin Lane Series

By
Kelley Griffin

https://www.KelleyGriffinAuthor.com

ISBN: 9781706341314

Cover Art by Amor Paloma Designs, LLC
Edited partially by Ellie Maas Davis, Pressque, LLC. and by Wendy Waxmonsky

Produced in the United States of America

Griffin, Kelley
Entangling, Book One of the Kirin Lane Series

November 2019

Dedication

To the original *Wonder Woman*, Wendy Waxmonsky. Thanks for all your input on this series and for pushing me to be a better writer. Oh, and for being my person—the one who laughs at my weird sense of writing humor.

To Paloma Johnson, thank you for encouraging me and jumping in with both hands to help me every time I needed you!!

And to my husband, Stacy. Thank you for reading my books, being supportive and for being the most selfless husband a girl could ask for. The way you love me is the reason I can write romance. You make me want to succeed every day.

Dear Reader,

Thank you for reading this story. Kirin was my first love as a writer. She was the first character I could see in my mind's eye as clearly as if she sat across from me sipping coffee. She's wonderfully made, clumsy yet endearing, and vulnerable yet strong as hell, although she doesn't know it yet.

She and I share similar missing father issues and I think that's what drew her into my world. Take care of her over the next several chapters. She's special to me.

Thank you for reading my stories and please connect with me! I'd love to know what you think of this book! Please consider taking a minute to leave a review. It's one of the best ways to encourage others to read a new author.

XO~
Kelley

Find me on Facebook or Goodreads as:
Kelley Griffin Author
https://www.kelleygriffinauthor.com
IG as @kelleygriffinauthor
https://www.twitter.com/AuthorKTGriffin

Other titles by Kelley Griffin

Binding Circumstance

Chapter One

One arm shoved inside the business-end of a toilet was not how Kirin Lane pictured spending her Sunday morning. Goose-flesh crawled her elbows to both shoulders.

Five-year-old Little Jack sat cross-legged on the floor next to her, clutching his blanket. Curly hair, like his dad's was, hung low over his chubby, tear-stained face. He picked at the toes of his mismatched socks; Batman on the left, Hulk on the right.

Kirin's fingers searched the bend of the porcelain. She touched the plastic toy but couldn't grasp it. It taunted her like most things in life these days, just out of reach. Her mind wandered. *Was wearing Hulk and Batman socks together a comic book sin?* Jack would've known. *If only Jack was here.*

A shiver wracked her spine. Early spring in the one-stoplight town of Corryton, Tennessee was filled with three things: hikers converging on House Mountain, allergies caused by budding dogwood trees, and weather as fickle as a high school prom queen. Mother Nature's thermostat got stuck on either hot as Hell's back porch or cold as a stream in January.

Today, however, the water felt as if she stood barefoot in a bathtub full of ice cubes. She clamped her eyes shut. Her mama would've said, "K, somebody's walkin' over your grave."

When she opened them, Little Jack's eyes met hers. He whispered for the tenth time, "I'm sorry, Mommy."

Will stood at the door, hands on hips and an "I told you so" look on his face, as only a ten-year-old brother could have at such a pivotal moment. Kirin exhaled and nodded down at Little Jack, smiling to ease his worry. Yes, she felt frustrated with the little booger for dropping

Batman in the toilet, but it wasn't him she was angry with, and she knew it.

It was the flippin' phone. Damn thing rang at five in the morning and caused a chain reaction of crazy. Number one, it woke all three of them, but number two it caused a sleepy Little Jack to stumble into the bathroom to potty while holding his favorite toy. Ergo Batman in the toilet. And if she was honest, it wasn't so much the *phone* as the news on the other end that flared her anger and tied her stomach in knots.

Her fingers stretched and spread while the toy danced around, teasing her. Calling a plumber on a Sunday would cost double. Money they didn't have. Her boys would have front row seats to witness their mama's breakdown. She blew the wispy strands of blonde bangs off her face. They'd escaped the messy bun she'd wrangled her hair into as she'd hurried to catch the phone. Her lean budget numbers raced through her mind. She had no choice but to get the toy out.

The man on the phone had asked for Kirin *Terhune* Lane. Nobody called her Terhune. She hadn't used her maiden name since nursing school, twelve years ago. And that was only because of her damn birth certificate. She needed no part of *his* name.

Tiny hairs on the back of her neck had stood at attention. She should've known right then, bad news followed.

"Your father, Sonny Terhune is dead," the man on the other end announced. She'd squinted at the clock, two in the morning, California time. As if reading her mind, the man apologized for the hour but stated that Mr. Terhune's orders indicated to notify her the moment it happened.

She didn't even know her father had been sick. How could she? Bastard. He hadn't spoken to her in thirty-two years. And now, he wanted her contacted the *instant* he died? Delusional old fart. No way in hell she'd mourn for him now.

Back then, she'd been a gullible, string-bean, almost-eight-year-old. Naïve and trusting. *He'd send for her,* he'd said. *Bring her to California with him.* Right.

And besides that emotional mess, *this* wasn't her job. Plumbing, electrical, removing dead wildlife from the yard or sticking her hand in cold, dark places, all were Jack's jobs. In the two years since cancer took him, she'd been responsible for all of it, and then some. Which was exactly why selfish anger crept up her spine like an army of ants.

Kirin's forefinger latched on to something tiny, hard, and plastic. A superhero's boot.

"Oh, almost!" she said.

Little Jack's eyes widened. His hands gripped his blanket tighter and he held his breath. She tugged the boot over the hump of the pipe. One plastic leg followed, then the other. Almost. The abdomen of the toy moved over the hump, then stopped cold. It wouldn't budge.

"Come on." Teeth clenched, she pulled and twisted harder. Unfolding crossed legs from underneath her, she braced her feet on either side of the toilet to birth the toy. Thank God, she'd cleaned this bathroom yesterday.

Two years ago when Jack died, sadness had engulfed her. Then came anger, aimed mostly toward him. He'd promised he'd never leave her. Promised he wouldn't do what her father did. But she was a logical woman. To blame him wasn't fair. It wasn't as if he'd had a choice. He could no more stop cancer than she could stop tripping over her own two feet. In her heart, she knew it wasn't his fault. But truth be told, she was tired of being responsible for everything and even more so of being alone.

Her mind sputtered. The man from California had said she needed to come to her father's funeral. No, he'd said she *had* to do so. He'd relayed information from her father's attorney and secretary. Both had strict orders to give Kirin her inheritance, an undisclosed, large sum of money and one tattered, Marine Corps Field Manual, but only if she came in person. A round-trip airfare ticket and hotel accommodations had been purchased in her name. At least his money paid for the funeral. She damn sure couldn't, nor wouldn't.

One thing was certain: Sonny Terhune was insane.

Realization hit—the cape. Batman's cape hung on the bend. Little Jack whimpered as the toy screeched and scraped through the opening. If she had to sacrifice the cape to save the man, she would.

Closing her eyes, she gave one last, long tug. The toy dislodged along with a half-gallon of ice water. It raced like a river down the front of her sleep shirt. Kirin yelped, pulling the soaked shirt away from her bare chest as Little Jack scrambled to stand.

"Oh, thank you, Mommy!"

She tossed the dripping Batman into the sink. Little Jack stood on tiptoes. His chubby fingers washed and dried the toy, then he flung arms around his mom's neck and kissed her on the cheek. A moment later, the thudding of socked feet padding down the hallway was followed by a quick slam of the boy's bedroom door. Doctoring Batman back to health, no doubt.

Soaked and trembling, Kirin washed her hands and shuffled past Will. She patted him on the head and trudged toward her closet. Digging into a pile of clean laundry, she found her warmest sweats and softest sweatshirt. She peeled off her nightshirt—slow like a Band Aid—then she stepped in. She leaned against the door frame and tugged on warm socks. An old-woman groan escaped her lips. Sitting cross-legged on hard bathroom tile for half an hour made her stiff and feel more like fifty-nine than thirty-nine.

Dry, and more awake than she wanted to be, she slogged downstairs toward the kitchen. Coffee fixes everything. Stopping at the sink, she robotically pushed the start button. Morning sun flooded through the six-paned window, as all noise around her receded. Fog poured like honey out of a jar through the thick woods behind her house. Two gray squirrels gave chase up a tree.

Her eyes closed as his words sunk in. Her teeth clamped shut making her jaw ache.

Her father was dead.

Breathe. Kirin opened her eyes and absorbed the shock. She expected grief, but anger filled every hole made by the man who'd abandoned her. A man whose sole job was to love his daughter. He'd never wanted her. It all came down to that.

She shifted her weight toward the kitchen counter to make way for Little Jack, who'd come downstairs and crawled between her socked feet to grab a wayward toy.

The mere idea of taking *anything* from him made her stomach sour. She had to admit though, the farmhouse needed a new roof. Jack's military life insurance had paid off most of the house and land, but she still had a mortgage payment and her nurse's salary barely covered everything else. Little was left for repairs, new clothes, or even new shoes for the boys unless she picked up an extra shift. She didn't know how much money her father had left her, but those karate lessons Will had been saving for might finally be within reach.

The wage she paid Rosa, the boys' sitter, pushed her right to her budget's edge. Then again, she'd cut lights and food before she lost Rosa. She'd stow her pride. He owed her, right?

She turned away from the window, sipping her coffee. She could feel Will's eyes surveying her. When she looked up, his fingers swiped at his iPad, but his eyes stayed trained on her. He'd inherited Kirin's stick-straight, blonde hair, general distrust of people, and cornflower-blue eyes. Those baby-blues narrowed at her now. No doubt he was trying to work out the emotional puzzle that was his mom. She'd explain some day. He didn't need to be burdened with her idiot-father issues. Especially when he struggled with missing-father issues of his own.

As her mind ran in circles, she placed her coffee on the counter and stared at her hands. Thin fingers, with nubby nails, like her mama's. A day didn't go by she didn't think about her. Her jolting death never made sense. How could a stay-at-home soccer mom in rural Tennessee die in a car explosion? Faulty gas line, they'd told her, but she'd never believed it.

Kirin drew in a deep breath. What a waste.

~*~

Rosa embodied the word tiny. The woman couldn't reach the top shelf of the pantry without a stepladder. Hispanic with skin the color of coffee beans, Rosa's tone was always snarky and sarcastic, and yet somehow filled with love.

Anyone with eyes could see how fiercely protective she'd become of Kirin and the boys. In two short years, they'd become family. She'd morphed into the glue they all needed after Jack died.

They'd met outside Morrissey's grocery store in the rain. The connection was quick, and before she knew it, she'd adopted Rosa the way she might have kept a loveable old cat. Rosa noticed small details like a CIA agent and could sniff out a lie like a machine. And she could always be counted on to comment on an elephant in the room.

This was why Kirin was baffled that evening as she walked from her car toward Morrissey's. Rosa and her sister had picked up the boys for a late afternoon trip to the zoo. The woman hadn't said a word. Nothing. Not a peep about Kirin's blotchy face or bloodshot eyes. Nothing about the scowl Kirin tried and failed to wipe off her face. The boys were even somber, their moods feeding off their mom's, and still, Rosa said nothing. No "Rosa inquisition" to deal with. To be honest, it was odd.

Rosa stood in the kitchen, uncharacteristically silent. She didn't even make eye contact. It was as if she already knew Kirin's news. But that was impossible. The only normal thing Rosa had done was grab the grocery list off the fridge and place it next to Kirin's purse. Eyeballing her as she did, so she wouldn't forget it, like usual.

Lost in thought, Kirin meandered past the parked cars toward Morrissey's and stepped out in front of a slow-moving car that screeched to a halt. The driver scowled and fluttered his hand for her to cross. She waved an apology and strolled into the store.

Kirin grabbed a cart and pulled out her list, shaking her head. Preposterous. There was no way Rosa had known. Maybe it'd been a rare day free of her normal snark. *Right.*

Morrissey's stood tall as the only grocer in Corryton. It took a full five minutes to navigate from one side to the other. The store looked like a cross between a Wal-Mart and a Rural King. The only place within fifty miles where you could buy a massive HD television and a baby chick only a few aisles over. Plus, it garnered the reputation as a gossip hub. Reunions between friends, smack dab in the middle of the store, were as common as grocery carts.

She meandered to the right, toward neat rows of fruits and vegetables, stacked in perfect pyramids on flat tables. Past the bananas she spotted the tomatoes, with a shiny one on top.

This was her day for everything to be out of reach, even without her hand in a toilet. She stood on tiptoes as if she were a ballerina and stretched out her arm to grab the gleaming one on top. *Almost there.* She'd ignored the wet floor sign, the fresh lemon smell and even the tiny, not-yet-evaporated puddles along the edges of the floor. Leaning over, her foot slipped as if it'd caught on a grease spot. Her body pitched toward the stack. The only option available to her free hand was to gouge the stack of tomatoes to stop her face from doing it. Tomatoes avalanched on the other side of the display like hundreds of bouncy balls, released together, thudding then splatting to the floor.

Customers stopped to stare. One hand slapped over her mouth to stop the curse words from flying out. Double crap. A grunt, followed by several choice words, flew out of a man crouching on the other side. Kirin rushed around the display, tiptoeing through tomatoes on the floor.

"I'm so sorry." She bent and touched the man's shoulder.

He rose quick and towered over her, then stepped back. His eyes narrowed in anger until they met hers. Then he froze. Deep green eyes widened as the corners of his mouth lifted in recognition, but the flicker died quick, turning back to a hard line.

Blinking a few times, he looked back at the sea of tomatoes lying on the floor and regained at least part of his annoyance. "What the...?"

"I'm sorry," she repeated, "An accident, I was trying..."

"To kill me, no doubt." His tone was light as he rubbed his shirt.

"No," she shot back, tight-lipped. "To reach a tomato."

She bent to pick a few off the floor, then placed them back on the display, all the while staring at this man as if he had three heads.

He nodded, then grabbed tomatoes too, monitoring her every move as he rose. He stifled a grin. Several of the fallen fruit had split, and one was flat out squashed to the floor. A nearby store clerk pushed a mop bucket toward them.

The man she'd accosted looked about her age, maybe a little older, muscular and trim like a firefighter. He reminded her of a tall, unshaven, James Marsden with light brown wavy hair, instead of black. Soft looking stubble lined his tight jaw. His rough hands held four of the huge tomatoes, where hers could hold three at most.

"It's not safe to climb the tables, you know," he stated matter-of-factly as he reached down, scooping another stack of fruit and placing them back on the stack. "Especially at your height."

Mid-grab she froze, then straightened, glaring. He stood an entire head taller than her, and neither his dark green T-shirt holding in muscled shoulders nor his low-slung work jeans had a speck of red on them. If he hadn't been so high and mighty he'd have been attractive. Not that she noticed, of course. But his comment ran through her like a sword.

"I didn't *climb* the table."

He froze, eyes locked on hers as his lips curved upward. "You're right," sarcasm dripped from this man.

"And I'm not *that* short." She snapped. She hadn't meant to sound angry, but he'd pushed her buttons.

He stayed motionless for another beat before resuming his tomato picking. "No. You're absolutely right…you're super tall." He eyed her as one eyebrow lifted and a dimple pinched in on one cheek. She ignored the stupid-cute dimple and tried to stifle her own grin. Fine. He was right, she was short. She'd admit that, but dang it he could cut her some slack.

When he stopped moving, she leveled a look at him.

"I didn't need help, thank you."

She stood her ground even as he towered over her. His chest was closer than she'd realized. An invisible tractor beam pulled her body toward his. She swayed, grabbed on to the table holding the tomatoes, and played it off.

"Obviously." Amusement crossed his face as he bent to pick up more.

When they'd retrieved the last of the half-squished orbs in silence and placed them back on the table, he turned to face her. His eyes, dark and intense, studied every feature of her face. Stock still, chin high, she glowered right back.

She'd be damned if she'd look away first. His expression became a puzzling mix of humor and respect. If he'd been more compassionate, she wouldn't have reacted so snippy. Clearly he wasn't Southern. Everybody knows a Southern man could be run over by a woman in a two-ton Dodge truck, twice, and he'd say, "No problem, honey, I know you didn't mean to do it."

This guy had no dirt or stains on his clothes, and he'd picked on her height. On top of it all, he hadn't accepted her apology. His conduct was *very* un-Southern.

They resembled two angry alley cats. Arched backs and fur standing on end, neither willing to move first. His face held amusement, where hers held a bit of resentment. A small, crooked smile erupted on his face. It reached his eyes and softened her stance a little, but it also seemed smug, as if he knew a secret she didn't.

"What?" she barked, her arms crossed.

"Nothing." He crossed his too, imitating her. His full-on smirk infuriated her, and yet butterflies in her belly did backflips. She stepped back, needing space, when he continued, "You gonna pick out another tomato or stand there and gawk at me all day?"

Despite her anger, she bit her lip to stop the smile. Of all the nerve. Turning on her heel, she stomped to the other side of the table, made a big show of grabbing a huge tomato and waved it at him. She placed it in her cart, rolled her eyes and pushed her buggy toward the next aisle, away from the produce section. Shaking his head, he laughed as she walked away.

Deep breath in and shoulders back, she was proud of herself. She'd held her ground. It took two aisles to slow her breathing and erase her embarrassment. She'd focus on shopping, thank you. Twenty-four aisles and a heaping cart later, she stacked her groceries on the conveyor belt.

By the time she'd paid, she'd talked herself into, out of, and back into, attending her father's funeral. As much as she wanted to blow it off, teenage therapy told her she needed to go for closure. That book better contain some damn answers, and not be a dumb artifact from his glory days in the military. Shoulders back, she made up her mind. She'd fly into LA the night before the funeral, spend an hour shaking hands with complete strangers and come home. Her mama would've wanted her to go.

Spirits lifted with at least one decision made, she glanced around. She wasn't searching for the tomato disaster guy, but if she found him, she'd make sure he knew he was being ignored.

Groceries loaded in her cart and hot tomato guy nowhere in sight, she zipped across the parking lot, past the lights of the store and into the shadows, toward her dented SUV.

Movement caught her eye. The outline of a man. He darted between the parked cars. She stopped on a dime. Dread fell like a boulder into the pit of her stomach. She glanced around. She was all alone in the sea of cars, except for him.

Pushing her cart forward a half a foot, she darted behind a truck and crouched. Maybe he wouldn't notice her. He moved through the vehicles like a cheetah closing in on its next victim. He lifted each car door handle.

Lungs seized, she couldn't tear her eyes away. She raised on tiptoes to determine how close he was and caught sight of him. His face was dirty, his body too thin and his movements twitchy and fast. He crept in and out of the shadows. If he kept moving in his current sweeping pattern, he'd be on top of her in thirty seconds. As he got closer, she caught a better look at his face. Eyes with huge pupils that darted from car to car. He had to be high.

Move. She had to move. He skulked closer. Now, a few vehicles away. He'd glance her way any second.

She took a breath and with one hand on her buggy, she used her other to tighten the strap on her cross-body purse. She angled her body to turn the cart around and run, at the exact second, he whirled around and stopped.

His sinister eyes drifted from her face to her purse.

No. Hell no. She had no money except a few dollars for gas and an envelope of cash from Will's candle sales to benefit his elementary school. This was not happening. The world stood motionless. No wind, no noise.

It was as if he could taste her fear. She squared her shoulders, trying to appear brave. Her mind reeled. Run back to the store or try to make a run for her car? Or yell and try to scare him off. What if her voice didn't work?

He sauntered toward her. A smile spread across his meth-scabbed face, that revealed dark holes where teeth should've been. "What's wrong, honey? You look scared."

Hair prickled on the back of her neck. She stood taller, trying for badass, but she wasn't fooling anybody. He towered over the cars, making him at least six inches taller than her. Her legs were paralyzed, like logs sealed in concrete.

If she could run, she might make it back to the store. She could yell "No!" as she'd learned in a self-defense class. Could she make her voice sound menacing? Closing the gap between them, he stared from her face to her purse.

Damn, why didn't she run when she first spotted him? She'd not go down in a parking lot. She had her boys to consider. Feeling like a helpless victim infuriated and empowered her.

Kirin sucked in a deep breath, stood as tall as her five-foot-two frame would go, and changed her stance to a fighting position. She tried to yell, but her voice squawked out some sad, inaudible chirp that sounded like a cat howl. Yup. No scream in there.

She'd plant her feet and wait. When he stood within a foot of her, she'd take a swing, then follow it with a swift kick to the groin. Maybe it'd stun him or at least knock him back. Either way, it'd give her time to run with her cart toward the store. She might go down, but by God, she'd go down fighting.

She cleared her throat, "You'd better go the hell on!" Her voice sounded deep even to her own ears as she pointed at the man.

He let out "tsk" noise of disbelief. Three feet away, he bent to her level. He looked like a big cat tracking a tiny mouse. She stepped back, putting some space between her and her cart. *Come closer, scumbag.* Fists balled tight. *Aim for his head and not his arms.*

Quick shallow breaths rattled in and out of her chest as she focused all her energy on one thing: survival. Her arm cocked back, ready. Adrenaline pumped through both arms as she squeezed her fists. Hold on. Closer.

Like a jackrabbit on speed, he lunged. Quick, dirty nails scraped her shirt grasping the strap of her purse, while his other hand reached over and shoved the back of her head down to pull the strap over.

It knocked her off balance, but she swung. Her purse strap slid from her neck toward the crown of her head. His body angled to the side and back in such a way, the kick to his breadbasket wouldn't connect. Desperate, she shoved both hands into his bony chest with all she had. He stumbled back but didn't let go of his tight grip. Furious now, he growled and yanked the purse downward, causing her legs to buckle. Both knees slammed to the pavement.

Eyes open wide, she dug her fingers into his hand pulling the strap. As if she wasn't inside her body, she heard herself chant, "*No. No. No.*" Her knees dug into the pavement. She leaned backward with all she had. Gravel bits under her kneecaps tore and ripped her pants. He lifted his heavy work boot and cocked it back, poised to pummel her in the face.

She squeezed her eyes shut and braced for impact.

"Freeze!"

All motion stopped. When she opened them, a man stood over the top of her, stance wide with a gun pointed at the robber. Her attacker's fingers released the strap, and his arms shot upward. When he let go, the tension pulling her forward ceased, causing her rear end to flop back onto the pavement.

Her attacker froze, then stutter-stepped backward. The gun-toting man stepped around her and crept toward him, listening to his excuses. "I, I wasn't doin' nothing, just talking, that's all. Maybe she had a dollar she could spare." A shuffling sound of the thug's feet scooting backward accompanied his excuses.

"I said freeze."

The man complied.

"On the ground, face down, now."

Her rescuer's voice held enough anger and power she had to stop herself from laying down too. Once her attacker was face down with his hands behind his head, one of Morrissey's young security officers ran up.

"Sam, what the —? Hey! You got him!"

In a flash, the guard knelt in the middle of the attacker's back. The robber groaned as the guard grabbed one arm then the next and put his hands in a zip tie. His speed reminded her of a rodeo cowboy roping a calf.

The rescuer, "Sam" as he'd been called, holstered his gun then grabbed the thug's elbow and drug him to his feet. Within seconds, a crowd had gathered. Two of Corryton's finest in plain clothes snatched the thief and ushered him inside the store to wait for an on-duty officer. Since the drama was over, the crowd dispersed as fast as they'd gathered.

"Nice job!" The young security officer said, slapping Sam on the back and shaking his hand. His head snapped down toward Kirin. He sprinted around Sam and crouched in front of her. "Ma'am, you okay?"

Before she could answer, Sam turned to face her. *Double hell.* Tomato disaster guy. Of all the people in the world, it had to be him. His face was serious and solemn. His eyes registered recognition and something else. Something protective. His expression softened some as he reached around the guard and without a word offered his hand to help her up.

Swearing under her breath, she took his hand. She'd have noticed the electrical currents racing around her insides if she hadn't been so preoccupied with stupid things like not falling and breathing. Plus, she couldn't seem to pry her other hand away from the death grip she had on her purse strap.

"You alright, *trouble*?" His eyes lit with humor as he held on to her hand too long. The guard's gaze darted from him to her. Apparently okay with letting Sam take care of her, he excused himself to run back inside where the other drama unfolded.

Kirin swallowed. "Yeah. Perfect." Her knees shook. Every muscle in her body wanted to squat back down, right there on the pavement and sit, but her pride wouldn't let her. She stepped backward and stumbled. He held out a protective hand.

"You need to sit."

"I'm fine." She broke free from his grasp.

"Are you *that* stubborn?" He crossed his arms and cocked his head to the side.

"No, I don't want to *inconvenience* you. You were pretty pissed about the tomatoes and now—" Even as she said it, her body swayed like a sapling in a tornado.

Cutting her off, he shook his head and without warning, wrapped an arm around her waist and guided her toward the tailgate of a red truck, a few steps away, and lowered it. He nodded toward the tailgate. She stared at it as if it was ten feet tall. Even on her best day, she'd have to hoist herself up. Sam's eyebrows raised as if asking permission to help. She nodded. He lifted her and set her on the tailgate. As the truck and Earth swayed, she scooted her rear back.

"Trouble seems to find you, doesn't it?" There was light in his voice, but seriousness in his eyes.

Kirin shot him a long look as she wrapped her fingers around the edge of the tailgate, locking her arms to hold herself in place.

Sam strode to the front of the truck and back. When he returned he held a bottle of water and a small first aid kit. He handed her the water and pointed the box toward her knees.

She followed his line of sight.

Great. She was a hot mess. Her pants were ripped exposing gravel and blood-stained knees.

16

He shook the first aid kit as if to ask permission to treat.

She nodded. As he bandaged her knees, she opened the water, took a drink, and tried not to stare.

And failed.

Maybe she stared because someone was taking care of her, which hadn't happened in so long she couldn't remember the last time. But also because she was mesmerized by his hands. Strong, rough, hands calloused by work that gently cleaned and bandaged her wound. It stirred a longing inside. She had to stop the urge to touch his hair.

He glanced from her knees into her eyes, staring a beat or two too long. She grinned thankfully at him, and he returned it. As he gathered the paper from the bandages, she attempted to form a question in her fuzzy brain.

"Where did you come from?" Her voice trembled, whether from the proximity of this man or from her experience with the robber, she wasn't sure.

"My truck." He pointed to her water.

Too rattled to be stubborn, she took a sip. "You always carry a gun to the grocery store?"

"Drink more." He cocked his head to the side and grinned, big. He raised his shirt to reveal a defined set of abs cradling a pistol inside a holster hooked on the belt of his jeans. When he caught her staring, he shoved his shirt back down.

"You never know when you're gonna need to defend yourself against a woman and her tomatoes," he said and concentrated on squishing the bandage papers in a tight ball. One eyebrow hitched with humor.

"Funny." The parking lot spun like a tilt-o-whirl at the fair, and she swayed again but took another drink.

After a beat, he closed the first aid kit. His expression turned serious. "I'm curious … Why didn't you give him your purse?" His tone sounded clipped and tight.

She lowered the water bottle. Defensive, she answered, "Survival, I guess."

He stepped in, standing between her legs. Bending over, he surveyed her as if she was a puzzle and lowered his voice, "So, the contents of your purse are more important than your life?"

Kirin set her water on the tailgate, then crossed her arms. She didn't owe him an explanation, but she didn't want him thinking she'd fought the thug to protect a designer wallet or something frivolous. Then again, why did it matter what this man thought?

"No. But when you have a small amount of cash for gas and groceries for the week and its threatened, instinct kicks in." He stood tall and studied her again. A small grin tugged at the corner of his mouth.

With her arms crossed and no longer locked against the tailgate, she tilted backward. She would've been fine if she hadn't been so dang dizzy. Uncrossing them, she grabbed for the tailgate to steady herself, but overcorrected. Her body pitched forward like a great oak in the forest falling in slow motion. Toppling face first out of the truck was not how she wanted this man to remember her.

He must've seen her wobble. He sat and wrapped an arm around her shoulder quick to keep her upright. She closed her eyes.

Spicy aftershave and pine trees floated across her nose. She breathed it in. Sitting next to him, her heart flapped faster than a hummingbird's wing. She'd forgotten how it felt, sitting close to a man. Obviously, it'd been too long. A zing of warm currents ran down her body. The heat of his arm seeping through the back of her shirt caused reactions that should not be happening in public. She almost groaned until she sensed him staring. His body stilled and the flutter of his breath tickled her eyelashes. Her eyes flew open. Looking anywhere but at him, she chewed the inside of her cheek and fanned her face.

Her body picked that exact second to shake uncontrollably. The more she tightened her muscles to stop the tremors, the harder they shook. It rattled her teeth.

"You need to go get checked out before you go into shock." His voice had an edge to it. Sudden and angry.

"No. No, I'm fine," she lied. Truth be told, she didn't want to move away from him. Which was crazy. But his scent alone awoke places in her that were in perpetual hibernation. Her cheeks flamed. She wasn't even sure of this guy's name. His back straightened. Maybe the zing got to him too? He must've read her mind. He turned and stuck out his hand. "I'm Sam."

"Kirin." She shook his hand while attempting to stifle the tremors. Her hand fit inside his perfectly. The second they touched, she'd swear the parking lot lights got brighter. Splotchy hot spots spread on her neck. When he cleared his throat, she withdrew her hand. She'd held on too long.

"Nice to meet you, Kirin." His voice rumbled low and smooth. A heart-stopping smile unfolded across his face. He pronounced her name slow as if he'd been practicing it for years. She liked the way it rolled off his tongue.

Sam sat stone still. Guarded, but friendly. He was careful not to get too close or touch her too much. Clearly, he was hesitant about being next to her. No ring on his hand, but she'd bet her last dollar he had a girlfriend. When she glanced down at his left hand, he followed her gaze. A brief smile crossed his lips, then he looked away.

Damn. She couldn't be more transparent if she tried.

Note to self: *try* to remember how to flirt. And concentrate on sipping the water, not taking in the hot man. Her embarrassing shake slowed. But the real test would be standing without falling over.

Sam broke the silence and stood. "Where's your car? I'll load these for you." As he called back over his shoulder, he strolled toward her cart. Kirin's white 4Runner was parked two spaces down. She dug in her purse and pulled out her keys, and tossed them to Sam. He caught them mid-stride and pushed the button but was already steering the cart toward it.

Sipping her water, she nodded her silent thanks. He loaded her groceries with ease, while she ogled thick muscles in his back contracting under his T-shirt. She shook her head and concentrated on the water bottle. After returning the cart, he walked back to his tailgate and cleared his throat.

"Want me to follow you home?" He tucked his hands in his pockets.

"Nah, I'll be fine. More stories to tell the girls at the hospital tomorrow."

"Which one?"

"St. Mary's downtown. Labor and delivery. I'm a nurse."

"Ew." Sam's face scrunched, half-smiling.

"What do you mean, ew?"

"Screaming women in pain? Nope. Not for me."

"Hold on, you carry a gun and save complete strangers in a dark parking lot, but you're afraid of a baby?"

"Well, first, you're not a stranger. You tried to kill me with tomatoes."

His single dimple surfaced when he grinned wide, like now. Scratching at his blondish brown stubble, his gorgeous eyes lit with laughter. "And secondly, it's not the baby part that scares me, it's the woman writhing in pain, I can't take."

Absurd. That this confident, handsome man would fear anything. A silent strength surrounded him like a bubble. Her body relaxed. She'd felt protected and safe sitting next to him. He'd walk in front of a bus to save someone, even her. And she knew it. He shuffled from one foot to the other, as if conflicted.

Ignoring it, she smiled. "It's not *that* bad, and we do offer painkillers."

"A drug dealer? And I thought I'd helped someone nice."

She laughed. "I am nice! I help make this world better by bringing babies into it."

"I save women in parking lots. That's gotta earn something for me in heaven, right?" His tone sounded light, but the look on his face made his question seem serious.

She cocked her head sideways and slid him a grin. "Probably not. Besides, I'm pretty sure one good deed doesn't erase all the bad."

"You're assuming I'm all bad?" his eyes lit with humor and heat.

"Bad for me...yes."

He grinned wide, eyebrows up and nodded as if to say she was entirely correct. She hadn't meant it that way. *Lord.* After a few seconds, she looked down at her hands and caught sight of her watch. It was late, and Rosa would worry.

Kirin slid off his tailgate. They stood a foot apart, toe to toe.

"Thanks again, Sam." She reached out and touched his arm. She wanted to hug him, but that was too personal, and she didn't want to scare him off. She opted instead to brush past him toward her vehicle and give him an elbow in the stomach. He grunted and chuckled. She glanced back. Arms crossed and stance wide, he watched her as she walked away.

"You're welcome." Sam paused, "Hey, Kirin?"

"Yeah?" She spun back around and stopped.

"Try not to get into any more trouble today, okay?"

Kirin shook her head. "Not making any promises."

A smile crept up the corners of his mouth. She opened her car door and climbed inside. Sam stood next to his truck, waiting and watching as she backed it out of the spot.

~*~

God, he was a moron. She'd gotten a damn good look at his face and his truck. There was no going back now. His plan was shot to hell. Like the rest of his life, he'd have to wing it.

He'd thought she was attractive from a distance, but up close...*Jesus.* She was stunning. Her bright eyes mixed with a sexy smile and creamy skin. And she had spunk too. That was something he couldn't know from watching from afar. *Get a grip, Sam. She's way outta your league.*

He followed her home at a safe distance. Could've led her there, he'd done it so many times in the last two years. But he was far enough back, she couldn't see him.

His mind automatically began listing out a new disguise. Old habit from years of training. 1. Sell his truck and buy a new one, 2. shave the itchy stubble and 3. darken his hair. Or he could just sport a hat and workout clothes instead of jeans and work boots. That'd worked in the past too.

But something stopped him. He glanced around at the clean floorboards and Armor-all'd dash. This was a good-looking truck. Best he'd ever had and it fit him. It'd saved his ass enough times that it felt like the best friend he never had. And he'd owned it longer than any other vehicle. Besides, at forty wasn't it time to be himself for a while? So what if she saw him.

It didn't matter anyway. He knew what he was and what he'd done. A woman like that would never be with someone like him. Plus, she hadn't noticed him before so maybe she'd be just as oblivious now.

Sam scrubbed one hand across his forehead. One thing was sure, with Sonny gone, he'd need to be on his toes. His orders would come in soon enough.

~*~

A few blocks from the store, the gravity of the encounter with the robber hit her. What if she never held her boys again? What if Sam hadn't been there or she hadn't knocked over the tomatoes? And what if the meth head had hurt her or worse…abducted her in the parking lot?

But she was safe. Kirin prayed a heartfelt thanks to God, then switched the radio station from love songs to old eighties' rock, cranked it up and rolled the windows down. She had to clear her mind before going home. She turned off the main highway on to the two-lane county road leading to her house and slowed, staring in her rearview mirror. A red truck, like Sam's, had followed a few cars behind her the whole way home.

Being followed should have creeped her out, but it didn't. Instead, she felt protected and safe, giddy even. Somehow, somewhere she wanted to bump into that man again.

Arriving home, she parked her car, shut it off, and laid her forehead on the steering wheel. Another silent prayer of thanks.

Unloading the groceries, she relayed the night's events to Rosa.

"What did the man with the gun look like?" Rosa barked.

The tiny woman asked questions as if she'd been an interrogator in a former life. While waiting for Kirin's answer, Rosa heaved open the panel in the pantry floor that led to Jack's panic room, then tossed a twelve pack of paper towels down the short steps and into the inky black below. The familiar musty smell of warm dirt rose and filled Kirin's nose as she stared into the darkness after it. Batman's lair, they'd called it, for the first time gave her a renewed sense of peace.

It'd been Jack's domain and she'd habitually made fun of him about it. She hadn't ventured down there but a handful of times since he'd died. Rickety old stairs led into the spider webbed dark. Old metal shelves lined the walls of the tiny room except one, where his desk and computer slept. Creepy. She made a mental note to boot that old computer up soon. She hadn't done that in months. She glanced up and met Rosa's questioning gaze. Rosa closed the lid and waited for her answer.

"I guess he was about five-eleven, brown wavy hair with matching stubble. But the way he rubbed it, unshaven didn't seem to be his norm. And he had eyes…nice, green ones. And a dimple on one cheek…" Kirin trailed off, caught herself then cleared her throat.

"He had eyes?" Rosa's voice was filled with laughter. "Well, that's a relief. And a dimple?" Kirin's cheeks flushed warm under her nanny's gaze.

"Shut up. He was a regular-looking guy, I guess." Kirin turned to hoist the milk on the top shelf in the fridge. When she turned, Rosa stood with her hands on her hips and eyebrows up as if to say she needed more.

"Why do you ask?" Kirin skirted the subject.

She ignored Kirin's question and continued, "What type of truck did he drive?"

"Toyota. Why?"

"Just wondering," Rosa mumbled, squinting as if she struggled to figure out a math problem.

The sound of Will and Little Jack squabbling over who'd get to be banker in Monopoly echoed through the pantry. Rosa stood in the doorway with hands still on her petite hips and stock still.

"So?"

"So, what?" Kirin bent over and spoke into rows of cans she rearranged to make room for more.

After a moment of deliberate silence, Kirin rose and locked eyes with her nanny. Rosa was a damn master at staring people down for information. She should've been the head of the CIA or the Mexican mafia.

Kirin wasn't. She'd always break. Sticking her tongue out, she smirked. Undaunted, Rosa continued, "What happened earlier? You acted like somebody shot your dog."

"You got me, my invisible dog died." Kirin reached around Rosa to grab more cans from the bags on the floor.

Rosa huffed. "Why the sadness and don't tell me 'nothing.' I saw it in your eyes, and I *know* you."

Kirin stood and let out a long breath, sizing up her nanny. For someone so small, Rosa always had a way of being the witty, sarcastic mother figure in their relationship.

"My father died. I didn't even know he was sick, but the facility called early this morning saying he'd died. I haven't spoken to him since my mom passed, gosh, thirty years ago."

Had it been thirty years since her mom died? That didn't seem possible. Rosa studied her for a moment, then exhaled. Her shoulders deflated as she shook her head. "I'm sorry. I had no idea. Why didn't you tell me? When are you flying out? My sister and I can stay here with the boys while you're gone."

"That's nice, thank you, but I'm not sure if I'll go yet. I haven't made up my mind."

Rosa's body became rigid. She stood taller and pulled her shoulders back. Chin high, she announced matter-of-factly, "You're going—you have to go." Rosa spun on her heels and stomped out of the pantry. Kirin shook her head and finished putting the groceries away as Rosa grabbed her purse and left without another word.

~*~

Competitive like his mama, Will's world would end if he lost to his little brother at Monopoly. Little Jack on the other end of the spectrum, giggled, cheated, and took nothing seriously. After the second game, Little Jack struggled to keep his eyes open, and Will yawned at least six times.

With baths finished and pajamas on, both boys raced toward their bunkbed. Kirin turned out the light and the nightlights flickered on. When she was Little Jack's age, her father prayed with her every night before bed, back when they'd been a normal family. A tradition she continued with her boys. Not because of *him* of course, but because she'd liked the idea. He'd acted so different back then. Loving and fatherly.

Both boys knelt next to their bed. Little Jack knelt but then stood and clambered onto the bottom bunk, sidetracked by an out of place teddy bear. Kirin dropped to her knees and eyeballed him. He took one look at his mama's face, tossed the bear and climbed back down next to her.

Will started the prayer, "Dear God, thank you for this day…"

"Mama?" Little Jack interrupted. Will exhaled impatiently. "Who was your daddy?"

Will raised an eyebrow and nodded as if to say, good question, kid.

Kirin's heart sank. Of course. They'd never asked this question before. With no living or willing grandparents, neither wondered until now. They'd been more awake when the call came in than she'd thought.

"My father's name was Sonny. He lived in California."

"Why?" Little Jack swiped his nose on his arm.

Great question, boy. She had no idea. "Well, because…it's where he lived."

"Did we ever meet him?"

"No, baby, he never met you." She guided a wayward curl off his forehead and swallowed the lump forming in her throat. She'd tried. The battle between hating him for leaving and wanting him to want her, had always raged. She'd had a moment of weakness right after Little Jack was born. Sent a few letters and some pictures, but always with the same result. Zilch.

"Mom," Will began, "why can't we fly to California?"

Kirin bit her lip. She didn't want to tell them. It'd open a whole other host of questions, but she'd prided herself on answering anything they were brave enough to ask. Even if it was difficult.

"Boys, he died today. That was the phone call this morning. One day soon, I'll drag out some old pictures, okay?"

Will stared in the distance. A sadness crossed his face. Little Jack stared at his hands.

What that darn little kid did next, broke her heart, made her even angrier with her father, and made her heart swell, all simultaneously.

"Dear God," Little Jack said, "please watch over my Grandpa Sonny in heaven."

~*~

As soon as they fell asleep, Kirin dragged her tired body into a hot shower before slipping into bed. Sam's strong jaw and green eyes ran through her mind. After he'd saved her, his eyes had changed. They'd become kinder and lighter. The echo of his comforting voice was etched into her memory. His kind way of wrapping a strong, warm arm around her, even now, made her shiver. He'd saved a stranger in a parking lot and been compassionate and caring, like any human would be, she told herself.

Oh, but he had a snarky side, all right. His hesitation to stand near her was no doubt because of a girlfriend. Or an ex-girlfriend. Ex-girlfriend sounded better. Or maybe he hadn't been attracted to her. He'd done his duty as a concerned citizen. That idea made her heart drop a little.

But the way he'd flirted and smiled at her felt personal. Green-flecked eyes had bored into hers. And he smelled like a campfire mixed with spice. Manly. His green shirt stretched across his muscular chest. His smooth, low voice filled with his flirty way of bantering—

"Stop." She scolded herself in the dark.

Careful as always not to cross the invisible line onto Jack's side of the bed, Kirin flopped around. She wouldn't think about Sam or his cute dimple. Lying still in the darkness, the idea of letting a man into her life caused a shudder to run down her spine. Tugging the covers tighter, she closed her eyes.

Tomorrow, she'd book a flight to LA to make funeral arrangements for a stranger.

Chapter Two

A week later, after an endless plane ride and quite possibly the worst night's sleep in a California hotel, Kirin trudged up the terra-cotta steps of the funeral home in the rain. She smoothed her already stick straight hair. *Jesus, why was she so nervous?*

The rustling sound of her long, black skirt matched the click-clack of her uncomfortable heels. In no hurry to get inside, she slowed. Time had sped to this dreadful moment.

A man stood under the awning beside a large stucco-arched door at the top of the steps. He smiled. His nose had a familiar shape to it. Recognition crossed her face and her Uncle Shane's simultaneously. It'd been too long since she'd seen him but walking toward him and seeing the tears in his eyes almost undid her.

Each step closer to the door brought an angry tightness in her chest and a longing for a relationship with her father that would never be.

He was here.

Dead of course, but here.

She'd already talked herself out of her brilliant plan which was to get spectacularly drunk on the plane. She'd fantasized about getting off the plane at LAX, walking straight to the ticket counter and buying an immediate return flight home, for spite. Skip the whole damn thing. But in the end, she was here because of her mama. She'd have been disappointed in her.

The irony wasn't lost on her. He didn't care enough about her to be a part of her world in life but wanted her to be a part of his world in death.

When she reached the top of the steps, her dad's little brother smiled and wrapped her in a warm hug. "Little britches, it's been way too long. How ya' holding up?"

"I'm okay." She squeezed him back. Her only living relative left on her dad's side. Back when her parents were alive, he'd visited and played board games with her on the floor.

He opened the heavy door leading to the main part of the funeral home and ushered her inside. The sickly sweet smell of fresh flowers invaded her senses immediately causing memories of her mama's funeral to flood in. Back then, she'd been a broken, freckle-faced little girl sitting on the front pew of the church while her father greeted everyone in line. She'd worn the red and green plaid dress she and mama had picked out for Christmas Eve mass. She never much cared for the smell of fresh flowers after that.

Shaking the memory, she forced herself to focus. She'd never make it through if she got emotional. New plan. Ignore the anger.

High ceilings, arched doorways, and large crosses stared at her from every corner. Each room was decorated in a contrasting hue of muted reds and oranges. The funeral home's Spanish influences were apparent on every wall.

Graceful high-back chairs, warm lamps, and inviting couches sat every few feet. Tissues lay on each table, free for the taking. She wouldn't need those, thank you. A quiet calm attempted to overtake her senses, but her nerves were much too powerful for it.

A lanky, white-haired man in a navy suit sauntered up. He wore a funeral-home name tag and spoke in a whisper. "Terhune funeral?"

Her mind went blank, like a fresh-cleaned whiteboard. She couldn't remember what he'd asked, let alone how to answer him. She glanced down at her fingers, while her uncle spoke.

"Mr. Williams, this is Kirin, Sonny's daughter."

Kirin glanced up as Mr. Williams's face paled, then rebounded with a fake smile. "Your father spoke of you. I'm glad you made it. Follow me and I'll show you where to go."

Kirin's jaw clenched tight. Glaring at the back of his head, she followed him down the hall. Her father didn't *know* her. Why would he speak of her? And who talks to an undertaker? The absentminded funeral director must say this to everyone.

As she walked down a long-carpeted hallway, reigning in her anger, the last door on the left stood open. An incandescent triangle of light shone from the open door onto the hallway carpet ahead.

It was time. He was here.

Kirin stopped short. Her poor uncle had to sidestep around her, so he didn't knock them both down. He turned around in front of her, placed his hands on her shoulders and bent to peer into her face. He squeezed. "What's up, kiddo?"

Dead body in the next room. She couldn't recall if they'd agreed on the casket remaining open or closed. Shit.

She swallowed hard to give her dry-as-sand throat time to function. Coffee and a banana churned inside her stomach, threatening a reappearance. She hadn't laid eyes on him since he drove away when she was eight.

Uncle Shane mistook her silence for grief and hugged her again.

"Honey, it's about to start. Can you walk?"

Kirin nodded and walked into the room wide-eyed, like a frightened child in a haunted house. She scanned the room. *Breathe.* A sleek, silver casket stood off to one side, lid closed, *thank God.*

Another quick scan told her there weren't many present, except for small pockets of people talking quietly. A chill ran up her spine. She hugged herself as her gaze slid back over the room and stopped. At the far side, three men stood shoulder to shoulder and stared directly at her. They were dressed like undertakers...or maybe mobsters wearing matching dark-suits, menacing faces and shiny shoes.

Gooseflesh rose on both arms. She took a deep breath, placed her handbag on the front pew and took her designated spot in the receiving line. Only a handful of people shuffled through the line, but all knew who she was. Which again, felt strange. Other than she and her Uncle Shane, everyone else introduced themselves as "an associate." It was odd. Nobody introduced themselves as his "friend" or even his "golf buddy." Did he have no one?

After a few moments, the sparse line of people thinned out to only one straggler. A woman, who held one hand on the casket and stared off into space.

Uncle Shane glanced from Kirin to the three men and back. His eyes narrowed as if to say, 'What's with them?' Kirin shrugged. She had no idea. Why would you attend a funeral and not speak to the family?

He shook his head, gave her arm a squeeze then sat down in the first pew. This left her to stand awkward and alone with the woman who had yet to approach and the casket which held her father. She pretended both weren't there.

Smoothing wispy hairs from her face, she concentrated on the space around her. Twelve crosses stood guard in this one room. Twelve. Wringing her hands, she counted people to busy her mind, when a blinding white smile from the back of the room caught her attention, then trapped her gaze.

Two of the black-suited men stood still as if carved out of ice. The bright smile came from the short, tanned-skinned man standing between them. He dripped in gold jewelry, with salt and pepper hair and stared at her as if he was starved, and she was a juicy steak.

His movements were calculated and slow as if everyone had been paralyzed except him. His tailored suit coupled with bright yellow tie, pointed chin, and up-turned nose made him appear smug. His cocky, wide-stance and unwavering eyes were locked on her.

When her gaze landed on his, he winked. Knots cramped her stomach. Weird man. Politely, she turned to shake the hand of the lone straggler who'd finally approached her. The woman held a white cloth which she dabbed at the corner of one eye then shook hands.

She looked regal and thin, wearing stylish clothes and long, gray, swept-back hair tied in a loose bun, reminding Kirin of an elegant but aging supermodel. Her pale blue eyes were the same color as Kirin's, but shifty. And even though her eyes said she'd been crying for days, her smile made her appear much less intimidating. She had a grip though. Sheesh. Fingers so thin shouldn't be able to squeeze that tight.

Whispering, she introduced herself. "Kirin, I'm Janet. I was your dad's secretary. I'm so sorry for your loss. The hospice center told you I've got a book to give you, right?"

Janet leaned back, never offering to let go of the hold she had on Kirin's hand. She lowered her face to peer into Kirin's eyes, waiting for a reply. Kirin tried to let go, but the woman's grip was not budging.

"They did. I-I can't imagine what he'd have left me. He didn't know me." Kirin's voice wavered for the first time all morning and her eyes shot downward. When a tear threatened to let loose, she sniffed and lifted her chin, finding the man with the yellow tie still staring at her. His smile faded. His lips formed a thin sneer as he stared from Janet to her.

When her attention turned back to Janet, the woman examined her. Her fleeting half-smile didn't touch her eyes. "Meet me at his office before your flight home this afternoon, okay?"

Janet's voice held a quiet confidence, honest, and kind. What could a book tell her other than how little her father knew her? What she wanted to do, was turn her back on this damn book, like he turned his back on her. She could do it. She could walk away and not discover what it held to prove her point.

Who was she kidding? No, she couldn't. Curiosity would always win. It was her Kryptonite. "Sure." She nodded. Janet smiled, a real one this time. A tear slid down her cheek as she turned to leave.

Movement caught her eye from the leader as he leaned over to whisper something to a short man on his right. She'd bet they were related. Both were stocky and tan, but the other man had a silver scar running down his right cheek. The scarred man nodded toward Janet as she walked out of the room.

Chapter Three

Only in LA would a funeral service take less time than ordering fast food at a drive-thru. She was grateful, though. Had Southerners ran the funeral, she'd still be knee deep in the prayer service and late to her next two stops.

Uncle Shane's flight back to Montana left earlier than Kirin's, so he offered to drive her to meet with her father's attorney, then drop her off at Sonny's office building before heading to the airport. She'd call a cab after she met with Janet.

She examined him as he drove. He reminded her so much of her father. Well, if her dad had been the outdoorsy hunter type instead of a geeky numbers guy, that is. Yet, they shared the trademark Terhune, turned-up nose and inky black hair with a receding hairline. Well, at least from what she remembered of her father. Shane's black hair was slicked back on both sides of his temples with a few gray sparkles dotting each side.

A self-proclaimed "bachelor to the rapture," Uncle Shane married once, in Vegas. He was the youngest of her father's siblings, and the only one still alive. Their sister Maggie had died when Kirin was a baby. Fell out of a window or something crazy like that. Her uncle rattled on about his busy Montana tour-guide business as they drove away from her father's attorney's office. Kirin laughed at his tall tales as he drove.

"I took on a quail hunting tour last week, I shit you not, filled with professional cheerleaders. Some sort of team bonding exercise. No joke. It was like handing grenades to a room full of two-year-olds. Half of them were so scatterbrained, I didn't give them ammunition. They kept shooting like they had rounds." His eyebrows danced as he laughed at his own joke. Smiling, she shook her head.

"You're not right." She poked him in the arm.

"True."

At the next stoplight, his laughter died down and his face faded to somber.

"Kirin?"

"Yeah?"

"You know your dad was a good man, right?"

Good men didn't leave their only child to be raised by relatives. Good men didn't leave town weeks after their wife died. Good men kept their promises.

When she didn't answer and leveled a look of disbelief at him, he continued, "I'm serious. A good man in a crap situation."

Uncle Shane parked his rental car in front of The Chapman Building, took a deep breath and turned toward her. "Look, I know. He separated himself from me too. I remember how bad it hurt. But, you saw those guys back there. You think they looked normal? They were his friends?"

She had to admit, she'd wondered the same thing. Her father had been a decent investment broker, a numbers guy. And before her mother died, she'd would've described him as a cautious, corny joke-telling, caring dad. But that was before.

She closed her eyes. Opening them a beat later, she hooked her purse over her shoulder and shook her head. "One thing I know for sure, there's no way in hell I'd let somebody else raise my kids."

He let out a defeated breath. "I know. But what if he had no choice?"

She scooted to the edge of the seat and narrowed a look at him as if he'd lost his mind. "How would he have had no choice?" Turning she pointed a thumb back the way they came. "That attorney insinuated he'd be sending me a *large* check. You're telling me he was too poor to put his daughter on a bus?"

Uncle Shane exhaled, ran a hand through his thin hair and smiled sadly at her. Then he pulled her in for a last embrace. "Look, all I'm saying is those men … they weren't his fishin' buddies."

Kirin returned the hug, then shrugged. "And now, we'll never know."

They both got out and met at the trunk. She gathered her bags and hugged him one last time.

Kirin waved as her uncle drove away. She'd promised to call him when she got back to Tennessee. He'd acted as if he wanted to say more but didn't. She'd never believe her father was forced to leave her. He was nothing more than a deadbeat dad. And now, she had to retrieve Mr. Deadbeat's book.

~*~

Exotic red flowers danced in manicured beds flanking the ornate door of The Chapman Building. Obviously, this was the money district. Glancing around, she couldn't swing a dead cat without hitting a Bentley or Rolls. Women, tan, thin, and dripping in diamonds strutted down the spotless, tiled sidewalks to go shopping in clothes that cost more than her 4Runner.

As she reached the door of her father's building, an angry California wind kicked up, wrapping long strands of Kirin's blonde hair around her face and into her mouth. She choked and gagged, then dropped her bag to free up her right hand. She swatted at her hair like a ninja.

Frustration coursed through every vein. She'd gone to the damn funeral and now she wanted to go home. Every second longer she stayed stung like a slap-in-the-face reminder of a life with her father she never had. He'd made moving to LA more important than his only child and to be honest, she played the part of the jealous little sister.

As she made it to the door and swung it open, her stomach growled. Way past lunch time. With the time change, her boys would be sitting on the floor or playing computer games while Rosa started supper. Perfect time to text them and check in.

Typically, doing anything while walking had always been a stretch for Kirin. Considering her uncomfortable heels and the fact she wore a skirt and towed a rolling suitcase and a loaded-down purse, this could prove disastrous.

She texted Rosa, "How's it going? Finished with funeral, headed to airport in 10. Miss you guys."

Kirin locked her phone and dropped it into the black hole of her purse. She stomped over to the directory and searched for his name:

Michael "Sonny" Terhune and Associates, 13th Floor

She stared at it for a beat. Weird. For one, most buildings had no thirteenth floor, but two, he'd been an important man. One with his own floor of a building. So why weren't there more people at his funeral?

Kirin wandered into the elevator. Distracted, she glanced inside her purse and pulled out her phone to check if Rosa responded. Without warning, her right heel caught the threshold of the sliding elevator door and launched her headfirst into the elevator. She landed on a tall guy, wearing a hoodie pulled down low, covering most of his face.

He caught her around the waist and stood her upright. Clearly aggravated, he let out a loud "huff." Under his navy hood, she couldn't make out his face but when he released her, he crossed his arms in an angry stance.

Her fair cheeks flashed hot. She mumbled an apology toward the floor and spun toward the opposite side. Staring down, she said to the woman in front of the number pad, "thirteen, please."

Self-conscious, she rubbed the back of her neck feeling judgmental eyes boring into the back of her head. Especially the man in far back corner. Kirin glared down at her cute but hazardous shoes, as if they could understand how angry she was at them. The silver elevator door closed with a thud.

Three people rode the elevator, but the tension made it feel stuffy and overcrowded. Other than her, there was a heavy-set, red-headed woman who looked to be in her late fifties, and the hooded guy she'd accidentally tackled. He'd moved as far away as possible to the other side of the elevator in the corner shortly after he'd caught her.

The redheaded woman reeked of money. From her freshly blown out hair and Prada bag to her shiny manicure and bright red lips, she even smelled expensive. Pampered. She also appeared to talk to herself, until Kirin spotted the shiny earpiece and telltale blue light.

Kirin stared straight ahead, awkwardly trying to pretend she wasn't forced to eavesdrop on the woman's entire conversation.

"What?" her voice screeched high. "No! I wouldn't have sold the property to him, *ever,* because…"

She turned to glare at Kirin, no doubt because she listened in on the woman's conversation. *Hello.* As if she could help it, they were stuck in a ten-by-ten box.

She hesitated, then whispered dramatically, "He's dangerous." Ms. Expensive squared her shoulders and stretched a little taller. "And besides, I didn't want to sell it before, but now, my mind has been changed." The red-headed woman turned toward the man in the navy hoodie and shot him a smile.

Kirin twisted slightly to look at him. He hadn't changed his *screw off* stance. He stood like an iron statue, with his hoodie angled perfectly so most of his face was covered.

The elevator dinged on the tenth floor. As soon as the doors opened, the woman pointed her nose to the sky and waddled off. Hoodie man stayed put. Feet wide, arms crossed, he carried the pissed off attitude until right before the doors closed.

Suddenly, he darted past Kirin through the closing elevator doors, narrowly escaping from being crushed. Kirin tried to get a look at his face, but his sudden movement had startled her, and she couldn't see his face.

When the elevator pitched back to life, something else was in the air. Remnants of cologne. An earthy smell. Man, did she like that cologne. Sam's face crossed her mind. She closed her eyes and took a deep breath in, making a mental note to research that scent.

~*~

The smell of garlic permeated the worn red carpet of the Italian restaurant. It was a scent that took him back to his childhood, back when he was innocent. Sam trudged down the dimly lit hallway like he was heading to the gallows. And in a way, he was. Behind the last brass doorknob on the right stood a roomful of people he loved yet didn't trust. When he reached the door, he closed his eyes and exhaled. Just last week, his life had made more sense. Now, he was risking his life for a woman who didn't even know he existed. But he'd made a promise. A promise he couldn't back down on, not that he ever did.

Head held high and confidence turned on, he turned the handle and entered the lion's den.

~*~

The floor numbers illuminated in sequence leading to the thirteenth floor. Kirin would miss her flight back home if she didn't move this meeting along. Janet had better be able to talk fast. She set a timer on her phone for ten minutes. Ten minutes tops and she was out of there, book or no book.

When the elevator door opened, there was a tiny waiting room anchored by a large wooden door. Two chairs, no windows, and a door. Nothing else. The door didn't even have a doorknob. Kirin tried for nonchalant as if she stepped off an elevator into a tomb every day. Her stomach clenched. How do you get inside? Two cameras pointed at her head from the ceiling.

A buzzing sound rang out and the door creaked open slow like she was in a scary movie. Shoulders lowered and chin raised, she took a deep breath and walked through. Janet rose from behind a sleek, gray desk. She smiled at Kirin and strolled toward her.

When Janet reached her, she pulled her in, hugging her tighter than expected, then she held Kirin out at arm's length with misty eyes. She looked at Kirin as if she were a lost child who'd returned home. Janet released her then grabbed a dirty, green book from the desk, placing it in Kirin's hands. Words tumbled out of Janet as if she'd get caught with a note in school. "Here. Put it in your purse. Don't let go of it, until you get home."

Her eyes switched from happy homecoming to fearful in a snap and the quiver in her voice rattled as she spoke.

Kirin turned the book over in her hands. It was short and thick with yellowed pages and a torn camouflage cover. It's spine wrinkled like a skinny, old chain smoker. Battered, it looked as if it'd been through several wars, not winning any of them. Janet's voice dragged Kirin's gaze back to her face.

"Kirin. Listen. And I mean *really* hear me. Your dad adored you. I understand it doesn't seem possible to you right now, but someday this will all make sense. I can't do this for you. This is your journey, not mine." Grasping Kirin's shoulders, she sighed. Dread swept across her face. "Your dad and I married in secret long after your mom passed away. I posed as his secretary, so we could stay close without anyone suspecting."

Kirin's back straightened. She interrupted, "Wait...you married my father? Why in secret?"

Janet sighed, speaking as if she chose her words carefully. "Associates of your dad's. Let's just say, they didn't appreciate him having a home life."

Kirin's eyebrows furrowed as she stepped back, slightly out of Janet's reach. Her brain caught up as disappointment slammed into her chest. He'd married again. She wasn't told. Once again, left in the dark by her father.

Janet ignored the question in her eyes and kept talking. "Keep your eyes open, and always be wary of strangers, especially anyone who asks about the book."

Kirin looked down at the mongrel book in her hands, "Why would anybody ask about this book?" Janet pulled Kirin in for one last tight hug.

"Read it." She whispered plainly in Kirin's ear, then turned and walked through another mahogany door, shutting it behind her with a click.

What the hell? Standing there, mouth open and dumbfounded, she tried to soak it all in. What brand of crazy was this woman? And who in the world would ask about this stupid book? And why did they have to get married so secretly they couldn't even send a damn note to his daughter?

Alone in his office, she looked around. Not one personal item of her father's. And not a picture of her anywhere. What a fool. Kirin clamped her eyes shut. No bullshit tears, not for him. The trip was a huge mistake and it ripped open the never-ending scab once again. She pinched the bridge of her nose, considered throwing the book back on the desk and leaving, but as she stared at it, the realization hit, the damn book was all she had left of her family.

Home. Adrenaline kicked in along with a fierce need to hold her boys. She wasn't anything like her father. She'd never leave them, no matter what the excuse.

Kirin shoved the ragged book inside her purse, grabbed her bag, and ran back through the still open door and onto the elevator. Down thirteen floors, away from the memories, she hit her Uber app and waited with her head swiveling side to side.

One hand fiddled nervously with the zipper on her purse. Back and forth. The sound alone soothed her mind. Stupid trip, stupid book, and stupid hope that somehow this experience might change anything she knew about her father.

A few feet away, a crowd of people gathered at the corner waiting for the light to change. When it did, the crowd all moved together except one man. He stood on the sidewalk and surveyed her. The afternoon sun glared in her eyes and cast a shadow over his face. His stance told her it wasn't a coincidence.

Her ten-minute timer's shrill alarm made her bobble and catch her phone. When she glanced back toward where the man had stood, he'd vanished.

A chill ran down her spine.

One thing was clear, someone had followed her.

Chapter Four

Saul Calamia strutted from his blacked-out limousine toward the glass doors of the state-of-the-art hospice center. He cut a look toward his new driver. The kid didn't open the door fast enough, and he had to stop. The boy stared at his shoes as Saul passed.

The pungent smell, even inside the most expensive nursing home in all the South, made him ill. God, how he'd tried to move his mother to a nicer one in L.A.. One where he wouldn't have to get on a plane to visit every week. But she wouldn't hear of it.

Rounding the corner toward her room, his phone buzzed.

"Calamia here," he barked.

"Mr. Calamia, Joe Johnson returning your call." Exasperation laced the man's voice.

Smug bastard. The head of the University of Tennessee never answered when Saul called. Every week, the same conversation. And every week the same answer. This week the man's mind would be changed. Or else.

"Mr. Johnson, I take it you received my last offer?"

"I did." Mr. Johnson took a deep breath. "Mr. Calamia, as I've stated before we cannot sell the Eugenia Williams's estate. It was left with strict instructions to be used only by the University."

Saul stopped short, making his bodyguard sidestep around him.

"Mr. Johnson, my last offer of eight million is more than generous for that crumbling manor. It will need millions more to restore it."

As Mr. Johnson droned on about the University's position, a young boy pushing an elderly woman down the hall in her wheelchair gave him an idea.

"Mr. Johnson," Saul interrupted, "My mother, sir, has terminal cancer. She hopes to see this property restored to its heyday before she dies. Now I have crews standing by, ready to start construction. Think of what the university could do with eight million dollars. Did you get the envelope I sent over? That's for you, personally."

Mr. Johnson cleared his throat. "Mr. Calamia, I did receive it, along with a warning from the man who handed it to me. I don't take kindly to bullies. And there's no need to pay me. I've told you I'll bring it up at the next board meeting in a week. Understand, their vote is final."

Damn Nicky. He should have sent the pimply faced kid who couldn't intimidate a fly.

Saul walked slow and spoke through gritted teeth, "My brother has an odd way of speaking sir, but he means no harm. The money is for your time. I'll expect a call by Friday."

Saul hung up then texted his attorney, Matthew, to contact the board members and sway them. If they couldn't be bought, maybe he'd send Nicky their way too.

The moment he stepped into his mother's room, he transformed. Gone were the pressures of adulthood and the ugliness and death of the business his father forced on him. It was only him and her, and in her eyes he was her hero and still twelve, not sixty.

"*Cuore mio!*" his mother said in a tiny Italian voice, "Come close, Sauly. I want to speak to you."

Lately, she'd struggled with flashbacks of life when Saul and Nicky were boys. She blurted out in a loud whisper, "I think your father is kidnapping girls. And maybe...he's a killer."

Saul's face remained unchanged, but his eyes widened. She didn't seem to notice. "Mama, why would you say that?"

"A woman knows. I've got to run to the store. Watch little Nicky and don't let him torture the cats anymore, okay? Be a good boy. Keep your dream, *passeroto.* From now on, I don't want you going anywhere alone with father."

Saul nodded and glanced at his hands. His father had been dead for years, but truth be told, if cancer hadn't gotten the bastard first, Nicky would've. He'd pressed both boys into service. Nicky had loved the business. Getting paid to "help" young, attractive Mexican girls into the US legally, then selling them to the highest bidder. Double paid. Saul had never wanted any part of it. But he had to admit, the money and the power had made him the man he was today.

She'd mentioned his dream again. Every week lately, she'd spoken of it. He was to be a pilot. Respectable. A white-picket-fence kind of man with plenty of kids and the love of his life beside him. It'd all died when she did. Stupid to think about it now. Who fell in love at nineteen? Nobody. The career he never wanted gave him respect and fortune, two things a silly emotion like love couldn't buy.

When he looked back at mother, she was asleep. It was excessive even for him to fly six hours for a three-minute conversation with her. When his phone buzzed, he read the incoming text twice, then dialed the number and took it in the hallway.

"Matthew? What the hell was that text about? Why can't I get into my accounts and get my money?" He growled, low and menacing.

His face turned hot as rage raced through him. After a beat, he spoke, "Oh, he did, did he?" Saul yelled and paced like a caged lion. Sweat beaded at his hairline. "Well, too bad Sonny's already dead. I might have liked to witness that go down. So, what the hell do we do now, Matthew? Codes? What codes? I don't have any codes. How could Sonny have hidden my money from me without someone knowing it?"

He stopped pacing and lowered his voice. "His daughter? No, he didn't speak to her at all. Why would she have anything to do with this? All bullshit, Matthew. The existence of the book was a rumor, nothing more."

A nurse walked by giving him the stink eye. He spun toward the wall and spoke low, "Well if my codes are in that damn book and she has it, you can bet your sweet ass we'll get it back. And Matthew, if you'd like a paycheck this week, you'd better find out how to get my fucking money."

Saul slammed the end button on his phone and stomped back into his mother's room.

She sat up, staring at him. No doubt she heard every word. A sad look crossed her face.

"Any luck on getting my house?"

How the hell was he going to cough up eight million, when he didn't have access to his money?

"We're close, mama, real close."

"You know my father was a friend of Mr. Williams. Eugenia was my age but was too snobby to speak to me. My childhood dream was to live in that mansion. I begged my father to buy it before he died. Eugenia left it to the University out of spite. I want to die there, you know, Sauly. And it won't be long."

"I'll get it for you, mama, I promise." He kissed her on the head, grabbed his jacket and walked down the hall, muttering to himself, "No matter what it takes."

Chapter Five

Boarding the shiny 747, Kirin found her seat. Her body melded into the uncomfortable chair. She prayed nobody sat next to her. She needed to stretch out and sleep. Something she hadn't managed in days.

As the other passengers filed in, she clutched her purse with the book inside, hyperaware of everyone around her. Damn that crazy Janet. She'd spooked her and made Kirin suspicious of everyone boarding the plane.

The airliner doors closed, and no more passengers filed in. She took over the seat next to her. After takeoff she stretched her legs out. With her purse tucked close to her chest and her eyes squeezed shut, she tried to stop the questions racing through her mind. She needed sleep. Ordering her exhausted mind to shut down, she drifted off.

~*~

Concord Park was a lush, wooded forest filled with winding hiking trails, busy tennis courts, dirt baseball fields, and a bustling lake. She and Jack took the boys to play there every weekend until he'd been too sick to go.

Their favorite spot was down a winding gravel road leading to an open grassy area with picnic tables and a small playground.

Below the playground, a small marina sat with a quaint, little country restaurant inside. They served Southern-comfort food like pinto beans and cornbread, gravy and biscuits, fried chicken and meatloaf with macaroni and cheese.

They'd celebrated her graduation from nursing school there, right before she'd agreed to marry him.

The restaurant had floor-to-ceiling windows overlooking the glimmering lake. It gave a panoramic view of the boats coming in from their long day of playing on the water. The sun sank slowly, dipping into the water and casting long shadows across the grass.

Kirin sat atop one of the picnic tables overlooking the lake. Will and Little Jack played on the slide. Turning, she smiled. Jack sat next to her. His curly mop, in need of a haircut as always, hung down on his forehead. Their shoulders touched as he sported his easy-going smile. His long legs stretched out past hers and the wind caught in his curls when he spoke.

"Love," he whispered, "it's time to let go."

"Can't," she said, "I still miss you."

He wrapped long, muscular arms around her and for a moment she swore she could feel them. His sparkling green eyes, the same color as Little Jack's pleaded with her.

"You need to be happy, our boys need to see you living life again."

He kissed her forehead, hopped down off the top of the picnic table, and jogged down the hill to play with the boys. The sun had all but set and as Jack lifted them into the air one by one, their giggles rippled on the wind toward her. She smiled, feeling at peace.

She didn't want to wake. Her stomach nudged her when the flight attendant asked the row ahead of her if they wanted food.

Food. Kirin pushed herself to sit tall. It was late in the flight and the stupid-expensive crackers and water she'd eaten in the airport left her with a rumbling stomach.

"Ma'am, would you care for a drink and a snack?"

"Yes, please. Could I have tomato juice and pretzels?"

"Sure thing, sweetie."

While asleep, her purse with the book inside, had slid on to the floor. She snatched it up like it had gold bars inside. She glanced around, feeling paranoid and silly, then flung it into the empty seat next to her. She practically inhaled the drink and snack. Weird dream, yet somehow comforting. Most likely it meant she'd lost her mind. She'd pick it apart later. Or the better option, ignore it completely.

Kirin finished her snack, threw away the garbage and checked her phone for messages. Two unread texts came through before boarding the plane. One came from Rosa saying she and the boys were busy making a cake to celebrate her return.

The second text read, "Private Number."

Give back the book and no harm will come to your boys.

She read it three times.

Blonde hairs on her arms stood at attention. She felt exposed as if all eyes stared at her and vulnerable, as if she rode a roller coaster unharnessed. She laid the phone in her lap and crossed her arms protectively. Eyes darted from passenger to passenger as if someone on the plane sent it. Her hands trembled. Fear turned to rage.

She pressed the bridge of her nose. A headache along with a protective, mental list began to grow; 1. Arm the security on the house *every day*, 2. Bring one of Jack's guns up from the safe room and hide it in the kitchen, and 3. Call Will's school and remind them she, Rosa, Aunt Kathy, and Uncle Dean were the only people authorized to pick him up.

Her mind spun out of control. How did they get her number? She'd take it to the police. Surely, they could figure this out.

Locking her phone, she slid it inside her bag. She couldn't get answers until they landed anyway. If she let it, her mind would run wild and she'd be a paranoid mess by the time they landed.

Jaw locked tight, she glared out the window at the blanket of soft clouds below. Her eyes darted to her purse holding the book. She needed to dig into it. Now. Damn her father. Why would he put this burden on her when he had to know it'd lead to trouble?

Kirin grabbed the sweater she'd brought in case the plane was chilly and draped it over her chest. Glancing around to ensure nobody saw, she took out the book and placed it on her lap, the sweater covering half of the book. Kirin looked at the passengers in front of her, then back down to the book. She opened the cover slow as if a rabbit could jump out.

A woman, a row over sneezed and she froze.

Good gravy get a grip, Kirin.

Folding over the first few yellowed pages, nothing seemed out of the ordinary. Her mind drifted to the safe room as she turned the pages. For the first time since they built the house it gave her a sense of security.

Her gaze fell toward the book she was only beginning to loathe. Maybe she'd leave it down there too.

A few rows back, a passenger dropped a large hardback novel on the aisle floor. Even with the engine noise, the loud crack caused passengers to turn, disturbed from their quiet conversations or sleep.

She gripped tight to the book and turned. An elderly, white-bearded man shook his head, then leaned over and winced as he retrieved his book. As he bent, she caught a quick look at the man directly behind him.

Eyes locked.

And for a long few seconds, she couldn't look away. As the plane banked to the left to begin its final descent, he turned his head to look out the window, cutting his glaring eyes away from her at the last second.

As the sunlight skittered across his face, a sparkling scar running down his right cheek confirmed her suspicions.

Leaving no doubt who sent the threatening text.

Chapter Six

Turning slow toward the front of the plane, Kirin shoved the book in her purse and zipped it securely. She wrapped the strap tight around her arm twice and stared straight ahead. As the flight touched down and came to a halt at McGhee Tyson, the passengers rose to gather their belongings.

She stood with knees wobbling, and tied her sweater around her waist, then secured her crossbody purse tight. Her eyes darted and searched but found nothing. He had to be there. She hadn't dreamt it. Back and forth through the throngs of passengers, she examined each row. He'd somehow vanished. She waited for her turn to exit the plane.

Shaking, she ambled toward the front of the plane and onto the narrow, uphill jetway leading the passengers toward the airport.

People bottlenecked behind an old woman using a walker. Passengers grumbled behind her. She glanced ahead over the top of the woman's white tuft of hair. Nothing.

A soft alarm rang out. A blue-suited airport worker raised a narrow garage door and passengers grabbed rolling packs off a cart.

All the bags looked similar, black, overstuffed rectangles, each with four dirty wheels. Hers had a pink, polka-dotted ribbon tied to the handle. Easy to spot.

Kirin grabbed hers, lifted the handle and locked it. Glancing back down the jetway, two wrinkled-suited men exited the plane below. Her stomach took a nosedive.

One of the suited men towered over the crowd. He had to be over six feet tall, yet baby-faced with fawn colored stubble. He was the larger of the two men, but not nearly as intimidating as the shorter man. Dumpy, heavy set with salt and pepper hair, the second man's hollow eyes showed zero emotion, only determination. She stopped at the top and squinted down the jetway toward the plane, trying to get a better look.

Yep. A visible scar on the right side of his face.

Neither man carried bags. They strolled around the slower moving passengers, heading right for her. Their eyes all the while focused on their target.

She darted around the woman with the walker. Swiftly, down the wide, glossy airport hallway she scurried toward the exit and security, as fast as her hazardous heels could take her.

Both feet ached. She maneuvered around slower moving passengers saying, "Excuse me" as she darted in and out of foot traffic like a Frogger game. The look of sheer hatred on the scarred one's face when she glanced back, told her she hadn't imagined it.

He wore a permanent, pissed off frown. The baby-faced man looked apologetic. Both men speed walked and were gaining on her.

Kirin used her free hand to gather her skirt. She sped to a jog. Her head swiveled from side to side. No place to hide. Her only choices were the bathroom—where she'd be trapped, a Starbucks kiosk and the tiny store with only a handful of shelves.

Passengers stared and scoffed as she ran past. She didn't care. This would be much easier if she could call a timeout and kick off her heels. One glance behind her told her it wasn't a good idea. She knew they couldn't have had weapons. They'd been through security like her. And yet, she didn't want to find out what they could do to her without weapons. Especially Scar.

The men sprinted and closed the gap to ten feet. Her chest heaved. Her rolling bag squeaked out its displeasure at being dragged behind her at this speed. Looking back, Scar's mouth twitched in premature celebration. His eyes were intense. Something in the way he looked at her wratcheted-up her adrenaline. Now, she was full-on running.

Her head swiveled back and forth, searching for the way out. Kirin darted to the right, in front of two passengers cutting them off short. They cursed her. A few feet ahead, the revolving door separated the main part of the airport from the family waiting area. Adjacent to the waiting area was security.

The sound of slapping footsteps and gasps from other passengers, told her the people behind her were pushed out of the way to get closer to her. Her fingers ached from clutching her skirt and the handle of her rolling bag so tightly. *Please God, don't let her trip.*

Her quick and flawed plan to get through the revolving doors faster, was to squeeze in with another person into the one-person compartment. It'd be tight, but it might work. And maybe if she could get to the door ahead of a few people, she could create some space between her and the men. On the other side, she could yell to the security guards to help her.

Running in her senseless, black heels, she stumbled a little and fell headfirst into a compartment with another woman, dressed primly in a navy business suit. Barely enough room for both ladies plus luggage, they were crammed into the small glass space, squished together like old friends.

The woman glanced sideways. A nervous smile accompanied by an annoyed, 'What are you doing?' look crossed her face.

Kirin let out a frustrated breath. The woman walked the pace of a slug. Kirin placed her hand on the glass and pushed the door faster. She would not lose her lead time. In her peripheral she watched Scar and Babyface reach the revolving door in perfect time for it to cut them off. His glare spoke volumes.

A few more seconds for her to figure out what to do. The two men were stuck behind a family two doors behind her, looking ticked. The revolving door opened to the other side and on instinct, she ran toward security.

As she emerged, the squeals of her sweet little boys echoed in the corridor off to her right. They'd come to surprise her.

Her motherly instinct changed her trajectory toward them without hesitation. It didn't matter if Scar and Baby Face came at her or took the stupid book. Hell, take it. But they'd be in for a rude awakening if they came near her boys. Her only thought was to protect them. She ran to them, dropped her bags and her purse and scooped them up, holding them tightly.

Rosa's smile changed in a hot second from a happy reunion to fierce worry as her eyes met Kirin's. She glanced up and somehow, without saying a word, grabbed Kirin's purse off the floor, and wrapped it around her body.

The revolving door opened, and the two men tumbled out, falling over the top of each other. Heads on a swivel, they searched the crowd. They caught sight of her at the same time a security officer noticed them, forcing them to compose themselves. She could swear Rosa growled as the two men passed between security and where they stood.

Scar veered around them, glaring. Never blinking, he stared into Kirin's eyes and straight through to her soul. A warning meant to intimidate. Cold gray eyes never left hers until he passed. Baby Face looked straight ahead as if he was embarrassed. Kirin swung the boys around. The two men strolled through the lower level glass doors and climbed into a waiting black limo.

Kirin crumbled to the floor bombarded with kisses and hugs. Little Jack spoke fast. "Mama, guess what we did?" Before she could answer, she caught sight of Will. His eyebrows pushed with concern. He searched her face then looked around. That boy always had a sixth sense. She snuggled him into her and whispered, "It's okay, buddy." He nodded.

Grateful, she smiled at Rosa who stood still and glared at the limousine through the window. Concern etched her face. Absentmindedly, she touched Kirin's head.

Little Jack's chubby fingers pulled her face back toward his and talked a mile a minute. "Mommy, you know what? We went to the park and to a movie and Rosa bought ice cream. I got chocolate. Can we watch the planes land, Mommy? Please?"

"Sure, sweetie." She smiled down at him and walked toward the large windows overlooking the tarmac. As her heart rate slowed, plane after plane landed. She concentrated on the squeals of delight coming from her boys.

"Mom, can we fly somewhere soon?" Will interjected as another 747 landed.

"Sure, we can." She stroked Will's head. He gazed at her. He looked as if he wanted to ask something else, but turned, squinting into the setting sun. He wrapped his arm around his little brother who bounced like a basketball as a 747 landed.

Kirin squeezed Rosa. Neither one mentioned the men or the fear. They herded the boys toward the door. As they walked in the parking garage toward Rosa's car, Kirin's head looked like it was on a swivel. She searched side to side, looking for the two men, but finding the rows of cars empty of anyone suspicious. Kirin threw her bags in the trunk and jumped in. Rosa locked the doors, placed her purse gingerly in Kirin's lap and headed for the exit.

The parking attendant cocked an eyebrow at Rosa as she handed them Kirin's cash. No doubt because they both glanced around as if the boogeyman would get them. Rosa doublechecked the locks before heading down the ramp toward home. This had spooked her too.

As Rosa drove them home, the boys chattered in the backseat. Rosa silently concentrated on the road, while Kirin's mind raced with questions. What did they want? How were these men affiliated with her father? Did he owe them money? It had to be the damn book.

She felt unprotected. Then, her mind wandered to Sam. She'd felt so shielded with him around.

Kirin smiled. Meeting Sam had shifted her paradigm. Angry as he'd been when they'd first met, he'd awoken something in her. Even if she never saw him again, he'd made her think about a relationship.

Kirin shuddered. Then again, she'd been fine all alone, hadn't she? Trusting men had never been her strong suit. Her dad had seen to that. She'd trusted him too much. God knew she didn't need to put her already damaged heart out there to be broken again.

Sam though. He seemed trustworthy, didn't he? He was most certainly her type. The only problem was, she had no way to reach him. She hadn't been brave enough to get his phone number or even slip him hers.

Maybe she simply wasn't ready to date again. In that department, she'd always been a big chicken.

None of that mattered now, she had bigger fish to fry. She had to discover what was so important about her father's damn book.

It had moved to the top of her to-do list.

Chapter Seven

Kirin groaned as she dragged herself into her closet. Grabbing her pink and white scrubs and Nikes, she trudged down the hall to wake the boys for school. Rosa was already downstairs making something in the kitchen that smelled like bacon-wrapped heaven. A warm, spiced-coffee aroma wafted toward her room. Today was going to be a much better day.

After devouring breakfast and hugging Rosa and the boys so tightly they all complained, she ran out the door, jumped into her car and drove to work.

A bright spring sun peeked around the tall, shiny downtown Knoxville buildings as Kirin drove into the parking lot. She locked her car and trotted to the elevator to push the button for labor and delivery. She couldn't remember today's code and had to ride the elevator for three minutes like a stalker before she could get a nurse on her floor to text her back.

What were they all doing?

When the code came through and the doors opened, six nurses crowded around a massive bouquet of red roses. She stepped off the elevator toward them. They scattered like smiling roaches.

Her BFF Stacy sauntered over like an old gunslinger. Her other bestie, Laura, scampered around Stacy and grabbed Kirin, hugging her. Stacy had a huge smirk on her face, but Laura's face was, as usual, unassuming.

"How'd it go, hon?" Laura's eyebrows pushed together on her round face as she held Kirin out at arm's length to get a good look at her. Laura was Kirin's Christian influence. She always took the high road and never talked badly of anyone. She'd make a comfort food and bring it over if a friend had a cold. The opposite of Stacy who was tall, dark, and flirty, with a love of new shoes that trumped her love of gossip.

"I'm fine," Laura's doubtful expression made Kirin add, "really."

Stacy leaned her tall frame against the nurse's station, sizing up Kirin with her head cocked sideways. Her eyebrows lifted as a devilish grin unfurled.

"Meet anybody new?"

"Well…yeah. Why?"

Stacy pointed to the flowers.

"For me?" Kirin's voice sounded too high and raspy.

She hesitated, then walked over and grabbed the already tattered card. She was positive everyone on the OB floor had inspected it.

The card read, "Glad you made it home." It was unsigned.

Her mind raced. Was this Sam? How did he know where she worked? Had she told him? Shoot, she'd been so shaken, she couldn't remember.

Or could this be from *them*? She leaned more toward believing this was the work of the black-suited men trying to intimidate her than her handsome, aloof savior in the parking lot.

She stood stock still and stared at the blood-red flowers. She shook her head, halting her racing mind.

Stacy stood across from Kirin, head still cocked to the side, obviously puzzled by Kirin's reaction to the flowers. She rhythmically tapped her foot waiting for an answer.

In the nick of time, one of Kirin's assigned delivery rooms buzzed for help. She shot Stacy a smug grin and pushed the call back button.

"Yes, ma'am?"

"I need my nurse, please, in room 304," a small shaky voice croaked.

"I'll be right there," Kirin smiled brightly at a frustrated Stacy, who promptly stuck her tongue out like a toddler.

No time for stories. Babies don't wait to be born. She walked confidently down the hall feeling Stacy's glare on her back and grinning to herself. For the moment, she'd won.

Kirin waltzed into the room. This was her playground. This was where she felt most confident and where she'd gained most of her self-worth. For years she'd fantasized about her father witnessing her in action. In her dream, he'd beamed with pride. It was silly, she knew.

But each time a new father held his newborn, she'd wondered…had her father vowed, like she had when her boys were born, that nothing would ever hurt her? The first eight years of her life he hung on her every word. Those memories faded and were then replaced by years of silence. And now she'd never know what she did to make him leave.

Kirin took a deep breath and shook the memories before greeting her patient.

"Good morning," Kirin sang, smiling. She popped open the dry erase pen and scribbled her name on Emily Hall's whiteboard.

"I'm Kirin. I'll be your nurse this morning. Who's ready to have a baby?"

Emily and the young man next to her both raised their hands like they were six. Kirin laughed but noted they looked exhausted and terrified. She reached out and shook the young husband's clammy hand who introduced himself as Chris and turned to Emily.

Emily was a twenty-four-year-old, first-time mom. Panicked from the word go, she yelled out whenever any twinge of pain shot through her.

Her husband wasn't much better, running to get ice chips and texting relatives the play-by-play of every contraction. Emily's contractions had lasted all night and neither had slept. Chris's demeanor ran the gamut from wide awake and terrified to snoring.

"We'll take good care of you today."

The young woman nodded at Kirin nervously. "Now, let's get your vitals and check your progress, okay?"

Emily's face softened and her shoulders lowered six inches. Kirin had always had a way of calming the chaos when she walked into a labor room. It was her special gift.

As she checked Emily's vitals and progress, which was something she could do with her eyes closed, Kirin's mind raced back to the flowers. As much as she'd wanted to pin them on Sam, she knew they were a threat. A threat meant to scare her.

Chris cleared his throat. "Is there something wrong with her heart?"

Kirin looked down at her hands. Lost in her own issues, she'd held the stethoscope there too long. Both the patient and her husband tracked Kirin's every move. She snapped it up and folded it around her neck.

"Oh, gosh no, I was just listening … good, strong heart young lady." Both soon-to-be parents relaxed. *Get it together Kirin.* Heat crept into her cheeks.

She recorded the vitals and reassured them, without eye contact, that at three centimeters dilated, her progression was normal.

Emily wanted to wait for her epidural, so Kirin put the anesthesiology department on standby before leaving the room.

"Try and rest between contractions. I'll check on other patients and be right back."

Emily's half-asleep husband Chris jumped up. His voice was high-pitched with fear, "But what do I do if she starts to have this baby and you and the doc aren't here?"

Why were guys so scared of childbirth? It's not as if *physically* they had to do anything. Kirin reassured him, "She's got time, don't worry, and if you need me, press the buzzer and I'll run right back."

As Kirin left the room and walked back to the nurse's station, Laura and Stacy leaned against the counter like gang members waiting to jump her.

After some prodding, Kirin told them about her weekend. She recounted the creepy men at the funeral, Janet, who gave her the book and her run-in with Sam and the tomatoes. And later how Sam saved her from the crackhead mugger in the parking lot. She made extra sure to keep her voice even when she told them about him.

Stacy was the first to speak. "Umm-hmm." She narrowed her eyes as if she'd found a Prada purse at a garage sale.

"What?" Kirin narrowed her eyes.

"Was he hot?"

"W-what?...No...I don't know, maybe." Kirin stammered, "He was insulting at first, but after he'd captured the robber, he was kind. Caring even." her voice trailed off.

Laura piped up as her gaze drug over the flowers. Her usual grin turned down in confusion. "So, did Sam send you the flowers?"

"I don't know," Kirin's voice lowered.

Her heart wanted it to be Sam, but her mind screamed out a warning. The black suits had sent her a threat. Hell, they had her cell phone, how hard would it be to discover where she worked?

Under the fluorescent lights, Stacy leaned an elbow on the counter and smirked.

"What?" Kirin demanded.

Stacy shook her head, then turned and walked backward, grinning. After a beat she called out, "Glad you're back in the game."

Kirin shot her a look as Stacy's face lit up with a mischievous grin. She knew Stacy was mentally scanning through her list of old boyfriends to find Kirin a blind date. She shook her head no and Stacy's grin widened.

As most nurses dispersed, Kirin was left alone with the flowers. She saw them now, in a different light. Slightly wilted and the color of day-old blood, they sent a chill up her spine. She should just hand over the damn book. But what if the book was the only leverage she had with these people? If she gave it to them would they leave her and her family alone? Something told her no. She knew deep down, when they'd chased her in the airport, they didn't want to talk. The scarred one looked as though he'd take pleasure in hurting her. She hugged herself.

The buzzing from a patient startled her and she yelped. She pushed the button and her voice shook.

"Yes?" Kirin replied.

"Miss Kirin," squeaked the weak female voice.

"Yes, Emily?"

"Can I get that epidural now, please?"

"I'll call right now. Hang in there."

Delivering babies connected her intricately with the parents. She could help deliver babies all day long and be happy. In her element, she didn't have to feel like her father's cast-off. Here, she knew she was worth something.

Kirin called and got a script for the meds, then buzzed the tech in pharmacy and ordered the epidural. As she marched into Emily's room to prep her for the procedure, her mind spun in circles.

Crack open the tray and lay out the alcohol swabs...*I've got to make time to dig into the book*...move chairs so the anesthesiologist has room... *why would my father put me in this position?*...Sit patient on the side of the bed with her legs dangling down...*I don't want to read the damn thing from cover to cover, but I have to.*

When Dr. Watkins shuffled into the room, Kirin touched Emily on the shoulder and smiled reassuringly. She'd already explained the importance of remaining still while the Doctor administered the epidural.

Dr. Watkins was as round as he was tall and known for being a crochety old fart. It was widely believed he made a point to berate and demean at least one nurse per shift. Most of the newer docs walked the patients through what would happen. Not him. His demeanor was more reminiscent of an old country vet shoving a cold thermometer up a horse's rear.

Abruptly, Emily yelped, and her body jerked. Kirin's head snapped up and met the angry eyes of Dr. Watkins. The smell of rubbing alcohol stung her eyes. He'd swabbed Emily's back without warning her or Kirin, and she'd jumped.

"Nurse Lane," he growled, "keep that patient still." His voice was tight and angry.

Their eyes locked. Kirin gripped Emily's shoulders tighter and whispered, "Remember, it feels like a sweat bee. Tiny pinprick, that's all. Close your eyes, grit your teeth, but don't move."

Emily nodded. Her husband Chris held her hand and stared at the doc's hands in horror. Emily held her breath as the doctor gouged a needle next to her spine. Emily's entire body stiffened, and one knee jerked outward.

Kirin froze. She'd witnessed this happening once before, and it was due to a wrong needle placement.

Dr. Watkins swore an oath under his breath, then growled, "Young lady, if you move even a centimeter you will be paralyzed. Nurse, wake up and get a hold of your patient!"

Kirin sprang to action. Careful so she didn't jar her, she wrapped her arms around young Emily and squeezed to hold her still. Tears ran down Emily's cheeks.

Sweat beaded on Dr. Watkins' slick head over his brow. This wasn't supposed to happen. She'd been preoccupied with the damn flowers and the damn thugs and not concentrating on her patient. And this old doc was too impatient and set in his ways to do this intricate work. It wasn't all her fault, but she'd be partly to blame if he paralyzed her. Kirin held Emily tighter.

Dr. Watkins pulled the sterile guide needle out slightly then reinserted the catheter tube less than sixteenth of an inch away, found the correct spot and inserted the tube.

A sigh of relief flooded the room, halted only by Dr. Watkins slamming the syringe back on the metal tray. The father-to-be jerked at the noise.

"Nurse Lane. Meet me outside," Dr. Watkins said through gritted teeth.

He gathered his things, scratched his name on her file and stomped out the door. Never uttering a word to the patient. Kirin smiled reassuringly at Emily, laying her back on the bed and covering her up. The couple held hands and shot her pity glances as if she was trudging to the gallows.

No sooner had she crossed the threshold out into the hall, Dr. Watkins lit into her.

"Young lady, where are you?" He yelled, but didn't wait for her answer, "Your mind should always be on your patient. Normally, you're one of the few nurses on this floor I don't have to worry about. Get it together, Nurse Lane, or find another career."

Dr. Watkins huffed, then stomped past her.

He was right, she was to blame. She wanted to add this to the long list of items she blamed on her father, but she couldn't. This was all her. She'd let her personal life threaten her work. She wasn't a crier, but tears stung her eyes. She stood for a full minute and stared down the empty hall.

Nothing felt safe anymore. These men and this stupid book had knocked her off track. Well, no more. With her fists balled, she swore. Even if she hated him, and his damn book, she knew what she had to do. She had to defend herself. She'd fix this. No matter what.

Chapter Eight

Heading home after her shift, toting the massive flowers to the car, Kirin passed one of the doctors she'd delivered with late in the day.

"Hey, Kirin," he called, trotting toward her.

"Hey, Dr. Tucker"

"I wanted to tell you not to worry about *the curmudgeon*, Dr. Watkins. Somebody peed in his bran cereal this morning because he's been hostile to everybody. It wasn't you. You're always on target with your patients. The way you take charge of the room and handle it with ease, amazes me."

Flattered, she smiled and stuttered, "Well...thanks, I appreciate that."

"Another thing," he continued, "I saw Stacy in the cafeteria, and she tells me you're dating now. So, I wondered if I could take you to dinner some time. Are you busy Saturday?"

Going. To. Kill. Her.

Kirin's mind scrambled. Quick as lightning, she found her way out.

"I...I'd love to, but I can't. My boys were invited to a birthday party and I've already promised them we'd go. I'm sorry."

"Hey, no problem."

Dejected, he turned and walked back to his car. It was a true statement, but still, a pang of remorse hit her as she climbed into her car. He was a good doctor and a nice guy. She hated letting anyone down.

Starting her car, Kirin pulled out her phone to text something verbally abusive to her so-called friend Stacy, when she remembered the incoming text she'd received on the plane. The warning.

Kirin buckled the flowers into the passenger seat and drove straight to a cell phone store. The young, pimple-faced techie behind the counter said there wasn't a way to trace it back and no way to block incoming texts without knowing the number.

Her mind ran wild with scenarios. Not a good way to finish out the day. Yes, she was paranoid and yes, she'd seen too many silly movies, but she dumped the flowers in the first dumpster she came across on her way home. Could be a tracer in there; better to be safe than sorry. She kept the card though, just in case.

~*~

After dinner, homework and showers, the boys drifted off to sleep. Kirin settled into comfy pajamas and nestled in at her desk to catch up on emails. A new message dinged from her dad's attorney. He needed one more paper signed for her inheritance.

She read it. Then deleted it.

Sure, she was strapped, and God knew the house needed some serious work, but wouldn't accepting the money mean she forgave him? Well, she didn't. She was fine, thank you.

More than fine. She didn't need money from someone who didn't care enough about her to be a part of her life. Someone who'd left her a tattered and torn Marine Corps Field Manual to remember him by. He must've been crazy or demented if he thought this stupid book would help her to know him.

Kirin snatched the book out of the chair next to her bed, as if it was to blame. She'd thrown it there the night before when she'd unpacked from LA and it'd stared at her from the corner ever since. She opened it. On the third page in, below the ISBN information, she found a neatly scrolled note she hadn't noticed until now.

It read:

Kirin keep this book and yourself safe. I did this all for you and I hope that someday you can understand. Please find the truth inside these pages. I love you, princess,
Love, Dad

Princess.

Kirin stared at the page and choked back tears.

Her dad called her princess before her mom died. When had he written it? Years ago or recently? *Find the truth.* What truth? Why did these words seem so cryptic and even more troubling to her, why did she care?

"Okay, Princess, your turn."

Daddy called out while treading water in the deep end. Her knees trembled. Her pink painted toes curled protectively around the edge of the scratchy diving board.

"I can't!" she yelled down to him. "Daddy, I'm scared."

"I'm right here," he pleaded. "And I'll catch you. Just jump, honey."

"Do you promise you'll catch me, Daddy?"

"Always."

Wiping tears on the back of her sleeve, Kirin skimmed over the book until her eyelids grew too heavy. She fought to keep them open, searching each page for something, anything. Curling into bed, she pulled the covers over her and fell asleep with the lights on, clutching the book.

~*~

The rest of the week flew by in an absolute blur. She tried not to think about the two mobsters but could swear they followed her every move. She wished Sam would magically find her phone number and call. Every night before bed she spent skimming her dad's book, halfheartedly.

Saturday began with noise coming from the boys' room. She opened one eyeball. They'd bolted out of bed with a clatter remembering it was their buddy Sean's birthday party.

Kirin met Sean's mom, Sarah, right after Jack died. She exercised after work one day trying to pretend her world wasn't falling apart, and Sarah had smiled on the stationary bike next to her. That's all it took. They struck up a conversation and became fast friends. Sarah was in her early thirties. A sweet, round girl who never wore much makeup. She'd been kind and understanding, listening about Jack.

Sarah's son, Sean, turned five and Kirin promised she'd bring Little Jack and Will to the party. Sarah lived west, in a nicer upscale neighborhood where the houses all had brick mailboxes with tiny little lights on top, surrounded by flawless grass.

Her beautiful home and lawn made Kirin's farmhouse and pitiful excuse of a flower garden look homely.

She'd dressed Little Jack in a nice red polo shirt and tan cargo shorts with the bribery of cake and a treat bag. Will wore his usual Saturday outfit of head-to-toe second-hand Under Armor shorts and t-shirt. He snatched his basketball at the last second, 'in case the party was too babyish.'

Little Jack bounced in his seat, and Will stared as their car pulled up. Everything from the stylishly covered porch to the large oak tree in the lush front yard was draped in blue balloons and crepe paper. A huge blow-up slide was anchored on the tiny swatch of grass in the front of the house. At least fifteen screaming kids ran around it like bees on a beehive. Jack and Will took off the second they got themselves unstrapped from the car.

The boys were fearless like Jack. Well, on second thought, maybe like her after fighting the crazy man at the store.

She smiled as Sam's handsome face traveled across her mind. How she'd love to sit and have coffee and find out more about him. And get lost in his deep, green eyes.

A loud gasp snapped her back to the present.

It came from a woman only a foot away. Kirin followed the woman's gaze in time to witness her ten-year-old catch air as he flung himself and his little brother down the twenty-foot slide. They both laughed hysterically at the bottom. She pretended it didn't scare her.

Kirin grabbed the present out of the car and walked through Sarah's open door. She shuffled quietly into the front living room. Sarah's house was understated but had a classic elegance to it, like Sarah. Kirin was green with envy.

Creamy lamps were placed atop the beautifully handmade wood tables. Pale peach curtains danced from the breeze of the open windows. Every piece of furniture coordinated with the theme. The pictures looked as if they were painted for that room. Kirin knocked her shin on a chunky wood table as she gawked at the room.

Sarah trotted in carrying a towel. She squealed when she saw her friend as if they were in the third grade. "You're here!"

Sarah hadn't been this excited since Kirin agreed to take a belly dancing class with her at the gym.

"I have the *best* news!" she cried.

Sitting, Kirin grinned wide. Sarah had hinted a few weeks ago, they were trying for another baby.

Sarah's brow furrowed, puzzled. "You can't know this news," Sarah said, with her hands on her hips.

Apologetically, Kirin nodded, "Sorry, go ahead."

Sarah fell silent for a long minute wiping something sticky off her fingers as if trying to heighten the suspense and then smiled before tumbling into her well-planned monologue.

"I've found… the *perfect* man for you."

Kirin exhaled, "No—"

"Kirin, he's amazing!"

"Please, no—" Kirin begged, but got cut off again.

"Nope." Sarah said. "It's already set up. Next weekend. His name is Pat and y'all will meet at Downtown Grill and Brewery for a beer and dinner. He's hot. You're gonna fall for this one. He's a ranger with the TWRA. He has an amazing personality."

The Tennessee Wildlife Resources Agency guys always looked as if they'd jumped into a creek with all their clothes on. And they always had some stinky half-dead animal in the back. *Great.*

And 'amazing personality' was always code for homely.

But she knew Sarah well enough, there was no point resisting until she stopped talking. Kirin sat still, staring at her friend as Sarah rattled off the guy's resume like an auctioneer.

"He's funny…and oh, he's one of Tim's Private Wealth Management clients, which means he's loaded. He's tall with brown hair and a great smile. He's ruggedly cute. Yes, you're gonna thank me."

Kirin groaned. She was armed and ready to barrage Sarah with her host of reasons she didn't want to go on a blind date when her phone rang. It was Rosa.

She stared at the phone for a beat. Rosa calling her on a Saturday was odd. She hoped nothing was wrong. Kirin held up one finger and excused herself from Sarah, walking into the foyer.

"Hello?" she stammered.

"Kirin?" Rosa sounded out of breath and…different.

"What's wrong?"

"Uh, nothing," Rosa's voice sounded strained and unsure. Rosa continued, "Are you guys okay? Everything all right with you and the boys?"

"Of course," Kirin scratched her head, "We're at Sarah's house. It's little Sean's birthday. Where are you?" The noise on the other end of the phone sounded as if she stood in the middle of interstate during rush hour.

"Oh…ah, out shopping."

Now, that was a damn lie. Rosa hated shopping as much as Kirin did, but before she could call her on it, Rosa interrupted, "Kirin?"

"Yeah?"

"Be careful. I moved your book. It's where we keep our treats."

The line went dead.

"What the…" Kirin said aloud to nobody and raised her free hand in exasperation.

Something was wrong. Rosa had acted strange since she got back from LA. She was on edge. And she'd hidden the field manual in random spots. At first, Kirin thought she was losing her mind when it wouldn't be where she'd left it the day before. It hadn't dawned on her that Rosa moved it every day.

Rosa had to know something about this book and the mystery surrounding it. Maybe one of the black suits had approached her? But surely Rosa would've mentioned it. Kirin's belly twisted. If they were bold enough to walk up to Rosa, then they'd have no problem getting closer to her boys. She needed to corner Rosa and make her talk.

Her world was bordering on bizarre. From the anonymous text on the plane, to being chased inside the airport, and the delivery of the blood-red roses, she felt uneasy in her own skin. And now, with Rosa acting odd, Kirin felt threatened.

And scared.

~*~

Sarah's party for Sean went off exactly as planned. First the slide, then a water balloon toss, piñata, cake, and finally, treat bags. The boys said their thanks and goodbyes and ran for the car.

Little Jack scrambled in and buckled himself into his booster. Sarah must have thought Kirin needed a reminder about her embarrassing blind date. In front of several other women, she stepped out onto the porch and yelled across the front yard, "Don't forget.! Six o'clock, Friday. Your *new* man will meet you there!"

Kirin narrowed her eyes at her friend then stood and yelled across the top of her car, "Great." Sarah smiled broadly.

As Kirin opened her car door, a balloon from the party tied to the top of the slide popped. It sounded like a gunshot. All the young guests outside shrieked with shock and delight, while Kirin dove into her car like a stuntwoman.

Locking the doors and feeling like an idiot, she pulled out of Sarah's neighborhood and sped home to find answers.

Chapter Nine

Through the rearview mirror, Kirin smiled while Little Jack fought his heavy eyelids. Will's face was etched with concern. He peered out the window and commented several times how fast the trees zoomed past. It was naptime for her youngest and Kirin's skin crawled on high alert. Something in Rosa's voice spooked her. Her words were choppy and quick as if she'd seen a ghost.

As Kirin raced home, a blur of red in her rearview mirror caught her eye. She didn't even slow down. Sorry, Sam. No time to see if this was him. She was on a mission.

Kirin pulled into her long, tree-lined driveway as the red truck continued down the main road. She slipped into her garage and shut the doors tight. Ushering the boys inside, she activated the alarm system and laid Little Jack down for a nap. Will plopped onto her bed and started a movie but was out minutes later.

Trotting downstairs, she headed to the pantry to check for the book. Inside the tiny room the light attached to a motion sensor, engaged. The illumination flickered on as it warmed. The top shelf behind the vegetable cans hid an empty spot Rosa and Kirin used to hide treats and chocolate. The little scavengers had never found it. So far.

Raising up on her tiptoes, she reached behind the cans as her fingers touched the tattered binding of her father's book. Her hand slid from the book to something cold and hard. Steel.

A gun.

Rosa had stashed one of Jack's loaded guns in the pantry.

Kirin's hand recoiled as if she'd touched something hot. She stood with her mouth open, lost in her own questions.

Rosa hated guns. Why would she put it there?

What was so important about this stupid book that made her father's secretary afraid to hand it to her? Those strange men ogled her at the funeral as if they knew something she didn't. And why had they chased her at the airport? So aggressive for a public place. They must've wanted the book badly.

Or her.

Even as Kirin shook her head in confusion, she knew. In the pit of her stomach, she knew something lurked inside the book. Something others wanted.

Information "they" didn't want her to find and her father desperately wanted her to figure out. She'd already scanned the book halfheartedly but noticed nothing out of the ordinary. It appeared to be a regular old worn-out *Marine Corps Field Manual*. Determined to figure this out, she made coffee, sat down in her favorite yellow chair and meticulously searched each page.

She took her time. Reading every line on every page. And there, she noticed something strange. On one page, between the lines of the manual, she found a long string of neatly handprinted numbers: three numbers and a dot, three more numbers and a dot, one number and a dot, then three more numbers. She scribbled them in her notebook.

This sequence felt familiar, but she couldn't place it. It'd take digging to figure out what those numbers meant, but at least she'd found something. Then oddly enough, three random pages had been ripped out of the book. Page 43, 167, and 288 were missing. She read the text before and after the missing pages to determine if they had any significance but found nothing.

Also, toward the back of the book was a handwritten name. It'd been carefully inscribed between the lines to mimic the typesetting of the words above and below it. She'd missed it the first few times she'd read over the book.

Manfred Pitts.

Strange name, but it had to be a clue meant for her to find.

Both boys rustled awake, so she stashed the book under her chair with the notepad tucked inside. She promised herself she'd give it top priority later that night after the boys went to bed, but as luck would have it, like much in her life, it didn't work out that way. After the drama of the day, a carb-loaded dinner and impromptu root beer floats, she couldn't keep her eyelids open.

~*~

Sunday morning after church, Kirin grabbed a steaming coffee and the book and headed for the table to eat brunch with the boys. The warm morning sunlight poured in over their antique breakfast table.

While the boys gobbled eggs, she sipped her coffee and glanced out the back window toward the forest. In the distance, she noticed a doe at the edge of the woods connected to her backyard. The doe's fur was the color of honey. Young, graceful, and elegant. Carefree, she munched on grass, then popped her head up and froze. She stood stock still staring at something off into the distance. Kirin stiffened, anxious for her. After an entire minute of no movement, the doe must have finally willed herself to move. She turned and galloped back into the woods.

Maybe that's what she'd looked like when the crackhead guy came toward her in the parking lot, and Sam came to her rescue.

Sam. Why did he cross her mind more and more? And then it hit her. Sunday was shopping day! Oh, please let him be a creature of habit like her. She made a mental note to dress up for the store. Just in case.

~*~

Showered and dressed in the tenth outfit she tried on – her favorite jeans and a pink shirt, Kirin crept down the hall to check on the boys. They'd been eerily quiet for several minutes, which usually meant trouble. Leaving them alone was like leaving a lion in a cage full of chickens. There was bound to be feathers everywhere.

Kirin peeked around their door. Little Jack hummed while working on a superhero's puzzle, and Will had earbuds in with his nose stuck inside a Harry Potter book. Veggie Tales played on a CD in the background.

She backed out into the hallway to listen and froze in her tracks. A shuffling sound floated up from the kitchen. And *singing*.

Rosa was singing. That was something she'd never heard before.

Kirin snuck halfway down the stairs. Rosa's head was inside the fridge cleaning out leftovers with pink earbuds wrapped around her dark hair. Kirin called her name. She knew Rosa heard her, but the woman ignored everything and kept singing. Rosa was avoiding her and her questions.

Kirin had straightened her long hair, brushed her teeth, and added makeup for a chore she hated. Normally, Rosa would not only notice, but would have a snide comment.

Rosa glanced at her once but continued to ignore her while singing. It was odd. She'd never pass up poking fun at Kirin if given the chance. Kirin felt as if she stood inside some alternate universe.

Kirin stood like a statue leaning up against the counter, narrowed eyes, staring at Rosa from across the room until curiosity finally won.

Kirin stalked toward her like a big cat and stood right behind her until Rosa turned and screamed.

"Ahhh!" Rosa pulled the headphones down to her neck and glared at Kirin, who grinned widely.

"What?" she yelled, grabbing her heart. "Are you trying to give me a heart attack?"

"No" Kirin answered softly, "I need answers." Kirin didn't move out of her way when Rosa tried to sidestep her.

"Your list is right there on the counter," Rosa pointed to the list with the hand that wasn't holding her heart.

"You know that's not what I want."

Rosa held Kirin's gaze and narrowed her eyes as if trying to decide how much to say. After a deep breath, she cleared her throat, and picked up a jar and spoke. "Oh, I got spooked. I ran back by the house because I'd forgotten my sweater and you left the backdoor open. I knew you weren't here, but I thought I heard footsteps upstairs." She fiddled with the jar, stalling. "I grabbed a gun from the panic room, hid it in the pantry and ended up leaving it on the shelf. The noise turned out to be the wind hitting the heavy curtain in the boys' room because their window was cracked open."

Rosa flashed a quick, albeit fake smile then spun around Kirin, carrying the jar.

This wasn't the truth. The way she'd told the story, rattling it out, way too fast. And her tone was sweeter than McDonald's sweet tea.

There had to be more to it, so Kirin pressed on.

"And the book?" she demanded. "Why does it keep moving from room to room?"

Rosa searched Kirin's eyes for a second and then laughed.

"I must be cleaning up and carrying it around, sorry about that. I *know* how much that book must mean to you since it was the only thing your father left you."

Rosa waited, no doubt for a show of remorse over not cherishing the book, but none came. A quick spark of anger crossed Kirin's mind. Who was she to make her feel guilty?

Although, she had to admit to a fleeting pang of guilt. Yes, it meant so much to her she'd barely picked it up and flung it off her bed several nights, treating it like a pair of dirty, old socks. Remembering the gut twisting feeling of not being wanted her entire life, that small shred of guilt vanished.

Rosa stared at Kirin with a serious face. Kirin stared right back then shoved her misplaced anger in her pocket. Something was off. She shook her head, grabbed her keys, purse, and the grocery list and headed out the door without another word.

Rosa followed into the garage and shut Kirin's door. She handed the stack of neatly folded reusable bags through the open car window. Rosa hesitated, as if she wanted to say something else, but finally resigned herself to one ominous warning.

"Be careful."

"Always am." Kirin replied.

Rosa shot her a look of disbelief and Kirin laughed.

As she drove in silence to the store, questions pinged in her mind. Why did it feel as if Rosa knew something she wasn't telling? What was she holding back and why?

She was damn sure going to find out.

Chapter Ten

Kirin drove toward the store like a Nascar driver. She winced and slowed when her tires squealed taking a corner too fast. Butterflies danced in her stomach. Giddy as a fifth grader with a crush, she parked and stepped out of her car. Nervous energy hummed in her veins as she walked toward the store. Concentrating on the pavement, she wracked her brain to think of something witty to say should the opportunity present itself. It was then something caught her eye, and she raised her head.

Sam stood by his truck a few paces away, leaning on it casually as if he was waiting for a parade. Jeans, boots, and a dark green polo that brought out the green flecks in his eyes.

"Hello stranger," he teased in a chipper voice.

Kirin smiled too broadly. She had to rein it back in. It was as if they'd planned a meeting. Sam fell easily into step with her, shoulders touching.

Kirin's smile, embarrassingly, crept out ear to ear. She didn't care. He looked genuinely as happy to see her as she was to see him.

"Do you always stalk women going into the store?"

"Only women who try to kill me with tomatoes."

For a moment, she was helpless and lost in his rugged good looks and kind eyes, until she walked smack into a taller woman coming out of the store. The angry woman mumbled something inaudible. Kirin's face flushed warm. Sam laughed and grabbed two carts.

Over the next several aisles, Kirin struggled with focusing on Rosa's list. Something about Sam took her mind and twisted it until she couldn't remember what she was supposed to do. She placed food in her cart, not caring if she grabbed what was on the list. Rosa would think she'd lost her mind. But the more they talked, the more she was attracted to him. And she didn't want that to stop.

Kirin crouched down in the frozen food case to pick out some veggies from her list. Sensing his eyes on her, she turned her head toward him. Sam stood still, watching her. Slowly, she stood back up.

"Problem?" her tone was lighthearted and playful, with her hands fisted on her hips.

"You keep getting prettier every time I see you."

"But you've only seen me once before today." She pointed out, raising an eyebrow.

"No. More than that. I just hadn't spoken until you tried to kill me."

Kirin glared at him, but a tingle fluttered in her chest. He'd noticed her.

Sam pushed his cart forward. He shook his head as if he argued with himself then stopped a few feet ahead and waited. He turned back toward her.

"You comin'?"

She nodded, pushing her cart alongside his as they continued shopping. The girlfriend or ex-girlfriend must've been conflicting him. She hoped for ex, but either way she wasn't a homewrecker. She'd have to play more aloof. Then again, he didn't seem like one to cheat.

Kirin's mind wandered over the next few aisles as they chatted about schools they attended, friends, and kids. Every time she'd try to get information about his past, he'd turn the conversation back to her. She managed a few gems. He'd never been married, no kids, and liked animals, but honestly, at that point in the conversation, she'd been too busy trying to stay neutral and yet getting lost in his face. Nothing was sinking in.

~*~

He'd flirted and she'd laughed as they walked toward the checkout. What the hell was he doing? Everything about this felt wrong and right at the same time. His heart and other body parts seemed to be leading his mind. He'd have to shut that part down quick.

He'd never been this invested in a target before. Never gotten to know anyone on a personal level. He heard himself asking about her family and friends like he stood outside his body and watched. He'd been doing this kind of work way too long to make such rookie mistakes.

He blamed Sonny. Meddling old fart.

Part of him didn't want the evening to end. In the checkout line, her cart was lined up in front of his. She stared at the magazines, wringing her hands and biting her lip. She was cooking something up in that brain of hers. *Oh, God.* If she asked him on a date, what could he say? His heart said hell yeah, but his brain pinged more warnings. He hadn't planned for this and damnit he was a planner.

Sam scrubbed his face. He needed a diversion. Grabbing the first thing he saw, a Hershey's bar, he tossed it into her cart, and it landed with a hard thud. She turned and narrowed her eyes. One pretty eyebrow shot up as a mischievous grin unfurled.

The chocolate bar teetered on top of a box of mac and cheese. The next thing he knew, she grabbed up big handfuls of candy bars and barraged his cart with them. Sam stood open-mouthed for half a second before grabbing them up, just as fast, and tossing them back into her cart. All the while, people around them stared. They were in the throes of a juvenile full-scale bar war. He felt like a kid. And it felt amazing and foolish at the same time.

Finally, they called a truce. Both leaned over to empty all the candy out of their carts. Sam cleaned his quick, then leaned into her cart at the same time she did to help. Her blonde hair spilled down past her shoulders and smelled like sweet juicy apples. Her smooth face and pink lips hung dangerously close to his. The electricity of having her mouth so close to his made him hold his breath. They stilled at the same time. She stared at his mouth.

This wasn't the first time a target was attracted to him. He knew how to be detached and aloof, he'd done that gig his whole life. But how the hell do you turn it off when you feel it too? This was a first.

Sam willed himself to snap out of it. He turned on his acting as he whispered, "They're staring at us." A grin spread wide across his face.

She wanted him to kiss her. He knew that slow flutter of the lashes and half open mouth look—he'd seen it many times before. But this time…he wouldn't have minded it. Not at all. And that shocked the crap out of him.

Kirin blurted out, "Wanna go for coffee sometime this week?"

His eyebrows wiggled in amusement. She looked shocked at her own words. He stepped back, and involuntarily smiled at her eagerness. Before his brain could say no, his lips defied him. "I'd love to."

~*~

Kirin volleyed back a grin, trying to remind her feet to move ahead in line. She'd had an epic loss of coolness and chided herself for sounding so desperate. After they'd both checked out and loaded groceries into their cars, they met back at the cart return.

Her palms sweated and her knees wobbled as she walked toward him, biting her lower lip. It was the way he looked at her. And the way they'd made an instant connection.

Sam handed her a strip of paper and pen to write her number down. As she wrote, he stood close enough that their shoulders touched. He didn't offer his number, nor did he promise to call. Handing it back to him, he held on to her hand and the paper for a moment, leaned in and whispered, "See you around, Kirin."

"I hope so," she replied, turning to walk back to her car, she smiled to herself.

Still mentally doing backflips as she buckled her seatbelt, her phone buzzed. A blocked number.

Leave the book by the cart return.

A chill ran down her spine. She'd gotten so wrapped up in Sam, she'd forgotten the dark suited men were still out there. She didn't have the book. It was at home. Safe. Kirin locked her doors. She wrote back.

Wrong number.

The text bounced back as not delivered. Kirin looked over where Sam's truck had been. He was gone. She drove home with her head on a swivel, looking for anyone following her, but found none.

Once home, Rosa still acted odd. Headphones still in, she sang and rearranged coats in the closet. Kirin went inside and put the groceries away. She ran upstairs to check on the boys who played a noisy game of tag in the playroom. Kirin got pulled into the action and chased them until they giggled in a pile on the floor.

Rosa yelled her goodbye from the bottom of the stairs, and the door clicked behind her. Smart woman. She snuck out before Kirin could ask more questions or get any answers.

Kirin trotted downstairs to start dinner, still happy from her encounter with Sam when a tuft of gray hair peeked through her screened back door. Three knocks. Kirin smiled. Arthur would never enter, even after all these years, without knocking and wouldn't dare come in without permission.

"Come in," she sang.

As he opened the door, his old black lab curled up on the bottom step, waiting patiently for the scraps from the table he knew would come.

Arthur's Sunday overalls had a freshly ironed crease down the front of his legs. Slowly he placed his red cap on the counter as he juggled two ripe cantaloupes in his free hand. Kirin wiped her hands and relieved him of one. He smiled back, grateful. She placed it on the counter then looked down and noticed his fingers.

Without thinking, she said out loud, "Your hands are dirt stained."

As soon as the words flew out, she winced and slapped a hand over her big fat mouth. *Damnit, Kirin.*

In an instant, two little boys were at Arthur's side, inspecting his hands and looking up at him, demanding an explanation. Kirin shot Arthur a look of apology.

"Now, boys," he raised his hands in surrender. "I've only been tillin.' I might have planted a few new herbs, but y'all don't like to plant those anyway."

Arthur touched the top of Will's head. "My instincts tell me our cold nights aren't finished with us yet. The big planting will probably come next weekend. And I'll need two strong boys to help me then."

Will smiled, and Little Jack squeezed Arthur's leg. Will took off like a shot racing his brother back to the dining room to finish a puzzle.

Slowly and with a grunt, Arthur sat, wrapping his legs around the bottom of the barstool.

"Ms. Lane, how are we today?"

"We're good. How's your arm?"

As if on cue, he rubbed his left arm. "Couldn't complain, ma'am, nobody to listen and don't do me no good anyways." He smiled wide. The deep lines on his tanned face curved together in unison.

"Ms. Lane," he began again, "did you know every spring a new family of fawns is born at the edge of the forest? A mama doe was there this morning, but something spooked her."

"I saw her, too." Kirin grinned at him as she peeled potatoes.

"New beginnings, Ms. Lane, that's what Spring is all about. But you gotta be wary for the danger. That doe could sense it. I think we could learn a lot from animals. People gotta learn to slow down and use their instincts to see the danger."

Arthur always had the best advice as if he somehow knew what was about to happen. *New beginnings.* As usual, he was right. This spring was about new beginnings for her. But she also felt the danger on the horizon. She'd remember his words and use her instincts.

Arthur interrupted her thoughts. "Ms. Lane, can I help you do anything? You're always a feedin' me."

Same question every week. Same answer.

"Nope. Who else would teach my boys about farming and living off the land? It's the least I can do, and besides, we enjoy your visits."

Kirin dished up spicy grilled pork chops, garden green beans with ham bits, potatoes, and a salad. Big glasses of chocolate milk gleamed on the table, producing smiles on two little boys' faces. She'd have to buy a cow from Arthur soon or go broke. The boys liked their milk. Bribing them with the chocolate variety was the best way to get them to eat the salad.

Aunt Kathy and Uncle Dean had used bribery to get her to eat during her non-eating phase, right after her mama died. Aunt Kathy reminded her so much of her mom. Same red hair and infectious laugh. Although it'd taken her aunt a long time to laugh again after her mama died.

Little Jack's squeal of delight brought her back as he and Arthur played a game to see who could stuff the most green beans in their mouth at once. Mature, big brother Will shook his head and shot her a look as if to say, "look at those kids."

Arthur swallowed his mouthful and spoke as Kirin picked up empty plates and carried them to the sink.

"How you doin' on beef, Ms. Lane?"

Kirin thought for a second as she placed a plate in the dishwasher. She answered, "Fine, I think. The freezer's still pretty full and I've only used a few of the roasts."

"When you run low, you let me know. I've got two freezers full."

"But this time," she said pointing at him, "you have to let me pay."

"No, ma'am." Arthur rose to refill his coffee cup. "I made a promise. Besides, Jack helped me too." His voice trailed off as he concentrated on the dark liquid falling into his cup.

Jack had been there for Arthur when his wife passed. He'd sat with him through the sadness, then anger and even a few embarrassing drunken nights. He'd helped him work through pain, putting up new fencing to busy his mind and hiring men to fix the angry holes he'd made in the barn.

Kirin smiled lightly. She knew that pain. Like Jack's death, Arthur's wife's had been expected, but it didn't make it any easier to accept. Death was death no matter if it was expected or a jolt. She learned that lesson from not only losing Jack, but her mama too.

Every day she longed for answers about her mama's death. Her Aunt Kathy was locked like a vault. Her mama's sister didn't smile again until Will was born. Who could blame her? She'd lost her only sister and gained an angry eight-year-old in the shuffle.

Her aunt and uncle doted on Will and Little Jack. Which reminded her to text them to ask them to keep the boys Saturday night for her blind date.

Ugh! Blind date?

Kirin gripped the sink. *Crap.* She'd completely forgotten. A wave of panic roiled in her stomach as her face flushed. Arthur stood then stepped toward her as Will jumped up and ran to her.

"Mom, you okay?"

"Oh, I'm fine honey, I just got dizzy."

Her little man of the house hugged her.

Why had she agreed to this? Damn peer pressure and her inability to say no, that's why. Her head already spun with wanting to meet up with Sam somewhere other than the grocery store. She needed no second man in this already ridiculous situation. It was reckless to worry about dates and handsome men in grocery stores when clearly someone was after her family.

She'd worry about the date later.

First, she had a true late-night date with some caffeine and a dog-eared *Marine Corps Field Manual*.

Chapter Eleven

After dessert, Arthur asked again if he needed to stay and help, but as usual, she refused. He bid them farewell and walked back across the backyard to his house.

Kirin put Little Jack in a bubble tub and Will into the shower. Little Jack's devilish smile almost made up for the fact he'd soaked the bathroom floor. After prayers, both boys fell fast asleep. Kirin trotted downstairs to retrieve her hot honey-tea. She knew what lay ahead of her, to scour the rest of the book.

She had to discover if there were any other clues.

As she grabbed it from its new spot on top of the fridge, a note from Rosa caught her eye. Her dad's attorney called again, and Rosa promised him Kirin would return the call the next day. Kirin snatched the number off the fridge, crumpled it, and jammed it into the top of her purse.

Something else she didn't want to deal with right now.

Curled up in her yellow comfortable reading chair she set her steaming cup of hot tea on the table and opened the old book.

"Guidebook for Marines." The green camo cover wore a black crinkle down the center. It looked as if it spent time in several wars and won none. Her dad had called it the "Green Monster" back when she was young. The spine of the book was badly worn, unreadable, and coming apart.

The first time she'd dove into it, she found three pages missing; page #43, a section about the history of the Marine Corps, page #288, adjusting the site on a rifle, and page #167, which looked to be the beginning of the chapter on sanitation and hygiene.

History, guns, and hygiene. The life of a marine recruit, she guessed. But did they tie together to mean something?

As Kirin flipped through the pages and read more about a marine recruit than she ever wanted to know, she froze on a page with her father's handwriting. He'd had been a lefty but the nuns in Catholic school back then considered left handwriting wrong. So, he learned early on to write with both hands. It showed in his cryptic writing slanted slightly to the left. In his later years, he'd sent her birthday cards with nothing written inside except, "Love, Dad." And as he got older, she'd had a harder time deciphering those words.

This was written neatly in black ink between the lines, and it read, "Manfred Pitts, Savannah Georgia." A great clue. Manfred Pitts might have been a friend of his. Or he could be someone she shouldn't trust. Holy hell, why was this so hard? Couldn't he have simply told her what to do?

Oh right, that'd mean he would've had to speak to her.

Kirin could remember none of his friends' names from when she was little. She wrote the name down in her notebook with a question mark.

He might have had nothing better to write on, but something about the careful script told her he meant for the name to stay hidden. Lost in thought, Kirin ambled to the main family computer sitting atop their antique secretary. Her plan was to google the name and discover what she could. At the exact second her finger hit the power button, her house phone rang. Kirin yelped like a bee stung her. Nobody called her house this late. Her hands trembled as she answered the phone.

"Hello?"

Silence.

"Hello?"

She hung up and checked the kitchen clock. Five after eleven. Her hands shook even more. She tried to navigate Google but couldn't focus. She stuffed the book and notebook in her purse and powered down the computer. The empty phone call had rattled her more than she wanted to admit, but it was time to fall into bed and start again tomorrow. It took over a half hour to settle her mind enough to fall asleep.

The following week went by way too fast. Between listening to Stacy and Laura's theories about her upcoming blind date, helping babies come into the world, and Rosa avoiding her questions like the plague, Kirin's days ran together.

When Friday arrived, she hurried through the day dreading when she'd walk through the restaurant door and meet her blind date. Sarah hadn't given her much to go on, his name was Pat and he was a client/friend of Sarah's husband, Tim.

Tim was Pat's investment banker and occasional golf buddy. According to Sarah, Pat had kind eyes and a great smile. Tim told her Pat was hard working, well off, and loyal. *Loyal.* That's how they'd described him. Stacy read this to mean something entirely different. She'd said it meant he wore a mullet and had jacked-up teeth.

Kirin dropped the boys off at Aunt Kathy and Uncle Dean's. Uncle Dean was a robust and hairy man with a great sense of humor and a wicked prankster mind. He could short sheet a bed while you were in the bathroom brushing your teeth.

Years of living under the same roof taught her to always check the kitchen faucet for rubber bands *before* turning on the water and to always spin the hard-boiled eggs before cracking them. She'd learned both these lessons the hard way.

She knew she was in trouble when her aunt and uncle ran out to meet them and Uncle Dean wore a Darth Vader mask and cape with his lightsaber drawn. Both boys squealed with delight and barely kissed Kirin goodbye. By the look of mischief on her uncle's face and the way he whispered conspiratorially to Will, she was in trouble. She shot her uncle a disapproving look and he responded with a guilty smile.

Kirin flew home, showered, shaved, and tried on everything in her closet. This outfit was too tight, that one revealed too much, this tight shirt sent the wrong message. Ugh. If she didn't leave in the next five minutes, she'd be late.

Hair and makeup done, she settled on a white, knee-length skirt and baby blue scoop neck top, along with some slightly uncomfortable but cute wedge heels. She ran downstairs, grabbed her purse and keys and stared at the book lying on the table, taunting her.

The Green Monster. She glared at it, then threw it into her purse and ran out the door.

Chapter Twelve

The college town of Knoxville boasted a recently renovated downtown area, which turned electric at sundown. The sun's orange glow shimmered off tall glass buildings as the city bustled. Young urban couples were refurbishing old abandoned lofts above the eclectic stores. Downtown came alive with the dogwoods in the spring and the first shot of warm air brought out most of the city dwellers, crowding the streets.

The day was a mild seventy degrees. As Kirin found a place to park, nerves wracked her body. She wanted this date to be over. She'd much rather be strolling toward a date with Sam, but he'd never called. Maybe he only took her number to be kind. That thought hurt her heart more than it should have.

The place Sarah chose for them to meet was a popular hotspot. A mahogany, rectangular-shaped bar anchored the middle of the restaurant. Beautiful wood floors surrounded it, and the whole place smelled like a thick, juicy steak. Sarah had mentioned several times the restaurant vibe was casual and not stuffy. The food was rumored to be outstanding.

Kirin backed into a parking spot inside the parking garage, shut off her car, and stifled the urge to check her teeth in the mirror. She'd glanced over as she put the car in park and noticed a man sitting alone in the car next to her. A few feet beyond his car, she spotted a group of young women walking together. She'd step in with them to get to the restaurant, so she wouldn't have to go alone.

The restaurant was a short jaunt from the parking garage. Her heart pounded as she rounded the corner and the sign came into view. She could feel nervous sweat mist her temples. Kirin squared her shoulders, pulled open the heavy wood door and walked straight to the hostess station, not looking at anyone. The perky hostess scanned the list for his name. Why didn't she think to get his last name? The hostess had no one on her list named Pat.

It was okay. After all, she was five minutes early. She added her name to the list then sat on a long bench in front of a giant window overlooking Gay Street. Couples passed by headed for the movies or dinner, holding hands. It made her long for Sam. How she wished she'd asked for his number. Why hadn't he called? Maybe the imaginary ex-girlfriend was back.

She people watched, bounced her knee and picked at her fingernails until she spotted a clock. He was now twenty minutes late.

Just then, a handsome man walked in carrying a Mast General Store package. She sat up straighter. Until his family of four ran up and embraced him before being called to their table. Kirin exhaled.

She stood to stretch her legs and craned her neck to look around the bar. Had they seated him and not told her? Hell, she couldn't even look for him because all she had was a vague description and his first name. A new hostess strolled up. Kirin asked if she'd seen a man seated who looked as if he waited for someone. The young woman halfheartedly looked around and replied no.

Kirin headed to the bathroom to check out the tables herself. No one was obviously dining alone, so she trotted into the bathroom, washed her clammy hands then walked back out. She touched her watch and it lit up in the dark hallway. He was now twenty-five minutes late.

She needed a drink. She walked back toward the front of the restaurant and slid onto a stool toward one end of the bar. Seats on either side of her were empty.

Several people chatted near her while two senior citizens squinted as if the dim lighting bothered them. At the other end of the bar sat a tanned man, wearing a bright button-down with sunglass circles on his face. He knocked back the second of two shots as if he'd lost his best friend. He looked like a car salesman. Three college soccer fans yelled at a nearby TV screen and downed beers, slapping each other on the back.

When the bartender noticed her, he shot her a genuine smile. "Finally, a pretty single lady at the bar; what can I get you, darling?"

Thanks to his loudness, all four of the men looked over at her, checking her out. Great, now she looked desperate.

"Can I have a Jack and Dr. Pepper, please?"

"Coming right up," he replied, flitting off to the other side of the bar. Kirin looked around the bar hoping to spot her date. She sent a text to Sarah, letting her know it'd been thirty minutes and the guy still hadn't shown up.

Mr. Bartender served her drink singing a Boyz II Men song piped in on the Muzac channel from the back of the restaurant. Kirin sipped the drink slowly. A tingle of anger took over, and she gulped it down instead. Checking her phone, it'd been thirty-five minutes. Sarah hadn't texted her back either.

She ordered another one. Maybe this guy walked in, took one look at her, and walked back out. After downing the second Jack and Dr. Pepper, Kirin chatted happily with the other barflies, striking up conversations with them and waving off the hostess when she told Kirin her table was ready.

The suited man at the other side of the bar raised eyebrows at her. She shook her head and took another sip. He was handsome for a middle-aged man, but very much not her type. After examining Kirin as she downed her two drinks, he sidled up with several cheesy pickup lines.

"What is a pretty young thing like you doing all alone?"

She couldn't help but laugh. Loud. She assured him that being a widow at almost-forty with two little kids made her the most un-datable person at the bar. She processed too late, he probably didn't want to date her. He only liked the way she looked in her skirt. She scoffed at the idea.

Her aunt and uncle made it perfectly clear with several not-so-subtle hints, they'd be keeping the boys most of tomorrow and hoped they wouldn't see her until late afternoon, if she happened to bring someone home.

What an absurd thought.

Hell, she couldn't even get a blind date to show up!

As Mr. Tanned Skin skulked back to the other side of the bar, Kirin ordered a beer to chase the liquors that'd made her light-headed and giggly. Somewhere in her inebriated mind, this sounded like a good idea.

She rose to situate her skirt. The room spun. Flopping back down, she thought an Uber wouldn't be a bad idea. It was only seven-thirty, and she was snockered. She barely registered it when a man sat down on the stool right next to her.

"Whatcha doin' all alone, tomato girl?"

She knew that voice. Kirin spun around to find Sam, grinning with kind eyes.

She couldn't have halted the face-splitting grin if she'd tried. She had to stop herself from throwing her arms around him and drunk-hugging him.

"Hey!" she cried. Even in her own head, her voice sounded too eager. She cleared her throat, trying not to seem so smashed but failing miserably. She followed his line of sight as he glanced at the empty glasses. His brows furrowed, and his tone was tight. "Having fun?"

She stammered, "Um, no. My blind date apparently …" She looked everywhere but into his eyes. "I guess he didn't like what he saw … and left."

Stating that aloud pushed her to the edge of tears. She swiveled away from him on her stool to collect herself and stared out into the restaurant. Two familiar-looking silhouettes sat partially in shadow across the restaurant. She couldn't be sure, looking through her alcohol goggles, but she'd swear it was Scar and Babyface.

Fuzzy brained, she ignored this for the moment and pushed down the anger boiling inside. Sam placed warm hands on her shoulders and spun her body back around. She couldn't look at him.

He pulled her chin up with one gentle finger and spoke. "Not a chance. He probably took one look and assumed correctly that he didn't deserve you, so he took his sorry ass back to the house."

She smiled at his kind words then swiped unfallen tears from her eyes.

They talked at the bar while she drank hot coffee. Sam nodded to the bartender and laid down a huge wad of cash to pay for her drinks. Kirin protested, fumbling through her wallet to pay but Sam grasped her hand and headed toward the door.

As she pulled her sweater from the back of her barstool, she searched for Scar and Babyface. They'd vanished. As Sam led her outside. Too much alcohol mixed with the cool night air and his warm hand wrapped around hers, made a chill run up her spine. When she shivered, he pulled her closer to him as they walked. She blamed her stumbling on some lame excuse about her shoes being too high.

"But you're not short, right?" His green eyes twinkled as he cut them toward hers.

"Nope. We don't wear them to seem taller."

He slid her a look.

"We don't! When a woman wants to look nice, she wears heels. My friend Stacy is 5'10" and she wears them." Kirin pushed her chin upwards. She could argue with the best of them, and except for her giggling and stumbling every few feet, it would have been nice to walk downtown, hand in hand with Sam.

Finally, they arrived at the parking garage and walked up the two flights to her car. Sam turned, held out his hand and demanded, "Key."

Kirin stopped short, dropped his hand and defensively replied, "I was gonna call an Uber."

Sam reached down and grabbed her hand once again. "How about I drive you home, and then I'll Uber back to my truck?"

Kirin protested, but she could tell by the grip he had on her hand, he wasn't letting go. She had to admit his warm hand and spicy manly smell were more than enough to convince her. She pulled her keys out and handed them over with a scoff.

Sam opened her door and placed her in the front seat. As he walked around the front of the car to the driver's side, she leaned back in the seat. Kirin closed her eyes and cursed herself for drinking so much while begging the vehicle to stop spinning.

He climbed into the driver's side, pulled the seat back to allow for his much longer legs and leaned over her, gently pulling the seatbelt across her lap and buckling her in. Eyes still closed, she muttered, "Thank you." She could feel his breath on her face. She held hers, still not opening her eyes. He kissed her cheek and started the car.

Kirin was a lousy drunk. She didn't remember the car ride home. She didn't even remember telling him where she lived or pulling up to the driveway. The first thing she remembered after the kiss was Sam taking her seat belt off and guiding her from the car to the porch. His strong arms around her waist. Inebriated, Kirin talked aimlessly, giggled, or fell dead asleep. Lousy drunk.

Much to her own amusement, she told Sam the correct key to open the door was the "silver one." After her short giggle fit, they finally made it inside.

God love him. He carried her, her shoes, her purse, and sweater along with her bundle of keys, all through the door. Once inside, she stumbled toward the kitchen bragging she could whip something up for him to eat. As she tripped over a toy of Little Jack's, she almost took a header right into the stove. Sam caught her, assuring her he wasn't hungry. He picked her up as if she were light as air and carried her toward the stairs.

Kirin wrapped her arms around Sam's neck and told him in a loud drunk whisper he was not only handsome, but he had the best smelling shirts of anyone she'd ever met. Kirin dropped her head on his shoulder and took in a big whiff of his clean fresh shirt and then promptly passed out.

The last thing she remembered was more like a dream and it was his hearty laugh and then another kiss on her cheek.

Chapter Thirteen

When she woke, the world was too bright. Kirin's head pounded and her teeth felt like they had socks over them. Her thoughts ran through the events of the night before: sitting at the bar, waiting for hours, and feeling dejected. And Sam rescuing her once again.

Sam. He'd put her to bed.

Immediately she sat up. Her face burned hot. With one eye squeezed shut and dreading what she saw, Kirin glanced down. Luckily, her shoes were the only thing on the floor.

Whew. Breathe. He'd only covered her up. She cringed. How pathetic she must've looked waiting in a bar for a blind date and drunk off her gourd. She made a mental promise to *never* drink that much, ever. And to apologize profusely if she ever saw him again. Even more disturbing to Kirin was the guy she was supposed to meet didn't even bother to call.

Who does that? Who lets a fragile widow be stood up? Okay, so she wasn't fragile, but *he* didn't know that! The more she thought about it, the angrier she got.

Until she smelled eggs.

Momentarily frozen she strained, desperate to hear some shred of evidence of who might be downstairs. Rosa wouldn't be there, and she hated eggs. Rosa would rather go on a three day shopping trip than cook for Kirin after a night of drinking. Instead, she'd fully enjoy cranking up the TV and the radio and fry smelly fish to teach the drunk a lesson.

Kirin tiptoed down the hall and crouched at the top of the stairs. She peered into the kitchen. A man stood at the stove, cooking eggs. She slunk back when Sam turned to grab butter from the counter. Kirin rose without a sound and snuck back into her room.

He stayed. Sam stayed. She clapped her hands silently and grinned ear to ear.

She tiptoed to the bathroom and about fainted when she saw her reflection.

My God. She looked like she felt, which was scary. With quick movements, she changed her clothes, washed her face, brushed her teeth and hair and rubbed some nice smelling apple lotion on her neck. Kirin's head throbbed, but she didn't care. She was half-mortified and half-giddy.

Breathe. Time to face the music and head downstairs. As she rounded the bottom of the steps, there he stood, smiling as if she was the most beautiful person in the world. Kirin shot him a shy smile, mouthed, "Sorry," and bolted past him.

"What for?" he crooned, following her into the kitchen. He stopped and straddled a barstool. Why did he have to look perfect? Fawn-colored hair tousled and sexy. Just-slept-in wrinkled jeans slung low with no shoes on. He looked as if he belonged in a Gap ad, not her kitchen. She had her back to him, facing the coffee pot. It was so much easier than looking him in the eye.

"For being a drunken basket case that you had to babysit all night," she said over her shoulder.

Kirin poured two cups of the fresh coffee he'd made and sat down at the island pushing a cup toward him. She stared into her coffee.

"I didn't mind it," he whispered.

Kirin glanced up at him. His eyes locked on hers. He smiled, then shifted his eyes toward the back window and out into the forest. His demeanor changed from jovial to serious in a flash. Kirin turned to see what he saw. She only saw her woods.

"So," she turned back and narrowed a playful look at him, "Exactly, how did you figure out where I live?" Before he could answer she blurted out, "And I know I was too drunk to tell you!"

He studied her for a moment then replied, "Your GPS has a home setting. I pressed it and hoped for the best."

Sam jumped up from his chair while still talking and dished them both up a huge plate of eggs and toast. Kirin was grateful for the food since she'd drank her dinner the night before. As they ate, her questions continued. "How did you know I was at the restaurant?"

He took a huge bite and chewed slow before answering. "I was downtown and thought I'd grab a beer, then I spotted you."

She chewed for a moment, then asked, "How'd you figure out the alarm code?"

"You told me that one, Kirin." He smiled.

Oh. She could accept that. She'd probably blurted it out. Kirin wondered what else she'd jabbered on about.

Smirking like he had her at this point in the conversation, he added, "You told me a bunch about yourself last night." The corners of his mouth turned up while he took a sip of his coffee.

Oh, *Lord*. Her face flushed. Her biggest fear was to overshare. She knew she got overly chatty when she drank. Laura and Stacy chided her about spilling all secrets after a few beers on their girls' night outings.

Kirin kept her eyes locked on her plate, trying to remain cool. She took a deep breath. "Oh yeah? What did I say?"

He took another sip. "Let's see … you told me about your parents, how your mom died, and your dad left. You talked about your boys, Little Jack and Will, and about the creepy black-suited men in the bar, your father's book, oh, and something about wanting to go out with me."

At this last part, he broke into a full-blown smile.

"I did not say that!" Kirin squealed looking up from her plate. He smiled and shook his head, locking eyes once again.

"You got me. I actually asked you."

"Really?" Was all she could say. After seeing her at her worst and saving her in a parking lot and a bar, she couldn't believe someone would still want to date her. Especially this handsome man. God, she could fall for this guy.

Smiling, she corrected him, "I don't exactly remember doing *all* of the talking."

He looked down and shook his head. Yep, he'd finally spilled a few details about himself while she stared at his beautiful face and forced herself to breathe while sobering up at the bar.

He'd never been married. Grew up in Colorado but moved to LA when he was seventeen. Both parents were gone, but he had one brother, Seth, who lived with his wife and babies in Illinois. His face scrunched up and turned serious when he mentioned his little brother She got the feeling there was some strife there.

From what she'd gathered he enjoyed anything if it was outside, like camping, hunting, baseball, and running. He had moved from city to city for his job, but he never mentioned what job sent him on these assignments.

As they finished their breakfast, sitting close together on the corner of the bar, their conversation turned quiet. Kirin stopped eating and stared at him until he noticed.

"What?"

"Thank you for saving me … again," she whispered while keeping his gaze.

He smiled and placed his warm hand over hers, closing in for a small kiss. Her phone, sitting on the counter, buzzed and ruined it. Stacy wanting the juicy details to her blind date way too early.

Kirin scooped up the phone and put it on silent. Sam stood and grabbed a dish towel. Kirin gathered dishes and put them in the sink. A small war ensued. They chased each other around the kitchen with wet dish towels, snapping them at each other.

Why did he bring out the kid in her?

After they cleaned up, she drove him back to get his truck. When they arrived, Sam leaned over and kissed her cheek. He held her stare and asked, "Wanna meet for lunch Monday? There's a little sandwich shop downtown I've been dying to try. Leroy's?"

"Sure," Kirin nodded, beaming and ignoring her loud heartbeat.

Finally, a real date with Sam.

Now, let's hope this one didn't stand her up.

Chapter Fourteen

At the red light, Sam scrubbed his face. He knew better. Staying over at a target's house wasn't something new. But this was more than obligation and he knew it. He'd grown fond of this one. The headstrong way she tackled any problem. And her uncanny ability to fall face first into trouble. But this was reckless. Unchartered territory. Every step in this chess game he played, needed to be carefully thought out and executed. And yet, he found himself flying by the seat of his pants with this woman.

The old Sam would've taken her home, made sure she was safe, retrieved the item he was sent for and vanished. Not stay, make her breakfast and kiss her. He was a damn fool. But, that was the real problem. He couldn't vanish. And even worse, he didn't want to.

And that was the scariest part of it all. He'd always had the perfect excuse to keep his heart closed. He *couldn't* get involved. But when she finds out who he really is, what if she decides she doesn't want him? He'll be crushed. He already felt more attached to her than anyone in his past.

His phone buzzed. The boss. *Shit.* Sam took a deep breath.

"Agent 4 …"

"…Yes, sir …No sir, haven't retrieved it yet … Yes, sir. I'll stay on it… I understand the importance … by the end of the week, yes sir."

~*~

Kirin couldn't have wiped the stupid smile off her face if she wanted. Yes, she fully got that as a single woman it was reckless to let someone she didn't know very well stay at her house. But … it was *Sam*. Someone she felt like she connected with on another level. He picked on her and protected her at the same time. She felt safe with him. And as hard as it'd always been for her to trust anyone, somehow he'd broken through that barrier super quick.

As she drove to her aunt's house, warning bells went off.

Something he'd said as she was sobering up. He'd moved around a lot. At least every two years and he'd been here longer than that. That tugged at her heart. *Don't get involved*, her mind said, *he won't be here long.*

She shook it off and pulled up the tree-lined driveway to her aunt and uncle's right on time. Little Jack and Will came running out as she shut off her car, with Aunt Kathy and Uncle Dean close on their heels.

Little Jack drew his lightsaber and pushed his Darth Vader mask on top of his head to speak, while Will strutted toward her, too cool to run. His arms were completely filled with a completed Star Wars Lego battleship. He looked so proud. Uncle Dean walked close on his heels, hands out as if he'd catch it if it fell. By the bags under both their eyes, she was sure they'd stayed awake until the wee hours putting it together.

She could hear them talking before she even opened her door.

"Mama!" Little Jack squealed. "We made cookies and put together a Darth Vader floor puzzle and watched movies all night!"

Kirin stepped out and Aunt Kathy squeezed her. "You're gonna have some tired boys today."

Kirin nodded toward her uncle. "Looks like you, too."

Uncle Dean nodded in agreement.

Kirin bent down to look at the battleship Will held. "Wow. How many hours did that take?"

"Not long," Will said, "Uncle Dean did most of it."

"Not true, boy. All I did were the wings and part of the tail. He's got an eye for putting things together, K. Maybe an engineer?" Uncle Dean was always trying to pigeonhole a career for Will.

After placing the battleship on the floorboard as if it were a carton of eggs, the boys ran back inside to grab their bags while she switched over the car seat for Little Jack. Reemerging from the car, her aunt smiled at her, eyebrows up.

"What?"

"Good date?" Uncle Dean walked up and interrupted, and then, embarrassed by what the answer might be, turned pink and excused himself to go help the boys pack.

Aunt Kathy brushed the lock of gray hair out of her eye and chuckled. "Well," she said, "nice guy?"

"Hmm. Well, whoever was supposed to meet me for the date decided not to show, but another guy I met in the grocery store happened to walk in, sit with me and take his place."

Kirin explained how Sam found her tipsy and took care of her. Conveniently, she left out the part where he'd spent the night. No sense muddying the waters. Even at almost forty, she didn't want her parents, or aunt and uncle in her case, to think she was a tramp, even if nothing happened. Aunt Kathy listened to her story and agreed whoever the first guy was, he was an inconsiderate idiot.

"Why don't you ask Sam to dinner? He and Dean can grill out steaks and we can get to know him."

Kirin didn't even have his number. "Well, we're not there yet," Kirin admitted, embarrassed, "But when I get to know him better, I'll bring him around to meet you guys."

The boys and Uncle Dean came outside. After thanking them and hugs all around, the boys climbed into the car. Uncle Dean hugged her especially tight. She looked up at him, puzzled.

"Be careful and call us if you need anything, okay?"

She narrowed her eyes at him. There was something he wasn't saying. She reached up on her tiptoes and kissed his cheek. As she drove home, the boys chatted happily about their stay. They mentioned learning to short sheet a bed and tying rubber bands on the sprayer at the kitchen sink. Pranks they'd learned from Uncle Dean.

Oh, boy.

Will hummed as he spoke of the sweet treats Aunt Kathy baked for them. When she turned the corner to pull into their long, gravel driveway, she stopped the car short.

There, parked in her driveway sat a shiny dark Mercedes. It was backed in and staring at her. Jet black mirrored windows hid any sign of life inside it. Not a speck of dirt anywhere. Panic hung in her throat. Was this one of the men who followed her? Maybe even the creepy leader?

Did they come to harm her or even worse, the boys? Or did they come for the book?

Will must've sensed her fear. "Mom? Why'd you stop? Whose car is that?"

"I ... I don't know, honey," she stammered.

Slowly, she pulled the car closer but kept the doors locked. She had plenty of gas and nobody could run these East Tennessee back roads faster than her. All the places she could hide ran through her head. Hell, she could drive some of the winding one lane roads up the mountain. They'd never catch her there, and she could lose them. She could outrun them and call the police while she drove. Instinctively, she plugged her phone in and dialed 911, but didn't hit the send button. Her stomach knotted the closer they crept toward the house.

They were about halfway down the gravel driveway when she noticed Arthur off to the side, rifle drawn and pointing at a short, thick, balding man in khakis with both hands up in surrender. Arthur's dog Duke stood a foot in front of the man, hackles up and barking.

She sped up. As she got closer, she recognized the man's chubby stance and wrinkled face. It was Walter Blankenship, her father's attorney. He'd called and left messages for weeks. Gone was the expensive suit and worth-more-than-her-car tie he'd worn the day she met him in California. Now, he looked more casual, more human somehow, and he looked terrified.

Deep breath. Kirin parked to the side, left the car running and locked the kids inside. She ran toward Arthur.

"What's going on?"

Mr. Blankenship was pale and looked like he was about to lose his lunch. "This old guy came out of nowhere! Said he was your bodyguard." Arthur waggled his eyebrows at her, clearly enjoying this.

Poor Mr. Blankenship. She'd avoided him for so long, he had to fly in from LA to close out the estate. He looked sad, scared and worn. She inhaled deep, guilt-ridden for having dodged him.

"It's okay, Arthur," she said as she signaled for him to lower his rifle. "I know who he is."

Arthur pointed at the man. "This ain't California, buddy. You can't just go snoopin' around somebody's house without attracting attention. You'd do well to remember that."

Mr. Blankenship glared at the old man, then nodded. Arthur tipped his hat to Kirin and called to Duke who happily followed him back to his house.

Kirin shook her head and apologized, then moved her car to the garage and shut off the engine. Mr. Blankenship wiped his face with his sleeve and followed her inside carrying a briefcase.

"Mr. Blankenship," she walked into her kitchen as the boys carried their things inside. "I've ignored your calls, and you had to come all the way here. This has taken up so much of your time chasing me down. Truly, I'm so sorry."

"Ms. Lane, please don't apologize. I came to settle your father's estate and give you some news in person. Shall we go out on the porch?"

"Sure," she stammered, "and please, call me Kirin. Give me a minute to occupy the boys then I'll meet you out back."

Kirin ran upstairs after the boys when she remembered her manners.

"Mr. Blankenship?" she called through the hall.

"Yes," he answered, sounding bewildered.

"Can I get you some iced tea?"

"That'd be nice," his voice echoed.

The boys were already entangled with Legos, so Kirin bounded back downstairs. Her mind spun with curiosity. She poured two tall glasses of half un-sweet and half sweet tea and headed out the backdoor.

It was midafternoon and were it not for the fans Jack had installed on the back-porch ceiling, she might have broken into an unlady-like sweat. In the distance, Arthur inspected his field with his horses, glancing at them from time to time. She handed Mr. B his tea and sat in a plump chair across from him.

He closed his eyes briefly and inhaled the mountain air. Opening them, he appeared mesmerized by the beauty of the land and horses. She gave him time to soak it all in and pretended she wasn't anxious. Finally, he spoke. "It's beautiful out here, isn't it?" he whispered it more to himself than her.

"Yeah."

His face was lined with worry. When he took a troubled breath, it dawned on her. Were the dark-suited men harassing him too? That thought made her stomach twist. What if they followed him to her house? She shuddered.

"Kirin," he said, pulling her back from her thoughts, "As I stated before, I have some news. Bad news." She nodded for him to continue. "Janet, your father's second wife, has died."

Kirin stared at him. She'd only met the woman the week before.

He continued, "Her death was … questionable. The police are investigating it for foul play. The initial cause of death was reported as an overdose, but anyone who even vaguely knew Janet would dispute that conclusion. The woman was a total health nut. She never took mainstream medicine. She only used herbs and natural remedies when she or your dad were sick."

Mr. Blankenship pushed off his chair and stood. Then he paced over to the edge of the porch and turned to face Kirin. "I know you didn't know her well, but she took great care of your father in a time when he was all alone. She almost had your dad convinced to fly here to get you and bring you to LA to live, but your father didn't want you in the middle of all that."

Your father didn't want you.

That's all she'd heard.

Mr. B. must've sensed he'd lost her, he stepped closer and squatted down in front of her, pulling her back to his words.

"Kirin listen to me. Your father loved you. He didn't want you in the middle of his mess. We had long talks about you and your wellbeing. Mostly, he talked of keeping you hidden and safe."

This made her sit up straighter. "Hidden from whom?" she demanded.

When he stood, his face scrunched up, filled with regret. Mr. Blankenship turned away from her, surveying once again, the back of her property.

"From the world," he answered softly.

He turned his head back toward her, pinning her with his eyes.

He whispered, "I believe Janet was murdered."

Kirin leaned forward, leveled a look at him and whispered back, "Why would those men murder her?"

By the look on his face, her question startled him. She wasn't dense. She'd made a few connections. Like her father had to be part of these men for them to come to his funeral. She'd guessed he must have gained their confidence over the years and then double-crossed them in the end.

Also, by the fear in Janet's voice, she'd presumed whatever they wanted was inside the book she'd been given. Kirin closed her eyes and pictured Janet. Sad. She'd been kind and gentle. Motherly even. Poor woman.

It didn't make sense. Scar and Babyface were in town. They had to know where she lived. It was public record for crying out loud. So, why hadn't they driven over, kicked in her door, and grabbed the book if that was what they were after? It didn't make sense.

Mr. Blankenship sat back down and took a sip of his sweet tea. Placing it back on the glass table he turned toward her and asked the dreaded question.

"Where's the book? I need to see it."

Her first warning from Janet had been not to trust anyone who asked about the book. She silently thanked her. Her hackles were up, all the same.

"Why?" Kirin stood, stepping back, then crossing her arms.

He shifted uncomfortably in his seat under her stare.

"Why don't you let me have it. I'll give it to them and maybe they'll leave both of us alone."

His eyes were bloodshot. The urge to have him leave overtook her sympathy. He needed to get out of her house. Now. He was hunted like her, maybe more so since he held the keys to her father's fortune, but she couldn't help him. She needed an insurance policy to keep her boys safe from these people. And the book was just that. She turned away from him.

"I ditched it." She said, then spun back around to face him. "I didn't want any part of my father's estate ... not the money, the drama, the headache, and certainly not his stupid book. It's been taken out with the trash days ago."

Mr. Blankenship stared at her. Probably trying to decide if he believed her. Shaking his head, he pulled out his briefcase and opened it, then snatched a small stack of bound papers and slammed the lid closed. The hilt of a black gun shone in the sunlight before it closed.

He needed to leave. Now.

After she signed the last of the papers, she grabbed her tea and walked toward the door, not caring she was being rude.

Mr. Blankenship placed the papers back in his briefcase. As he locked it he spoke. "I'm leaving my practice in California. I'm licensed to practice in three other states, so I'm headed to one of them to start over. Maybe, even retire."

She wanted to ask if he fled because of them, but she already knew that answer. He said, on his way to the door that his office deleted her address, but he'd send copies of the completed paperwork in a few weeks. As he stood at her door, he handed her a check for $1.1 million dollars. Stunned, she stood openmouthed. She hadn't expected more than a few thousand. He waited for her to look up and when she did, he gave her a quick nod and vanished out her front door.

~*~

That night, she had a vivid dream of spending some of the money on a lavish vacation with the boys. Lying on a warm, sandy beach, she gazed at Will and Little Jack making sandcastles and chasing waves. The taste of salt in the air and the warm breeze on her face calmed her. She sipped on a cool drink while waves rolled in, and she buried her toes in the warm sand.

In a flash, the sky grew dark. She stood to gather their beach toys and run back to the house before the storm hit. When she bent, gone were the towels and toys, replaced with only a single item, her father's book.

A scream filled her ears, and she turned. The man with the white smile from the funeral lurked a few feet away, his eyes trained on her sons. But this time, instead of a smile he wore a sneer. Cold eyes locked on to her two unaware boys. He took one step toward them, and her entire body lurched up casting her out of the dream, drenched and shaking.

When she'd finally calmed down enough to lay down and close her eyes again, the same sentence rattled on repeat in her head.

Protect them.

Chapter Fifteen

The morning began like any other typical Sunday. Racing around to get ready for church and trying desperately to keep Little Jack, Will and herself clean for a few hours while they attended mass. It all went off without a hitch until the "peace be with you" part where everyone shakes hands with the parishioners around them. It was at this moment Little Jack and Will broke out into a full-scale pushing and shoving contest.

Real peaceful.

She spent the rest of mass breaking up the fights, glaring at the boys and smiling at people giggling around them.

Back home, Kirin sat on the back porch and read the paper sipping hot mocha coffee while Little Jack blew bubbles and Will dragged a tiny skateboard with his fingers across every surface on the patio.

The sweet smell of honeysuckle blew in over the mountain, keeping them cool as the heat of spring sun began its relentless ray that would last well into October.

Arthur stood in his garden, talking to himself. No doubt planning what and where to plant his vegetables. He whistled so the boys would look up and notice him. They did and ditched their play to run across the field to meet him. He glanced over, and she waved.

"Ms. Lane, can we plant, today?"

"Sure!" she yelled back.

Maybe they'd learn the green thumb from him since she didn't have it.

Kirin sat back, propped her feet up and opened the paper, pulling out her favorite sections: Coupons, Real Estate, and the Living section. She flipped past the obituaries section then remembered they were supposed to post her father's obituary.

You'd think after handling Jack's arrangements, she'd be a pro at this, but she'd initially forgotten to put his obituary in the Knoxville paper where he'd been born, until her friend, Laura mentioned it. Who would've remembered him in Knoxville? She copied the one from the LA paper and put it in their local paper.

She turned to the last page and found his name:

Michael "Sonny" Terhune died of natural causes March 13, 2019. Preceded in Death by wife Nancy, parents Frances and Nelson, son-in-law Jack Lane and sister Margaret. Survived by daughter Kirin Terhune Lane, grandsons Jack and Will Lane and special friend Janet.

Reading Janet's name, who was alive when she'd written it, made her sad. Even though she didn't know the woman well.

After dinner, Rosa pulled in armed with a new grocery list. Her first thought, *Sam.*

Kirin ran upstairs to change and brush her teeth. The sun had begun its descent and a chill hung in the air, but she wanted to wear something feminine. A medium length white skirt to show off her legs, a pink shirt, and her brown flips. She added a touch of lip gloss and a quick squirt of perfume she instantly regretted. Rosa wouldn't miss questioning the perfume. Especially for a chore she knew Kirin loathed.

She tiptoed downstairs, trying not to call attention to herself. Even before she rounded the bottom of the steps Rosa's sarcasm wafted into the kitchen from the pantry.

"You smell nice for the store." She said "store" as if it was a smelly fish market. Rosa sauntered out of the pantry carrying cans. "Why are you dressed up?"

Kirin twirled around so her skirt filled with air. "Well, you never know who you'll run into at Morrissey's. And it's high time I start trying to look nice again."

Rosa snickered, "Yeah, right." She laid the cans down on the counter. Swirling around, she placed a hand on her hip and began the Rosa interrogation.

"So, I'm guessing you didn't like Mr. Right on Friday?"

Kirin's smile disappeared. She'd forgotten the sting of rejection.

She let out a sigh, "No, he stood me up."

Rosa stared into Kirin's eyes as if she didn't understand, so she continued, "He must have taken one look at me and run the other way."

She couldn't figure out how, but when Rosa asked her a question, she always told her darkest truth. The tiny woman had some superpower where she knew if Kirin lied anyway, so it was pointless to resist.

"He left me … sitting in the restaurant for two hours. Never even called to tell me he was delayed or that he wasn't coming. It was humiliating, but then a friend happened to walk in and sat with me. He ended up bringing me home since I'd sat there too long in the bar drowning my sorrows. I didn't have much time to sober up."

Rosa walked closer and lowered her voice to a growl.

"Who brought you home?"

"Sam," Kirin answered. "Remember … the guy I met at the grocery store. He saved me … again."

Rosa's scowl spoke volumes. She didn't approve of bringing some stranger to the house. Probably a good time to grab the list and walk to the door.

"Kirin," Rosa blurted out.

"Yes?"

"You look nice." She said it dry, then turned and trotted upstairs.

Kirin stood open-mouthed. A compliment coming from Rosa was rarer than a snowstorm in June. They usually volleyed harmless insults back and forth at each other, not compliments. Kirin smiled to herself on her way to the car, glad she'd at least approved of the outfit.

The winding mountain roads made for a fast ride to the store. She let the tires hug the road, turned up the radio and, enjoyed the butterflies in her belly. Pulling into the store, she surveyed the lot for signs of his truck. It wasn't there. She checked the clock. Six pm on the nose, the time she'd always arrived on Sundays.

She sat in her car pretending to be lost in old eighties' music, scanned the place like she was casing it. She'd sat there so long, the same young bagger walked three sets of people and groceries out to their cars. He gave her the stink eye on the third time he passed.

Her mind raced. Maybe he was inside, waiting? She hadn't thought of that. She gathered her things and speed-walked inside. Once there, she grabbed her cart and stared at her list, not reading a word of it. She hoped she didn't look desperate. Glancing over the top of her list, he was nowhere in sight.

Disappointment festered in her belly where the butterflies had been. She hoped he wouldn't forget tomorrow's lunch too.

She meandered through the store, half-heartedly checking groceries off the list. The feeling of rejection reminded her she needed to call Sarah and squash her matchmaking skills since Mr. Loyal hadn't even had the decency to call and apologize for standing her up.

Who does that? She still couldn't believe how much it'd affected her. She'd allowed it to injure her tiny shred of self-confidence. She was even angrier at this unknown man for making her doubt herself. Hell, she was smart, successful even, with two beautiful boys and a great life. Kirin raised her head higher. Nobody would be stealing her self-confidence again.

Her turn came to load her groceries on the conveyor belt. After she placed a flat of waters on the belt, she stood on her tiptoes to take one more look around. Maybe she'd missed him.

Three lanes away stood two familiar backs. Even without the dark menacing suits, she knew it was them. Shocked they were so close, she gasped and ducked down behind the candy bars and gum. She picked up a magazine to put in front of her face and peered over it, observing them through the holes in the display. Breathe.

They were close enough, and now turned sideways, she could memorize their faces. Babyface was probably six feet tall with dark eyes and a square chin. Scar was shorter, heavier and the skin on his face looked like a worn-out Aigner purse.

Luckily, they waited behind a woman with a notebook full of coupons trying to get everything for free.

Her big-boned cashier gazed at her with a sly grin and spoke soft.

"See an old boyfriend, honey?"

Kirin added the magazine to her pile of groceries and shook her head.

"How fast can you get me out of here?" She whispered.

The cashier pushed up both sleeves. "Honey, I'm the fastest one here. You're lucky you got in my line."

Kirin smiled gratefully, and without a sound helped the cashier bag and load the groceries. She put her debit card in the machine and begged the machine to hurry. The cashier turned to follow Kirin's line of sight.

That's when Scar spotted Kirin.

She swallowed hard and kept moving as if he hadn't noticed her. Scar elbowed Baby Face in the side. Both men stilled and stared at her as if she performed a circus act on a high wire.

Her hand shook as she took the receipt and thanked the cashier. The cashier looked from Kirin's shaking hand to her fearful eyes, then glared in the men's direction.

As Kirin pushed her cart toward the door, a man's gravel-voice rang out. "We've decided we don't have time to wait."

Their cashier yelled out, "Doris, can you get these guys down on three? They're in a hurry."

Kirin glanced back at her cashier, who winked in her direction.

"Sure, send 'em down here, I'll help 'em."

Kirin crossed the threshold of the store to the outside and took off in a dead run. She didn't even look around, she yanked open the back door to the SUV and threw in the groceries. She flinched when the sound of eggs cracking reached her ears. She even left her grocery cart sitting next to her car, something she judged others for doing. She sprinted to the drivers side, jumped in and locked the doors.

Her lungs burned. She'd held her breath loading the groceries. As she backed out, the two men, bags in hand jogged out of the store right behind the coupon lady. They looked around and stopped once their eyes found her car. She'd escaped them once again.

~*~

As they put away groceries, Rosa mumbled loud opinions to herself about broken eggs, squished bread, and how an entire bag of chips could be pummeled to dust. All due to *someone's* driving. Placing the last can on the shelf, Kirin turned as Rosa spun around and stopped. She pulled on the straps of her purse and eyeballed Kirin.

"What happened to the handsome guy at the store? Didn't you see him?"

"He wasn't there," Kirin answered.

"Oh," she sounded surprised. "Well, he must have had a good reason not to be there." She added, "Anyone not smart enough to see how wonderful you are must be blind."

Kirin gaped at her. Wow. Two compliments in one night, and perhaps one of the nicest ones Rosa had ever uttered without a hint of sarcasm. *Bizaroland.*

Kirin waved goodbye then she and the boys snuggled in for a movie. All the while, her mind flitted. She sure wished Sam had shown up at the store.

After the movie and showers, she put the boys to bed. They were especially tired since Arthur had them both pulling weeds in his garden and digging for worms most of the afternoon. Kirin trudged up to her room and logged into the computer with a glass of tea in her comfy UT orange sweats.

She hadn't been online for more than a few minutes when a popup at the bottom of the screen read: *Is this Kirin Terhune Lane, daughter of Sonny?*

She froze. Her world had been so strange since her father's passing. She was leery of everyone. Her mind went blank. What should she say?

The little box popped up again: *I was a close friend of your dad's.*

Hmmm, the question of her life lately, to trust or not to trust? She wrote back but didn't give away any information to this person.

What is your name?

It took forever for the reply box to pop up. Maybe the person typing was in the same quandary.

I'd rather not say, but I knew both of your parents well. They both trusted me. Your dad and I were bowling friends. He went on: *Your mama made the best pies, but only for close friends and family. My favorite was her apple.*

A grapefruit-sized lump formed in Kirin's throat. It was her favorite too. And even though she had her mama's recipe, she hadn't mastered making it like her mom did. Her mom had made it from scratch only for people she loved. He must have known this. He'd earned a little trust with that one.

Apple was my favorite too. What should I call you?

His reply was immediate: *Your dad called me "Kidd" when we were alone, but it had more to do with my farm than my age. I'm only a few years younger than your dad ... was.*

Alright. Kidd, what can I do for you?

No, Kirin, it's what I can do for you; I can help keep you safe from the people following you.

Kirin froze. Her heart thudded in her chest. He knew about the men in the black suits. She didn't know what to type so she stared at the screen until he wrote:

Are you still there?

She typed: *I'm still here, wondering what you mean?*

The box indicated he typed something else, but it took forever to come through. She examined the computer screen as if her life depended on it. Couldn't tear her eyes away. This might lead her to answers, or it could be a trap. She mentally ran through her nightly safety routine; she'd locked all the doors, shuttered the windows, and set her alarm. She was fine. Shaking, she raised her hot tea to her lips.

Finally, his message came through. *The artifact you were given, is it safe?*

Her eyes darted to it. It stared back sitting next to her on the computer table. Lately, she didn't leave the house without it. It was her security blanket. She wasn't supposed to trust anyone who asked about the book. She bit her lip and wrote back: *Yes, why?*

Right on cue, he typed: *Have you noticed there are a few items missing?*

YES! What does it mean?

As she tapped her foot waiting for a response, she bounced in her seat from either excitement or too much tea. No way she could tear herself from the computer. She would finally get answers that'd stumped her for days. His reply popped up. She read it several times to absorb the meaning.

Your father knew you'd have trust issues in life, Kirin. He gave those torn out pages to certain people, so you'd know you could trust them. I have page 43.

Kirin grabbed the book and ran to the bathroom, dropping the orange sweats and sitting, she flipped through the stupid book to find page 43 missing.

Tears stung her eyes. He knew she'd have trust issues. Of course he did. He caused them! She felt relieved to have at least one answer. But it both rattled and infuriated her. This stranger knew more about her own father than she did.

And if her father couldn't be involved in her life while he was alive, why leave her all these riddles in death? She got a hold of herself, walked back to the computer and sat. Kidd had typed several quick messages.

Kirin? Are you okay? Are you still there? I'm so sorry. Did I upset you?

She wasn't sure how he'd react, but she had to try. *I'd like to meet you.*

After several minutes of biting her fingernails, he finally IM'd back: *Not a good time, but soon. Must go, I'll catch you on here soon. Stay safe, Kidd.*

And with that, he was gone.

So now, she knew why there were missing pages, but it still didn't explain what she was supposed to search for or why these men were after the book.

She rose and stared at the words on her screen. She'd been tired before, but now, determined. She grabbed up the book, her notebook, and pen and sat in her recliner with every intention to continue her search for more clues.

Her tired body had other plans as she fought to keep her eyelids open.

Drifting in and out she wondered why every mystery in this book only revealed more questions about her father. Would she ever know the truth? And the even more disturbing question—was she capable of forgiving him?

Chapter Sixteen

It felt like minutes later when the morning sun peeked out over the trees. Kirin stood, her stiff shoulders ached. She had to laugh at herself for falling asleep so fast. She'd think about the book and Kidd later, right now she had a mission: look fabulous for her lunch date with Sam.

Kirin dried and straightened her hair and pulled on freshly washed baby blue scrubs.

The familiar click of the front door closing, and Rosa starting breakfast for the boys, meant Kirin was behind. She rushed around to finish. Rosa began her morning at the exact same time every day, and the boys slept through it all. The sweet smell of pancakes wafting upstairs with the gurgling of her old coffeemaker, made her smile. Her savior. Rosa made coffee.

Kirin crept downstairs and slid the book in her purse, then grabbed the creamer and a cup. She whispered, "Good morning, sweet Rosa."

Rosa cut her eyes as if Kirin had called her a bad name.

"Why are you so chipper?" Rosa's brows furrowed.

"It's a new day," Kirin said.

"Hmf," Rosa grouched. The woman was the polar opposite of a morning person. But the instant the boys' footsteps reached her ears, she transformed into this sweet, loving, grandmotherly-type person. She was like a street magician pulling a brand-new attitude out of her sleeve instead of a card.

Two sleepy boys ambled downstairs and sat at the table staring. Kirin hugged and kissed them both, grabbed her coffee and spun around stepping right on one of Rosa's feet. She yelped, and Kirin kissed her forehead.

"Sorry," Kirin grinned as she sidestepped her. "See you guys later."

Rosa called out over her shoulder, "Hey don't forget, Will's out of school and my sister and I are taking the boys out to lunch and to a movie today."

Both boys yelled, "Yay!"

"Thank you! Have a great time."

Kirin ran to her car, jumped in, started it, and slammed it into reverse. She hated being late. Rosa observed her through the front window and shook her head. Kirin laughed. Rosa was convinced Kirin had to be the worst driver on the planet.

She spotted a small red truck on the interstate on her drive toward town, and her heart skipped a beat. She sped up to catch it, only to be disappointed. A bald guy with a goatee sang to his steering wheel until he noticed her and smiled back with raised eyebrows. He must've thought she flirted with him. Kirin sped past.

Only a few hours remained until her lunch date with Sam. She could do it. She could focus on her work for a few hours, right?

Kirin strolled into the hospital and spotted Stacy and Laura talking at the nurse's station with a doctor. Stacy's face was somber. Kirin remembered reading a work alert late last night that a baby had been taken away from its parents because of meth in its system. Those were the saddest cases.

The morning dragged along with no new babies born but a crop of laboring mothers. She hated to leave them, but it was almost time for her break. As she made her final rounds before lunch, she checked her watch repeatedly.

St. Mary's hospital sat on a hill but was within a mile of some of the best hole-in-the-wall family diners. Leroy's was a favorite of hers. Named after the current owner's grandpa, it was only a ten-minute walk and patrons were usually lined out the door by noon. Her favorite item on their menu was their homemade strawberry shakes, made with real cream and strawberries. It reminded her of some part of her childhood she couldn't place.

Kirin checked in with her last laboring mom and let her know she had to take a break. Then ran and grabbed her cross-body purse. Adding a little lip gloss, she jogged out of the hospital and down the sidewalk. As she rounded the last corner on the way to Leroy's, she spotted him. Butterflies went into spastic fits in her belly. *Slow down. You look too anxious. Walk and breathe.*

He was here.

104

He wore a tight-fitting navy shirt and jeans. She watched as he searched the sea of people but hadn't spotted her yet. She couldn't tear her eyes away. He ran his hands through his hair then shook his head as if he'd had a mental disagreement within himself. He looked nervous, but his face softened as soon as he found her.

His eyes locked on target as a smile erupted as if she was the best thing he'd seen in days. Sam walked toward her to bridge the gap. When he was close enough, he reached out and grabbed her hand, intertwining their fingers.

His hands were warm. Tingles ran down her spine as he pulled her next to him. Closer than she'd ever been before, except maybe the night he'd carried her drunk butt up the steps in her house.

This was different, though. This felt right. They belonged next to each other. Before she could even say hello or ask why he didn't go to the store, he leaned in.

"About time. Don't think I could've waited much longer to see you."

Kirin could feel the layers of defense melting away. He'd torn down her steel wall of distrust by admitting he felt like she did. She grinned wide.

Letting go of her hand, he opened the door to the diner and led her inside with a protective hand on the small of her back. The clanging of plates and utensils, along with the chatter of hungry customers and the hissing of the grill made the small diner seem loud. The smell of burgers on the grill made Kirin's stomach growl on cue.

Sam grasped her hand again then pointed toward a table toward the back. Kirin nodded. He snaked around a few tables when someone called her name.

"Kirin?" Her friend Sarah, the matchmaker, stood sporting a goofy grin.

"Hey, how are you?" Kirin sang. Sam dropped her hand. She glanced over at him, puzzled. His demeanor had completely changed. His face was white as a ghost. Kirin turned toward him.

"Are you okay?"

Sam nodded, but something in his bright green eyes pleaded.

Sarah continued, "Well, I see my matchmaking skills are to be commended! I guess you two hit it off Friday night, eh? I told you, Kirin, I had the perfect guy for you."

Sarah's grin widened, so pleased with herself until she caught sight of the bewilderment on Kirin's face.

Everything at that point moved in slow motion. And then it all clicked together.

Sam had been her blind date. He'd stood her up.

He'd left her in misery, drinking herself into oblivion with the barflies. Left her there to think she wasn't good enough. Made her question her self-worth.

Kirin felt the heat and anger rise in her face, bright pink and hot. But wait, she was supposed to meet "Pat," not Sam. Kirin spun. A betrayed voice she didn't recognize, came out of her.

"I thought your name was Sam?" she spat.

"Wait … please … my full name is Samuel Patrick." Sam reached for her hand, but she snatched it away. He continued, "Some of my friends call me Sam and some call me Pat." Sarah looked confused, then mortified.

"Kirin, what happened?" Sarah whispered.

"I'll tell you what happened," Kirin pointed a finger at Sam. "This man stood me up, then sat back and laughed as I drank too much. I wallowed in self-pity until he swooped in to be the hero. He deceived me into thinking he was a nice guy, which obviously, he isn't."

Her stomach churned. She needed to flee. Get the hell out before the tears could fall. She'd been so stupid. Sam touched her arm. Instinctively, she jerked it away.

"Stay away from me, find a new grocery store, and lose my number!"

Sarah's horrified expression would haunt her. Kirin didn't have time to explain any further. The tears were welling up. She'd not be giving him the satisfaction of hurting her and watching her ugly cry. She turned to run, and this time Sam grabbed her arm. Hard.

"Stop. We need to talk about this. I screwed up and I didn't know how to fix it. This wasn't supposed to happen..." His green eyes pleaded for her to stay, but she freed herself of his grasp and ran for the door.

Kirin jogged the whole way back to the hospital's parking garage as tears stung her eyes. She cursed herself for being so stupid. What a naïve and trusting fool. *Trust.* What a shitty word. How does a girl orphaned by her mother, abandoned by her father and then widowed, ever have faith someone could be there for her?

By the time she'd run all the way to her car, she'd stopped swiping at the tears. She let them fall freely now. Kirin jumped in and locked her door, composing herself long enough to call work. She dialed the number and Stacy answered. She gave her a story about not feeling well and needing to go home for the day. Stacy read right through her, as usual, and demanded a phone call later with the real story.

Kirin hung up. Backing out, she half expected a red truck in her rear-view mirror. Part of her wished he'd chase her, so she could yell at him again, but another part dreaded it. His feelings were obviously not as developed as hers. Despite being so hurt, she knew. Knew her emotions ran deep for him. And she was well on her way to falling in love with him.

Well, she could bury those feelings, couldn't she?

"I'm such an idiot!" She yelled out to the void.

As she drove toward her house, she recalled Rosa and her sister had the boys out all afternoon. All she wanted was a hot bath and her bed, to cry herself to sleep and mourn this failed relationship. She'd harden her heart and get back to life before Sam.

She pulled into her driveway. Breath staggered in her throat from crying.

A man stood on her porch. She slowed and squinted. Her knee-jerk reaction was, "Bring it on whoever you are." She was in a mood to take on anybody in her way right now. Part of her hoped this was one of the guys in the dark suits. She was angry enough to kick some ass and make them wish they hadn't followed her.

Closer to the house she recognized his stance. Sam. He'd parked his red truck out of sight from the driveway behind the shrubs that bordered the side of the house. He paced on the front porch with his hands in his pockets, looking anxious and defeated.

Kirin parked on the same side and shut her car off. She let out a big breath, grabbed her purse and walked right up the front steps, past him to the front door.

He begged, "Please, listen to me. This wasn't supposed to happen. I wasn't supposed to fall in ..." He stopped short.

She wasn't listening. She turned the key and opened the door, placing her purse on the floor. Rosa must have forgotten to set the alarm because the normal one beep sound didn't go off when she opened it. Sam walked in, grabbed her around the waist, and covered her mouth in one quick move.

She'd been ready to pummel him with angry words and sling insults at him with her hurt heart, when he spun her around to face him. His eyes dark. He mouthed, "Don't say a word." He grabbed her purse and shuffled her to the right and into the kitchen. Right on cue, a muffled male's voice echoed down the stairs from her bedroom. Her body went stiff. She held her breath.

Someone was inside her house.

She couldn't make herself move. Her legs quivered and her mind processed what was happening at a turtle's pace. Part of her newly acquired badass attitude came rushing back. Shoulders down, her back straightened as she glared through her kitchen toward the stairs.

Hell no. This was her house! She struggled to get away from Sam's grip. Where was that damn baseball bat that always seemed to be underfoot?

Sam sensed her anger and grabbed her tighter around the waist, lifting her off the floor. He pushed her into the pantry off the kitchen. When he released her briefly, he walked straight over to the hidden trap door to the safe room, moved the box and the carpet that covered it without a sound, then opened it as if he'd gone down there a thousand times.

A different man's voice came wafting down from the stairs. Two men.

Her two dark-suited stalkers.

Part of her wanted to grab the gun stashed in the pantry and run at them shooting and screaming for them to get out. But under pressure, she may not be able to hit the broad side of a barn if she stood inside it, so that wouldn't work. Sam picked Kirin up and placed her on the stairs leading down to the safe room. He scampered right behind her and with quiet hands and closed the hatch door.

The safe room had been Jack's domain. All high tech and packed with everything needed for a three day stay. The space wasn't large, more like the size of a small office. But, the only thing *not* high-tech and perfected was the light fixture. It was a naked bulb hanging from the ceiling and when lit, it made the room look like a horror film.

As if on cue, Sam's head hit the bulb in the darkness with a pop. He must've hit it so hard it busted. A piece of broken bulb smacked the concrete floor, causing a tiny tinkling sound.

"Ow, shi—" Sam cursed under his breath, and then, "uh-oh."

Kirin grabbed a flashlight off a shelf and clicked it on. Blood trickled from Sam's head and landed on his hand. His body swayed. Apparently, blood made the strong man woozy.

Sam's eyes rolled back as he staggered to stay upright. Kirin reacted quick, grabbing tight to one arm and holding his back, she aimed his body toward a stack of tarps. He landed mostly on her and partially on the stack, but luckily his fall was quiet.

Kirin struggled out from underneath him and ran to the shelves finding a first-aid kit. Trotting back, she knelt on the floor and angled the flashlight toward his head. Quick fingers checked for tiny pieces of glass stuck in his forehead. She disinfected and bandaged his head. He stared into her eyes the entire time, grinning. At one point, he reached up to touch her cheek. She batted his hand away and kept working on his cut.

Kirin fought hard not to look at him. She didn't even crack a smile. When she was finished, she rose, jaw tight and determined to harden her heart before he melted it again. The low growl of the men's voices overhead snapped her back into reality. They had to be directly above them in the kitchen. Kirin froze. She could only make out some of the muffled words they said.

The deeper-voiced one said, "It's not here."

"It has to be," the other one answered gruffly.

Her father's book. Jesus. She'd left it. She swirled, looking for her purse. Please God, she didn't leave it upstairs, did she?

Sam whispered, "It's right there." He pointed at her purse sitting on the steps.

Wait.

How did he know what they were looking for? And how did Sam go right to the door to the safe room as if he'd been before? He'd grabbed her purse and threw it down there.

The deeper voiced one said, "Pat vowed we'd find it here."

A wave of nausea rolled through her body. The man upstairs had mumbled the words that broke her.

Sam had let them in her house. He had the code to disarm the alarm.

The thudding of the two men's footsteps moved above their heads from the pantry toward the kitchen.

She turned around and pointed the flashlight into Sam's eyes. She stared for a moment in disbelief. Sam glared right back. Why hadn't he yelled out, so they'd find her? And why go to the trouble of hiding her?

She was closer to the shelves where the guns were hidden. She could make it before he could. It was all a setup, and she'd trusted the wrong person. He'd let the enemy into her house. He wanted the book as much as they did. Kirin crept backward toward the shelf, careful not to tilt the flashlight. She turned her head for a split second and slipped a pistol in her scrubs pocket.

When she turned back, he was gone.

Kirin lunged toward the steps, as the flashlight slipped landing inside an open box with a thud. Light shone upward causing long shadows on the wall. It illuminated most of the room. Without a sound, Sam was behind her.

The men upstairs, who'd been rummaging through her kitchen drawers stilled at the noise.

Quick, Sam pulled her arms behind her, holding them with one hand as if she were under arrest. With his other hand, he reached in her scrubs pocket and relieved her of the gun, placing it back on the closest shelf. His breath was ragged. The familiar scent she was now determined to hate, invaded her senses.

Sam whispered into her ear, "I know you don't believe this right now, but we're on the same team. Please be quiet."

His free hand reached into his back pocket and pulled out his wallet. Sam set the wallet on a shelf, turning her body to face it. One handed, his fingers worked quick like a spider to open it and pick out a yellowed piece of paper. He unfolded it and held it out in a ray of dim light for her to see.

It was page 167 from her father's book.

Chapter Seventeen

When the voices and noises upstairs had long since disappeared, Kirin assumed the men had abandoned their search.

It was eerily quiet. Too quiet and the silence gnawed at her. He'd let her go once her heart rate had slowed, then cautiously moved to the opposite side of the room. She'd sat with her back against the opposite wall. She needed answers. Her eyes adjusted to the darkness, pierced only by a dying flashlight. Squinting, she could make out his shape. He sat on the ground like her.

She'd stewed in silence long enough. Her legs were asleep, and her arms wrapped protectively around her body. She'd been trusting, foolish, and stupid. Why had she wholeheartedly let him in? Hormones? But why hadn't he taken the book and given away their location when he had the chance. Her head swam with opposing theories.

Sam sucked in a deep breath and sighed. He spoke low. His voice was tight.

"This isn't gonna make much sense right now, but everything I'm gonna tell you is the truth." Clearing his throat, he continued, "I've been protecting you for the last two years."

She was glad he couldn't see her face. Her mouth dropped open and her mind went blank. *Two years.* Since Jack died. But she'd never noticed him until her father died. How? She felt exposed, but another emotion arose too. It thrilled her to know he'd protected her all that time. Thrilled her way more than it should have. Shut up, heart.

He continued, "It's part of what I do. I learn people's habits. I watch them. I know where you buy your morning coffee, and where you have your car serviced, and where you take the boys to the park. I knew where you worked before you told me and even where you go to church."

Sam rose slow, stretching his legs. "Obviously, I knew where you lived too. I'm sure to you it sounds creepy, but my job was to be invisible. You never saw me because I was careful. I only observed."

Sam ran his hands over his face. "And prior to a few weeks ago, you didn't seem to be much trouble."

Kirin stood then, fists balled, and her voice shook, revealing too much.

"So, the whole "date thing" was an act? You pretended to like me? And I fell for it. Do you get some sort of bonus if you get laid?"

Sam took a long step toward her. Even in the partial dark, she could feel his anger rolling off him. She stood her ground and didn't budge.

"It's not like that." His voice came in a low growl. "But when you assaulted me with the tomatoes, I should've walked away and become invisible again. But you'd gotten a damn good look at me. So, I had to change tactics."

Sam paced in front of her, arms flailing, but his voice remained quiet. "Then you go and fall ass-backward into a dangerous situation with the drugged-out guy in the parking lot."

She closed her eyes and shook her head. She could take a lot of things, but pity wasn't one of them.

He'd pretended to fall for her out of pity.

"Look at me."

"Oh, God and I thought..." Her eyes clamped shut and she turned away from him.

Sam took another step closer.

"Look at me," he demanded.

She turned and opened her eyes. He stood in front of her, but out of arm's reach. The fading flashlight bounced a soft light off his face, making his dark green eyes look lighter.

"I don't pity you. Not at all. Everything I've felt for you is real, whether you believe me or not. But relationships, they never work out for guys like me. Besides, none of that matters now. My job is to protect you. Having feelings for you isn't going to help you stay alive. I made a promise and I have to focus on keeping you safe."

Kirin crossed her arms and stared at the floor. She couldn't look at him but knew his eyes were trained on her. She shut her eyes in the darkness.

Something about Sam had spoken to her and she'd let her guard down. Trusted him. And that trust had been shattered all to hell. She'd allowed someone a few inches into her heart only to find he couldn't allow himself to love her. Angry tears pooled, but she couldn't focus on this. She needed other answers.

"How'd you know this safe room was here?"

Sam took another deep breath. "I helped Jack wire it for the computers."

He knew Jack. That took more than a moment of silence to swallow.

"Who hired you?"

"I think you know that answer, don't you?"

She did.

Her father. This had his name written all over it. From the little she knew of him, he'd be happy to keep her in complete darkness and not give her a heads-up that he'd paid a total stranger to protect her. Par for the damn course.

Her next question was much harder and part of her didn't want to know the answer. But she had to ask. "Did you let those men into my house? You work for them too, right?"

Kirin's voice broke at the end, which made Sam take another step, closing the gap between them, but he didn't touch her. His voice softened, "Yes, and not really. And that's all I can tell you right now."

She let out a psh sound of disgust. He'd let them in her house knowing she'd be with him on a pretend date and wouldn't find them searching for the book. He played both sides of the fence and she was sure he got paid handsomely for both. So what, he had a page from the book?

Was that supposed to mean she could trust him? Money can easily buy loyalty. She was sure the dark side bought him too. What if he dangled her and her boys like a carrot to string along the dark suits? Mama-bear anger hit her like a freight train.

She spun around to face him and yelled, "What if my kids had been here, Sam?"

Kirin's voice resonated off the block walls. She stepped toward him, fists clenched and one finger in his face. Her chest grazed his stomach and his body tensed at the touch. She pushed through the electricity zinging between them. She wanted to rip his eyeballs out. "Did you ever stop to consider them? Or Rosa?"

He had no answer.

She stomped around him, grabbed the fading flashlight off the floor and snapped the button to turn it off, but it was damaged from the fall and despite her best efforts, continued to shine.

As she struggled with it, she turned her head and growled, "I don't need you, And I don't need your protection. Stay away from me and my family. I don't want you around."

Anger and frustration made her tears fall faster. It infuriated her to cry when she was mad, but somehow her anger was mainlined to her damn tear ducts. She'd always been this way. She had no control over it. When she attempted to stifle a cry, she sobbed instead.

Sam wrapped his arms around her from behind and with gentle hands, took the flashlight. He unscrewed the bottom releasing the connection of the batteries. The flashlight died, and he tossed it on the pile of tarps.

He took her by the shoulders and spun her to face him in the dark, then pulled her in. He held tight. She pushed at his chest, but his arms were like steel, crushing her to him. Her mind wanted to scream for him to leave, but her broken heart was in complete control. She couldn't force her body to move away.

"I'm so sorry," he mumbled into her hair, then kissed the top of her head. He continued to say it as he trailed kisses from her forehead down her temple until his mouth covered hers. Warm and sweet but deeply stirring in places that hadn't been alive in years. As if someone had flipped a switch inside her, she changed from pushing him as hard as she could to pulling him to her. She didn't want him to stop. Her world felt complete when she was in his arms. She kissed him back until her mind gained control.

He couldn't love her. He'd already said it. Kirin shoved him with all her might. It did little to move him backward, but he stilled immediately.

Even in the dark, she knew she'd stunned him. Her lips tingled and stung as she wrestled away from his arms. She spun around to look for her purse in the dark. She could still feel the pressure where his arms had tightened around her. Her body ached to be held like that again. Finding it along the floor, she snatched up her purse, flung it around her body and started up the steps.

She stopped on the next to the last step and without looking back she fumed, "Don't protect me anymore, I'll take it from here, you're relieved of your obligation."

Kirin pushed open the trap door, walked through, and didn't look back once.

~*~

The shadows from sunlight coming through the windows were much longer than she'd expected. How long had they sat in the darkness? How long had she been in the dark about Sam? So trusting … so stupid. She wouldn't make that mistake again.

Rosa and her sister would be home with the boys any minute. When she crept back through the pantry, she grabbed the hidden gun and looked in the chamber to make sure it was loaded.

Numb from the losses of the day, she half wished someone was still there. She wanted someone else to hurt as much as she did. She shoved the gun in her pocket and sneaked around the house. As she checked the bedrooms, the rumble of Sam's truck speeding down the driveway and the crunching of gravel reached her ears. Kirin sat cross-legged in the hallway.

Angry and sad, she curled up on the carpet and grieved. Her inner voice made her stand and finish looking in each closet and each room. She had to make sure her family would be safe when they returned.

After Kirin searched every inch of her house, she ran downstairs and changed the door code. She had to remember to tell Rosa, so she wouldn't set it off. She whipped out her cell and made a few calls. The first, to a locksmith. She had no idea how they got into her house without a key, but those locks would change. Then she called a perimeter fence company, but they couldn't work her in for a few weeks. She toyed with calling the pound to buy a mean dog but decided she'd better not.

After hearing all about the movie and restaurant from two sleepy boys, Kirin made everyone dinner, put the boys to bed, and sat in the darkness as warm tears wet her pillow. She couldn't believe it'd been less than twenty-four hours when she couldn't wait to see Sam. And now he was gone. It would take some time to explain to her heart why her mind had to stop thinking about him.

Part of her didn't want to get past this. That stupid part was still under the delusion he could be one of the good guys in her story. Maybe he'd choose the light over the dark, and they could somehow still be together. *Get a grip, Kirin.* This isn't Hollywood.

Moonlight splayed through her window illuminating the green book. Without Sam to protect them, the dark suits might get wind she was fair game and come after her. She had to make it a priority to discover why they wanted it enough to put her and her family in harm's way.

She vowed, from this moment on, she wouldn't let the book out of her sight. She'd keep it in her purse when she was out of the house and keep it in the hidden safe when she was home and not digging through it.

What she needed more than anything right now was to talk to Kidd again. She had to know what she was up against. She also needed to find someone more tech savvy than her. Someone who would understand what the string of numbers meant.

Tomorrow, she'd find answers.

She had a bad feeling this hunt might take her places she didn't want to go.

Chapter Eighteen

Tuesday was just busy enough, she'd had little time to think about Sam. She'd put him as far out of her head as she could. She only wanted to wallow in her misery and be left alone. She was comfortable there. Misery was her old friend. They'd spent years rooming together, bunkmates really, if she was being honest.

Stacy and Laura both cornered her as soon as she got to work. She told them Sam had stood her up. She told them about confronting him in the restaurant and about how he was on her doorstep when she got home.

She didn't mention the men in her house. She didn't want to involve them in that drama, and she feared if anyone knew, somehow, they might use it against her and hurt her friends. Kirin's eyes welled up as an image of Sam driving away crossed her mind. She shuffled away after telling them it was over.

On her next break, she found Stacy and Laura whispering. They were plotting something. When they simultaneously stopped talking, Kirin raised an eyebrow at them.

Laura cleared her throat and smiled, "Well, your girl Stacy here thinks a night on the town is the perfect way to get over this man who hurt you." Laura shifted uncomfortably, "But I think a nice dinner at my house after I shove Adam and the kids out the door would be better, what do you think?"

Kirin hesitated. "I … I don't think I'd be good company for either."

Stacy stepped in front of Laura, pushing her rear end out playfully to knock Laura back.

"Hey!" Laura said, laughing.

Stacy looked as if they were planning espionage. She reached back and pulled Laura back into the huddle then lowered her tall frame to speak intimately with them.

"I think, we need to get Kirin to a club, have a few drinks, and get her mind off the guy who can't seem to remember his own name."

Stacy's thin eyebrows did pushups on her face, making Kirin laugh.

Laura smiled, then shrugged, "I'll be the DD. Come on, it'll be fun … like old times."

Kirin's face scrunched, "I don't know…"

Laura put a hand on her shoulder, "Think of it this way, how much trouble could we get into on a Tuesday night?"

~*~

Stacy scored reservations at Apollos, a restaurant voted number one in the city. After 10pm, the nightclub part of the building had bodies packed in as if they gave away hundred-dollar bills at the bar.

The boys were thrilled when Olivia, their favorite high schooler from church, walked in. Laura honked twice to pick Kirin up, and they headed to Stacy's house, so they could all ride together.

Stacy came dancing out of her house, with a big smile and arms waving like an orangutan released from the zoo. They were in for a fun night.

Stacy's fiancé Todd, who never talked much, stood in his normal pissed-off stance on the porch and glared as they pulled out of her driveway.

Kirin sat up front and stared at Stacy through the mirror in the visor. Her flamboyant attitude stilted temporarily. She whipped out her phone, typed something with fast fingers, then tossed it hard into her purse. With no provocation, Stacy talked aloud to herself, arms once again flailing.

"You know what? I'm a big girl. And I can do whatever the hell I want. If I want to go out with my friends on a damn Tuesday night, by God I'm gonna do it. I never go out anymore. Never! He's got the stick up his ass turned sideways."

Stacy snatched the compact out of her purse, flipped it open and looked herself over in the mirror, then continued as if she was already in a conversation nobody could hear. "… you know what, I don't care. I'm not letting this ruin our night. This night is about Kirin … and getting her laid."

Stacy's eyes locked on Kirin's in the visor's mirror. Kirin froze mid-lipstick application and sputtered, "Wh-what?"

Stacy horse-laughed. "Kidding. Just making sure you're listening."

"Oh my God, shut up," Kirin said, glaring at Stacy through the mirror, although her lips curved up in an unintentional smile. "We're not setting Kirin up with anyone, and nobody's getting laid."

Stacy raised her eyebrows.

"Okay, maybe you and maybe Laura, but not me. We're here to eat dinner and have fun. Kirin will be going home ... alone," she announced, finishing her lipstick.

"And forget about what's-his-name," Stacy added.

"Yeah and that," Kirin said, nodding.

Laura shook her head, smiling.

Stacy had talked Kirin into wearing a flirty, flowy dress with cutout shoulders and boots. She felt overdressed, but pretty.

As they walked into the two-story main lobby for both the restaurant and the bar, the hostess smiled wide at Kirin. Only at Kirin. *What*? Was there something on her dress? Kirin looked back at Stacy to find her head cocked sideways, surveying the hostess, and shrugging her shoulders.

Kirin zoned in on an enormous fish tank filled with all kinds of colorful exotics, something Apollos was known for, so she'd feel less awkward under the hostess's constant stare.

She tugged at her dress and glanced back. The woman continued to stare. When the hostess found their reservations, she talked and flirted with only Kirin as she placed them at the best dining table on the second floor. Kirin hoped nobody else noticed.

"Well, that was odd," Stacy said, elbowing Kirin after the hostess walked away.

"Tell me about it."

"If that dress caught *her* eye, imagine what it will do for the hordes of men here tonight," Stacy said as her eyebrows did pushups.

"Is it too much?" Kirin looked down and surveyed her dress. No cleavage showing, only shoulders, and legs. Compared to some of the tiny scraps of material Stacy used to wear when they went out clubbing, it was downright homely.

"Hell, no, you look amazing," Stacy said, flagging down a waiter for drinks.

Their table overlooked the nightclub on the first floor. They had a perfect view of the entire lit up bar and the pulsing dance floor below. Laura's jaw dropped, while Stacy bounced up and down in her seat like a three-year-old at Christmas.

Men were everywhere. Good-looking men. Kirin wondered if they'd stumbled upon "free beer and naked women night" as every eligible bachelor within a hundred miles was at the bar below.

Kirin sat closest to the short wall overlooking The Club. People buzzed down below like worker bees extracting honey. Their waiter sprinted up to the table and the girls ordered beers and an appetizer. Laura ordered her usual diet coke then whipped out her phone for the server to take a picture. Moments later, the waiter dropped the food and drinks as he flew by to greet the next guests.

Kirin took a long pull on her beer half listening to Laura and Stacy argue about the best band of the nineties and mesmerized by the flurry of people below. On the other side of the expansive square bar, she spotted a face she recognized. A face that sent anger speeding through her veins like lava. Downing the rest of her beer like a sorority girl, Kirin slammed it back on the table and rose. Her friends stared at her.

"Hey, anybody else need another one? Our waiter looks busy, so I'll run downstairs and get them. You guys need one?"

Kirin spoke quick. Too quick. Stacy's eyes narrowed as she glanced over the side of the wall toward the bar below. "Sure, honey. Go find us a *beer*." Stacy winked at Laura.

Laura fished in her purse for money, but Kirin waved her off, grabbed her ID and cash, and trotted through the restaurant and down the stairs.

The noise tripled as she walked down the grand staircase into The Club. She was stopped at the bottom of the stairs and had to show her ID. Flattery. Kirin moved through the crowd like a circus performer, sideways through a small gap here and on her tiptoes, there.

When she made it around to the far side of the enormous bar, she slowed her pace. She hoped he hadn't seen her coming, but he probably had. Kirin looked down the length of the bar where she'd seen his face. Gone.

She pushed up between an empty seat next to two girls. Several empty beer bottles sat like little statues in front of them as they continued what looked like an intense conversation. They didn't even notice her.

The woman behind the bar had more tattoos on her right hand than most people had on their whole bodies. She smiled and tilted her head back. "What 'cha need, hon?" she yelled over the music.

"Two Bud Lights, please."

The bartender jogged over and grabbed two cold bottles out of the freezer. As she uncapped them, she stood directly in front of where he'd been. The bartender dashed back with the bottlenecks intertwined between her fingers and slammed them on the bar. Kirin paid and tipped, then turned and stopped short.

Scar skulked back from the bathrooms, tugging on his too-tight jacket. His face angry, wrinkled, and somehow more sinister than the last time she'd seen him. The tell-tale scar glistened in the reflection of the dance floor lights. He eyeballed a tall woman's cleavage as he walked by her. Scar smirked as he ogled her. Climbing back up on his seat, he dug into his dinner placed before him.

The man shoved his napkin into his collar as if he starred in an old western. Anger coursed through her. This thug had broken into her house, chased her in the airport, and if she thought about, she was sure he was behind the cryptic texts. He'd made her feel unsafe in her own home. He might have been from the West Coast, but this was the South. He'd have better luck poking a stick at a black bear than going up against an angry Southern woman.

Feeling the brave effects of chugging her frosty beverage, Kirin turned. She took a deep breath, leveled her shoulders, and stomped toward him, carrying the beers.

Was it possible to break a bottle over someone's head like they do in movies? She smiled at the thought. He'd be sorry. Her mind raced with insults as she bridged the gap between them. She'd give him a piece of her mind, all right.

Grabbed.

Grabbed wasn't a strong enough word. She was *snatched* a few feet away from her target. Strong hands picked her up around the waist and in one seamless motion, she was relieved of the beers in her hands, which were placed on a nearby table. Her body was hoisted several feet away to the dance floor by an angry, green-eyed man. A man whose shirt smelled like spice and did things to her resolve. Slow-grinding romantic music played while he yelled at her.

"What the hell do you think you're doing?"

She pushed his rock-hard chest, but she might as well have been trying to move a house. He didn't budge, only glared, expecting an answer.

"I thought I told you to stop following me."

"Old habits die hard. Stop fighting me." He hissed through gritted teeth.

Her hands stilled on his chest as he swayed to the music, still glaring at her. Chin raised in defiance, she stared right back at him.

"I was only going to introduce myself. You know, Southern hospitality and all."

Sam bit down on his lip as one corner of his mouth hitched up. But his dark green eyes still held anger.

"I've never protected anyone so hell-bent on getting themselves killed."

When Kirin attempted to look around Sam to find Scar, Sam spun them around, so her back was to the bar. His eyes bored into hers as he nodded back toward Scar.

"That deadly man over there would take pleasure in choking the life out of you, right here in this bar. He'd pay his bill, spit on your lifeless body, and waltz out the door."

Kirin glanced toward Scar, who ate his food as if someone was about to steal it. Elbows out, head down and shoveling. The tattooed bartender observed Kirin and Sam with crossed arms and a furrowed brow.

She'd better make it seem as if she *wanted* to dance with him. Kirin swayed to the slow music. He pulled her closer. Her stupid heart flapped wildly. She told herself it was because of her run in with Scar. And not because of this man holding her.

Sam wrapped his arms tighter around Kirin's waist and for a second, she pretended it was real. After a few moments, she laid her head on his chest and breathed in the familiar scent of him. She stole a glance up at him. His eyes were closed. He was a good actor. She closed her eyes again. It was easier that way.

"Pretty dress." His voice was raspy and low.

"Thanks," she said into his chest.

The song ended, but they continued to sway. When Kirin opened her eyes to look around, Scar was gone. Sam held one hand on her waist as he leaned over to the corner of the empty table and grabbed the beers placing them back in her hand.

"Go back upstairs, eat something, then go *straight* home, got me?"

Unaffected. He was unaffected by her. She was only a target to be protected. A paycheck. Kirin shook her head and stomped around him to leave.

Sam grabbed her arm and pulled her back to him. Hard. Her chest pressed against the top of his abs. Sam pulled her chin up to look him in the eyes. He snagged a loose strand of hair and gently wrapped it around her ear, pushing her long hair behind her exposed shoulder. He grazed her shoulder with his fingers, sending electricity to her lower parts.

"You're killin' me, woman, you know that, right?"

Kirin shook her head no. Sam leaned down and placed a soft kiss on her cheek.

"Please, go home ... alone." He breathed into her ear.

Mind swirling, Kirin broke free and took the stairs two at a time. When she rounded the corner back toward the restaurant Todd, Stacy's fiancé stood at their table, red-faced and yelling. "...So you came here on *meat* night? You're telling me you didn't know it was men's night? Come on, Stace, I'm a whole lot smarter than that."

Stacy rose as tall as Todd. Her voice lowered to a growl. "You listen here, you little prick, I came here to cheer Kirin up, nothing more. You need to get your head outta your ass and realize that for some odd reason, I love you. I'm not going anywhere. And I'm sure as hell not out here trying to find a replacement for you. But if you don't stop acting like an immature ass, I just might."

Stacy sat hard, with her back straight as a rod, took a swig of her beer, and slammed it back on the table shoving a chip into her mouth. She never even blinked. Todd stared at her, grabbed her beer, shook his head, and left with it.

Laura sat still, wide-eyed.

Kirin placed a new beer in front of Stacy, then sat and waited.

Stacy shoved three more chips into her mouth as the restaurant resumed its noise level. She turned, glancing at Kirin as the color returned to her face.

"What took you so long and why are you so red-faced?" Stacy took a long pull of the fresh one, her hands trembling.

"Long line and I ran up the steps two at a time." It was partially the truth.

Stacy pulled her beer away from her mouth and shot Kirin a look of disbelief. Finally, she broke into a smile.

"He's good looking."

Kirin had just stuffed a chip loaded with spinach dip into her mouth and stopped mid-chew. Swallowing hard, she turned to Stacy.

"Who?" she replied innocently.

"The tall stubble-faced man who danced provocatively with you and kissed you. Would that be Sam?"

Kirin stuttered, "Oh...him. Well, yeah."

Laura leaned forward, eyebrows high and hopeful.

Sam would never stop protecting her, it was his job. She had to defend herself and her boys, but she needed answers even more. She wanted to know how far his loyalty ran with the black suits. And if she could trust him.

She had a dangerously sexy man sending her mixed signals. Kirin closed her eyes to drown out the thumping of The Club music. Was Sam that good of an actor?

Kirin sat, eyes closed, shaking her head trying to make sense of it all when Stacy's hand rested on the back of her chair.

"No worries, love, you don't have to know tonight. I'm glad he showed up, though. Prior to my dumbass fiancé showing up, you were smiling when you came up the stairs. That's a great start." Stacy winked at her and took another swig of her beer.

After they finished appetizers and more drinks than any of them were used to, the three paid their bill and headed to The Club downstairs. Scar was nowhere in sight. The three sat at a table, drank coffee and relived old times. Her stomach muscles felt tighter because of all the laughter.

Laura yawned making Kirin touch her watch. Midnight-*crap*. She'd really meant to do as Sam asked and go home early. Who was she kidding? No, she didn't. He didn't get to tell her what to do. And anyway, she'd had fun.

The three friends left the restaurant and Laura drove them home.

Kirin paid her babysitter, locked the doors and formulated a plan in the shower. Sam obviously knew much more about her situation and her father's business than she gave him credit for. Could she glean information from him? He knew her father and her late husband. He knew about the book, and he knew the goons following her.

Maybe he could explain why the book was so important. Might be worth buying him dinner to discover the truth. She'd have to figure out a way to shut off her heart to do this, though. She didn't want to believe it was real.

Then again, if Sam could pretend, she could play that game too, right?

Chapter Nineteen

Wednesday morning Kirin jumped up and got ready in a flash. She ignored her three-beer headache. Months prior, she'd signed up for a continuing education course in nearby Sevierville, near the Smoky Mountains. She needed the credit, and if nothing else, she might squeeze in a hike. The course would end at noon and she'd be too close to the mountains not to go. She packed a separate bag with hiking clothes and shoes, just in case, and then threw on a T-shirt dress, flats, and a sweater for her morning class. Comfortable and easy.

The sweet smell of spring wafted into her car window as she drove to her local quick mart for a hot cup of coffee. She turned the heat on. Spring mornings were often close to freezing. Later in the day though, she'd change it to A/C. Caffeine was mandatory for the headache and the forty-five-minute drive.

She pulled into an empty parking space right in front of the doors. Three spaces down sat a red truck. Of course. Sam knew where all her favorite places were. Here was her chance to make up and possibly snag an information-date. She checked her lip gloss in the mirror, told her heart to power down and walked into the store, shoulders back with a ton of confidence.

~*~

Sam filled his mug with coffee toward the back of the store near the drink machines. His head pounded from the loud music in The Club. His mind shifted to Kirin. Her long blonde hair sweeping across the back of that dress he couldn't seem to rip his eyes from.

And the brave way she stomped toward danger. Brave or careless, he couldn't decide. God she had a death wish sometimes. Had to talk Saul's brother off the damn ledge afterward. Took a while to get it through his thick skull that getting the book back took time.

His back was to the door, but he knew. Knew she was there. He could sense her and that was weird.

When she tried to creep up behind him, her perfume reached him before she did. He inhaled with his eyes closed, opened them and spoke.

"How was your date?" Even to his own ears, his voice sounded tight and angry.

"How did you know I was behind you?" Kirin whined, her voice playful.

He turned to face her, with curious eyes.

"Hi." She smiled big.

She must've gone home with someone from the bar. "So, I'm guessing *you* had a good night?" He sounded whiny, like a child who didn't get the ice cream flavor they wanted. Feeling defeated, he turned back to add sugar to his coffee.

It took her only a beat to catch what he was saying.

"No," she blurted out, then lowered her voice, "No, I went home alone like I was *told* to do. I'm just happy to run into you."

His shoulders relaxed, and he turned. His smile crept up automatically in response to hers.

Kirin put a hand on his arm. He stilled at her touch. "What if we called a truce? Let me buy you dinner one night this weekend, as friends? Maybe Saturday?"

His face lit up and then darkened. "I have to go out of town Saturday. I'm free Friday night, though."

"Perfect." She scooted next to him to grab the coffee decanter and shoved him with her hip. He stared down at her. A sexy smile played at her lips as he stirred his already well-stirred coffee.

She poured her coffee, set it on the counter and then leaned over in front of him to grab the creamer. He stilled. She was flirting. She elbowed him in the stomach as she passed back in front of him. Her smile unfolded faster, reaching her eyes. It knocked him a little off balance. The heat in his return gaze must've thrown her.

She stutter-stepped backward, cleared her throat then asked, "Where do you want to go?" she stared at her coffee as she added cream.

"How about my place? I'll make dinner."

Her brow furrowed and she chewed her lip.

"Uh, okay…but you don't have to do that. We could—"

"Nope. I insist. I can cook, ya know."

She swallowed hard. Her voice sounded higher than before, like she was nervous. "Okay. I'll bring wine and a movie, deal?"

Sam nodded. *Hell yeah.* Her eyes looked unsure, but he shot her a reassuring smile before walking to the front to pay for his coffee. They met again at the door.

"Until Friday," he leaned over and whispered, opening the door with his back and sticking a piece of paper with his address and cell number into her hand.

"Six?" Kirin yelled over the top of her car as he headed for the other side of the parking lot.

"Perfect." he yelled back.

~*~

Lord. A romantic dinner at his house. That wasn't in the plan. She wondered if he was only asking her to his house, so he wouldn't have to worry about her doing something stupid again in public. She didn't care. She'd bring an extra potent wine and make flirty conversation. She'd drag out of him whatever he knew about her father and his book.

But Kirin's heart kept interrupting. This was a real date with dangerous consequences for her fragile already busted up heart. She ignored that side totally. She needed answers and this was the quickest way to get them. Placing her sunglasses on her face, she cranked up the music and drowned out any fears about the date. She'd think about it again on Friday.

~*~

"Hello?"

"I saw you." The gruff voice she didn't recognize, laughed bitterly.

Had to be Scar. Kirin swallowed hard. Not one thing she'd meant to say to him at the bar was inside her head at that moment. And without her liquid courage, her brain emptied like a library at closing time.

"Next time, your little boyfriend won't be there to save you."

Two beeps indicated the call ended.

Kirin tossed her phone into the seat next to her like spiders lived inside. Her phone rang again, and she glanced over. Another unknown number. Nope. Not answering that one.

As she sped down the entrance ramp to get on I-40 heading toward the mountains, her phone beeped with an incoming text.

She didn't want to look, but damn, curiosity won out. She flipped the phone back over and glanced down.

"Where the hell are you goin'?"

She tapped the mic and spoke a text, "Who is this?"

The return text bounced back. "Sam, who'd you expect?"

Kirin dug the number out of her sweater pocket. Whew, it matched. She hit the dial button and put the phone on speaker. He didn't even say hello.

"Where're you going?"

"I have a class in Sevierville. Why? Wait, are you following me?"

"Duh."

A tiny shiver of delight ran up her spine. "Well, I'm not going to work today."

"Obviously." His tone was dry.

"You know if you have to follow me everywhere, you might as well ride with me, instead of wasting your gas."

"I'm fine. How long is your class, Kirin?"

"I think we finish at noon, but I probably won't be home until four."

"Why?"

"I'm gonna change and find a trail to hike."

"No." He said it as if he told a two-year-old she couldn't have another cookie. Her jaw tightened.

"You don't get to tell me what to do."

Sam let out a long-exasperated breath. "You're gonna get lost or fall off the side of a mountain *by accident*."

He was trying to scare her. Tight-lipped she replied, "I'll be fine. Go do whatever you need to do today." And hung up.

Why did it make her so angry and yet so happy he still followed her? It was his job. *She* was his job. It wasn't as if he protected her because he wanted to. She had to remember, he was paid to do it.

Kirin sped up. Anger pushed her accelerator.

~*~

Four long hours and a buffet of caffeinated drinks later, Kirin stumbled out into the sunshine toward her car. She smiled. The weather was in full cooperation for her hike; warm enough to ditch the sweater she'd brought, but cool enough not to sweat. She didn't care what Sam said, she wouldn't let them make her afraid of a little hike. She did, however, make a mental note to find a popular trail with plenty of people.

Starting her car, she pulled out into traffic. Crap. She forgot to change clothes. Looking ahead and in her rearview mirror, the sea of tourist vehicles moved along at a snail's pace, but she couldn't get back off the highway, she'd never get back on.

Sitting in traffic, she took off her flats and tossed them in the backseat. Then pulled her bag up front with her tan shorts, white shirt, hiking boots and socks inside. Traffic stopped momentarily letting some crazy person inch across three lanes of traffic to get to a Cracker Barrel. She used the stop to pull on warm socks and pull the shorts over her ankles.

At the next red light, a man on a motorcycle pulled up next to her. His helmet indicated his focus was straight ahead, but the facemask was blacked out, so she couldn't tell.

Aw hell. If she flashed him, she flashed him.

With one foot firmly on the brake, she pulled her shorts up under her dress to the tops of her thighs, momentarily exposing pink polka dotted panties. Great. Lifting her rear, she yanked them the rest of the way up, and buttoned them under her dress.

Motorcycle Man never flinched. She probably looked odd, but so what?

The top would take some maneuvering. If she were in her twenties, she'd have ripped off the dress and put her shirt on, mid-traffic, without missing a beat. Now, she was more self-conscious. Eyes were always on her. Damn her father and damn black-suited men, they'd made her paranoid.

Finally, through traffic but still wearing a dress, shorts, and hiking boots sitting inside her bag next to her, she took the bypass. She'd avoid the neon signs, theme parks, and shopping malls and drive straight to the hiking trails. She closed her eyes briefly to take in the sweet smell; pine trees, dirt, and fresh air, exactly what she needed.

She pulled over and parked at the first trailhead she came to with only a few cars parked in front. Locking the doors, Kirin crawled into the backseat and grabbed her boots to change. Her windows were tinted from the factory, which was to say *not* dark, but as she looked around. Nobody in sight.

Kirin flung off her dress, revealing her baby blue bra. No big deal, except she'd forgotten to get her shirt out of the bag up front. Stupid how five cups of coffee in the seminar messed with her ability to think clearly. She huffed in exasperation, pushed her whole body in-between the two front seats rooted around for her shirt. Please say she didn't forget to pack a shirt.

"Aha!" she said to herself and shook the shirt in celebration. A man with an amused smile wearing a hoodie, jeans, and hiking boots, leaned against the post directly in front of her car. Arms crossed, his grin was infectious. Clearly, he was enjoying the show.

Kirin draped her shirt over her chest and with her index finger made a swirling motion, telling her voyeur to turn around.

Sam's smug smile faded, as heat filled his eyes. Slowly, he shook his head no. The car immediately felt ten degrees warmer.

She changed fingers to give him a new sign and sat back to pull her shirt on. Why did everything seem to come so easy to him? And why did it seem she always was the one who looked stupid?

Stepping out of the car, she pulled a hair tie off her wrist and flung her hair in a loose bun, then turned to get behind her SUV to stretch. He didn't need to get the full show.

"You 'bout ready?" he yelled from the front of her car.

"You're an ass," she called back.

"What?" He chuckled. "I can't help if you like to get naked in your car in public."

At the exact moment he said it, an elderly man and woman started on the trailhead. The man turned to look at Kirin and snickered. Sam couldn't contain his laughter.

Kirin huffed past him, picked up a walking stick propped against the sign and stomped up the paved pathway.

He'd be damn lucky if she didn't push him over the side of the mountain for fun.

His long legs allowed him to catch up to her quickly and when he did, he nudged her with his elbow. She wasn't biting. She wished she hadn't seen the stupid-cute grin plastered on his face.

"What?" she snapped.

"Blue. It looks good on you."

Kirin stopped. Hands on her hips, she sent daggers with her eyes.

His face at first held confusion, then his eyebrows shot up. "Wait … no … I meant the *dress*. The blue dress looked good on you, not the bra. Well, the bra looked nice too, but … aw hell, I was talking about the dress."

Sam shoved his hands in his pockets then stared at the pavement. He looked so cute, like a scolded little boy with his flushed face. It melted her, how he tripped all over himself, making him seem more human and less perfect. She walked again, and after a beat, he followed.

"Umm-hmm," she said, glancing sideways.

"Oh, shut up, you knew what I meant."

"Pervert."

"Yep, that's me. A perv." He glanced ahead of them and behind them, then took Kirin's hand and switched places with her.

"What're you doing?"

"Putting you next to the safe mountainside and away from the jagged side that falls down a ravine. I've seen you walk, remember?"

Kirin stuck her foot out and tripped him. As he recovered she sped up and moved back to the side closest to the stream that hugged the trail.

"I'm obviously *not* the clumsy one," she pointed out, smiling.

His mouth twitched up, "Yeah? Except for *elevators* though, right?"

Kirin stopped cold. Her mouth hung open.

"That was you? You caught me in that elevator in my father's office building? Were you following me in California too?"

He shot her a look.

"I had no idea," she whispered to herself, staring into the trees. Stunned.

"I told you, invisible. I'm good at my job. And that was a happy accident. Two jobs colliding."

He walked again but she stood there, mouth open.

"You comin'?" he called over his shoulder. He picked up a rock and threw it down the side of the mountain into the stream below. She ran to catch up.

"Why were you mad?"

"What?"

"In the elevator."

"What makes you think I was mad?"

"You were. I know you."

Sam looked at her, staring for a moment, then shook his head.

"Well, first, you."

"Me? What'd I do? I didn't even know you then!"

"You weren't paying attention. You fell on a stranger in an elevator. What if I'd been one of the bad guys? It was like you were *trying* to get hurt."

"You *are* one of the bad guys." She elbowed him, but he didn't smile. "But you were there to catch me, so no harm done. Plus, it was the shoes."

"Right." He laughed.

"It was! I'd just left my father's funeral, so I probably didn't have my head on straight. Thanks for cutting me some slack on that one."

He looked down and nodded.

131

After a moment, he finished. "And Mrs. Westin. The wealthy widow on the phone, remember her? She had the bright idea that she'd sell a coveted piece of property to my boss, but only if I went to certain functions … as her date."

Kirin giggled. "Did you? I didn't realize you were a *full-service* escort."

She'd meant it as a joke, but Sam's body went rigid. A silent, icy wall hung between them as they hiked the inclined trail. She hadn't meant to hit a nerve but obviously, she had.

The trail narrowed to only one body distance across, making them walk in a single file line. Sam took the lead. To their right was a curvy wall of rock and to their left was a small stream ten feet below. The stream followed the path's every curve. The sound of swishing water increased with each step.

After a moment, she poked him in the back, and he glanced back at her. "Sorry. I didn't mean to offend you."

Sam waved it off like a gnat but didn't say a word. The muscles in his jaw contracted, hard as stone.

His long legs moved at an angry pace and tightened with each step. His body was angled forward, but his head swiveled back and forth as if a bear would come out of the woods at any second. Kirin moved in right behind him, hitting her stick on the partially paved trail and breathing heavy to keep up.

She tapped his foot with her walking stick, making him turn his head. She wanted to lighten his mood. Silent, he kept moving. She tapped it again, harder and he immediately stopped. She'd been staring at his feet and ran face first into the brick wall of his back. Finally, he laughed and without a word grabbed her hand, and pulled her in front of him, so she could lead.

The trails were several degrees colder than the parking area. For one, the canopy of trees blocked most of the sunlight and the higher you climbed the cooler the air. Add the rush of the cold mountain water in the stream alongside them and a waterfall about a mile ahead, and it was chilly.

Sam took off his sweatshirt and nudged her with it. Her heart melted a little. She shook her head.

"Take it. It's hot, and I don't want to carry it."

She turned and looked back at him. He was being kind. There was no way he was warm. Kirin nodded, thanked him and pulled it over her head. Immediately, she regretted it.

Jeez. It smelled amazing. It caused happy bodily reactions that shouldn't be taking place in public. She'd have to accidentally keep this.

The trail widened and flattened out, so they could walk side by side.

Sam's phone buzzed, and he looked at it, never slowing his stride. If she hadn't been a seasoned hiker, they would've had to stop before now. Keeping up with his long strides was a chore. She glanced at him. His eyebrows furrowed. At first, since he was breathing heavily she thought he was huffing because of the pace, then it dawned on her, he was reading.

Sam stopped and typed something furiously into his phone.

"Everything okay?"

"Fine," he said, through clenched teeth.

"You suck at lying, by the way," she stated, staring straight ahead.

Sam turned and leveled a look at her as he shoved his phone back into his pocket.

"Oh yeah? And how do you know I'm lying?"

"Your eleven."

"Pardon?"

"Your eleven," she stated slower.

"I heard what you said. I don't know what it means."

Kirin rolled her eyes. "The two creases between your eyebrows. They deepen when you lie. It's pretty easy to spot."

Sam reached up and touched the skin between his eyes. His face, perplexed.

Kirin laughed. She dropped her walking stick and sprinted ahead. The mist coming off the waterfall came into view. She glanced back over her shoulder. "Last one there's a rotten egg."

His eyes narrowed, and his smile widened as he chased after her.

The swoosh of rushing water grew louder. Around the next corner was the bottom of a ten-foot waterfall over mountain rocks. The water at the base was so clear and cold, the air around it held a halo of smoke. And the temperature had dropped fifteen degrees.

Kirin stopped to take in the sight of it, as Sam caught up to her and did the same. Even with his sweatshirt, she shivered at the cold air. She looked at him and felt guilty. Sam wore only a thin T-shirt and was forced to do the hike to follow her. When she pulled at Sam's sweatshirt to give it back, he let out a growl and shook his head.

Sam found a spot on a big rock with a perfect view of the water. She followed him over and sat down next to him. They sat, gazing at the waterfall for several minutes, both quiet and contemplating. Kirin's curiosity got to her.

"You okay?" she said.

"Yeah, fine, why?"

"You were angry texting."

"I was."

"Want to elaborate on that?"

"Nope." His jaw clenched tight.

Kirin stared at him. This was about trust. He obviously didn't trust her. She shook her head and moved off the rock and away from him. She stood several feet away, arms folded.

"Come back." His voice sounded playful.

"Why?" she spun back around, raising her voice over the sound of the waterfall. "You don't trust me. You tell me nothing about yourself and, yet you know *everything* about me. How is that fair? It's not. I'm damn trustworthy, and if we're gonna work together, you gotta let me in. You gotta have a little faith."

The elderly couple they'd seen at the trailhead popped out from behind the waterfall heading toward where Kirin and Sam stood. Sam motioned for Kirin to come back. She shook her head.

Arms still folded, she stood her ground.

Sam stood, brushing the dirt off his pants and walked over to stand next to her. For several minutes he only stared at the waterfall. Finally, he spoke loud over the noise of the water.

"My life is … *unconventional*. I rely only on myself. Before your dad, I didn't trust anyone, not even my family."

Sam picked up a rock and skipped it across the pool of water. He'd been fond of her father. A tinge of jealousy reared its head, but she couldn't tell if she was jealous of him or of her dad.

"I'm sorry," he said, turning toward her. "There are things I can't tell you, for your own safety. But I'll try to be more open. And I'll tell you what I can."

She was grateful he'd cracked open a little. "Thank you."

He volleyed back her smile. Sam walked back to sit on the rock, while Kirin kicked off her boots and socks to wade in the small pool at the base of the fall. Sam shook his head at her like she was a fool.

Playfully, she kicked water at him. A devilish grin swept across his face.

With one movement, he stood on the rock and jumped. His strategy appeared to be to land next to her in the wading pool with his boots on and splash her back.

His plan backfired. Epically. Everybody knew that the rocks beneath the water were as slick as trying to ice skate on snot. Apparently, he didn't. His feet shot out from underneath him and he landed flat on his back in shin deep water. He screamed like a four-year-old girl on a ferris wheel. And raced cursing out of the water.

Soaked from head to toe, her tall savior looked like a mortified, drowned rat. His face held shock at how badly his plan had failed. She tried to stifle her giggles but holding them in made it even funnier.

It didn't take Sam long to decide she needed to get wet too. He took one athletic step toward her and tackled her. They both fell into the icy water. This time the scream was hers, but she continued to laugh. Soaked and trembling, she was grateful when they descended toward the car and the temperatures rose a little.

They were mostly dry when they reached her car. She found towels in the back of her SUV. They stood with the back hatch open drying themselves off and nudging each other like two kids on a playground. When she turned to find her key to start the car and turn on the heat, he was gone and so was the key. The engine roared to life. Sam sat behind the wheel monkeying with the dials. It was such a caring gesture. She stared, gratefulness mixed with something else. It twisted her insides. She was sure she wouldn't need the car heat anymore.

He stood next to the open door and waited. Kirin closed the back hatch and sat in the driver's seat, looking up at him. She rolled the window down as he closed the door.

"Wait for me okay?"

"Sure."

Kirin pulled her visor down, so she wouldn't stare at him while he put his motorcycle gear on. She caught sight of herself in the mirror. Good gravy. She looked as if she'd run a 5k after swimming the English Channel in winter.

She stole another glance at him. The world was unfair. He looked perfect. He noticed her gawking at him and shook his head, grinning as he swung one leg over his bike and started it. With the black visor lifted on his helmet, he mouthed the word "Friday," smiled and pulled out.

Chapter Twenty

Will's first research paper was due Friday, so right after Thursday's taco dinner, she loaded the boys up and headed to the library. A win-win. She'd brought her notebook with the odd clues she'd found. She could do some research of her own while helping Will. Plus, she could keep an eye on the littlest turkey perusing through the children's audio books, sitting on a Mickey Mouse bean bag with bright pink headphones on.

The Powell Library was best known for its floor to ceiling stacked-stone square fireplace. The crackling fire always made her want to curl up on one of the reading couches with a novel. It reminded her of the huge fireplaces in Hogwarts.

Kirin reserved two computers; one for her and one for Will. When everyone settled in, she typed in the numbers she'd found, but it took her nowhere. She studied them, added them together and even looked for a common denominator. She tried assigning each number a letter to determine if it spelled something out, but nothing worked. Giving up, for now, she'd move on to the name she found. She googled: Manfred Pitts, Savannah, Georgia.

When she was young, before her mama died, they'd lived in Savannah for about a year. Well, at least she'd been told they did.

The only thing she remembered clearly about Savannah was St. Patrick's Day. Schools closed, and people everywhere were decked out in green, heading to the street parties downtown by the docks. Oh, and green Jell-O. To a six-year-old girl, green Jell-O was the bomb.

Kirin Googled the name but didn't get far. She'd found a seventeen-year-old Manny Pitts in Texas, and a Manfred Pitts in South Dakota who recently celebrated his ninety-first birthday. Neither of those were right.

She used a few different search engines. One hit on a computer business in Savannah whose sole proprietor was a Manfred Pitts. Pitts Web Design and Commercial Recycling

Kirin jotted the information down on one of Will's scratch papers, then typed in the website address.

The site had colorful graphics and eye-catching fonts. She searched through several screens, but no pictures of Mr. Pitts. Shoot. Looking at their rates she swallowed her tongue. Web design was not cheap. On her way home, she'd call the store and finagle more information.

Kirin helped Will find a few more information sources, checked out a few audio books for Little Jack and ushered everyone into the car. She dialed the phone number for Pitts Web Design

After three rings, a woman with a southern accent and a gravelly smoked-a-pack-a-day voice answered.

"Pitts Web Design, May I help you?"

"Yes, ma'am, can you tell me what your store hours are today?"

Her reply sounded as if she was bored. "Monday through Friday, eight to four and Saturday eight to noon and closed on Sunday.*"*

Next question. "Great, can you tell me if Mr. Pitts does the web designing himself or does he contract that out these days?"

"Yes, he does it himself. What type of business do you have?"

Crap, she didn't have a lie ready. *Think, Kirin.*

"Um … a catering business in Tennessee, with a specialty in … apple pies."

It was the first thing that popped into her mind.

"Oh, sure, dear, he can take care of that for you. Oh, and, honey, nobody 'round here calls him Mr. Pitts. Everyone calls him Kidd."

Her mouth dropped open. *Yes.*

Then the woman asked, "Can I have him call you, dear?"

"Oh, yes, please," Kirin answered way too cheerily. *Rein it back in.* Kirin gave the woman her name and number, letting the woman know how anxious she was to get started.

"Alrighty, I'll have him call you. Honey, you have a blessed day."

"Thanks, you too." She hung up and did a happy dance in her SUV.

She smiled the entire way home. Proud she'd uncovered more of the puzzle her father had left her, but those numbers still eluded her. Then it hit her, she knew the exact person to figure it out. Uncle Dean, the man loved games, pranks, riddles, anything he had to figure out.

She laid her notebook on the passenger seat and dialed his cell.

"Kirin? Everything all right?"

"Yeah. I've got a quick question for you."

"You still mad about the pranks?" Excitement bounced in his voice. She was sure this was payback for her teenage years.

"No. But if I find another slimy frog swimming in my bathtub, I'm going to start retaliating."

Uncle Dean chuckled. "That's not one I taught them. Good for them! Following in my footsteps." He laughed even harder. Finally catching his breath, he said, "All right, honey, sorry. So, what's up?"

She loved this man. He was fun-loving and ferociously loyal. For never having kids of his own and having an angry eight-year-old dropped in his lap, he'd always been kind, loving, and protective. He'd never treated her as a niece by marriage, but like his own child. She couldn't have asked for a better substitute dad, which made it all the harder to lie to him.

"So," she cleared her throat, "I'm reading this mystery and within the story, there's a puzzle. I can't seem to work it out. It's a random set of numbers with dots between. And I thought since you love puzzles, you might help me figure it out?"

"Sure, I haven't met a puzzle yet that stumped me. Wanna text it to me?"

She didn't know how secure her cell might be. If they could text her, they might somehow read her texts.

"I've got it right here, can I read it to you?"

Grunting, he shuffled papers around.

"Yeah, sure. Hang on. Ah, okay, I got it, shoot."

Kirin read the numbers to him and told him the avenues she'd exhausted so far, but none panned out. God, she hated to lie to him. Then again, the less he knew about it, the safer he'd be.

Now, she had only to discover who had the third torn out page. She prayed Kidd would call or message after dinner. Maybe then, she'd get some answers.

~*~

After putting the boys to bed and gathering everything she needed for work the next day, she ran upstairs and logged on to Messenger.

He was there waiting.

Kirin, you there?

I'm here.

How are the followers?

Haven't seen 'em in days. Maybe they gave up?

Not likely. Hey, an interesting thing happened today. A woman called my shop needing a website designed for her apple pie business.

☺ *Found a name in my artifact.* Her rapid fingers sent another message: *You know, this would be much easier face to face.*

He took forever to respond. His message finally popped through.

Do you like baseball?

Who doesn't?

Good answer. Braves game 1pm Saturday. Think you could get away?

Will you answer all my questions?

And then some.

Then yes!!

He replied. *See you soon, KTL*

See you MP, she typed back.

This was possibly more exciting than the pretend date with Sam Friday night.

Chapter Twenty-One

Friday night. She rushed home from work and ushered Rosa out the door early. The observant woman eyed her as if she'd stolen something. Rosa had prepared chicken and dumplings in the crockpot for their supper. While the boys ate, she ran upstairs for a quick shower. When she came back down, her phone flashed a missed text from her aunt, they'd be there in five minutes to get the boys. She'd asked them to babysit for a few hours while she went to Sam's house, but they'd insisted on a sleepover.

The doorbell rang and within five minutes everyone was gone, and the house was quiet. She was all alone, staring into her closet fighting with herself about what to wear.

If she picked something too revealing, he might think it was a real date. Her stomach fluttered. This wasn't a date. It was an 'information-seeking-meeting.' Right. Her mind needed to explain that to her heart. Plus, this was the guy who stood her up. She didn't need to go overboard with the outfit.

But she needed to look pretty. She still needed information. With several failed outfits piled on the floor, she grabbed a lime green skirt that hung a few fingers above her knee and a sleeveless white V-neck button-down with a sweater over it. Cute lime shoes, earrings and a dab of perfume topped it off.

She checked the time. Fifteen minutes to finish hair and makeup before it was time to leave. She'd typed in his address into her GPS. Only a ten-minute drive. No wonder he followed her so easily.

As the crow flew, it wasn't far, but navigating curvy backroads would take the entire ten minutes. She finished her hair and makeup, then changed purses to one large enough to fit the book.

Staring at it in her hands, she knew the safest place would be a safe deposit box at the bank or even a safe inside her home, but she was constantly looking through it. And somehow, it dawned on her, it comforted her. She shook her head, stuffed it inside her purse, and set off toward his house.

After several stops and turns, she was convinced her GPS was on meth. She locked her doors at a deserted crossroads. Thick trees lined all sides of the intersection. No street signs, and no signs of life. Her phone repeatedly told her to turn right, indicating she'd "arrived."

Her head spun side to side, as if she followed a tennis match. There was no flippin' driveway to her right! She was in the damn twilight zone. The woman's voice on her GPS repeated, "Arrived" until she told her to shut up, pressed end and tossed it in the seat next to her.

She inched closer to the intersection, still squinting. If she hadn't noticed bits of gravel in the road, she'd have never seen it. A long gravel driveway emerged, hidden by two overgrown bushes. She had to back up and swing wide to navigate her SUV between them. She winced, anticipating a scraping sound down both sides of her vehicle, but it never came. Those bushes had to be less than an inch away from her paint.

The gravel turned into two wide strips of dirt, with a neatly mowed line of grass down the center. It looked as if it'd been made by a covered wagon. She hoped she was on the right path, because there was no room to turn around.

She drove slowly, not entirely convinced she wasn't driving into deliverance. She checked the door locks again in a spot where the forest grew so thick it looked like nighttime.

A few hundred feet ahead, the trees thinned out to reveal a quaint rock bridge over the top of a small stream. From afar it looked old, as if she was being transported into another time, but upon closer inspection, parts of it were new.

Off to her right were trees covered in moss and to the left sat a bright luscious field with horses and a small barn. A few feet past the bridge stood a fence with a locked gate.

She crept toward the gate, rolled her window down and searched for some way to get in. Cleverly hidden behind a bush were a camera and a speaker. Both were invisible until you were right on top, like the driveway.

She leaned out the window and pushed the button, ready to turn around if this was the wrong place. Without a word the gate opened. She hesitated, then drove through.

The gate slammed closed behind her. She stared at it for a second in her rear-view mirror, with a sinking feeling of being trapped. This place was locked down like a prison. She wondered what sort of people Sam dealt with to keep him holed up on the side of a mountain.

The dusty road curved to the left ascending the side of the steep mountain. Spring clung to everything around her and the air smelled sweet. As she rounded the last turn, the ground leveled off and out from the top sprung a rustic cabin snuggled by trees and grass. Twilight settled in over the clear mountain range, and the view was spectacular. It was like something from a dream.

Thanks to getting lost, she'd arrived a few minutes late. She parked to the side of the cabin, shut off her engine, and opened her door.

The cabin glowed from lamps next to the windows. Thanks to the open front door and raised windows, she had a clear line of sight straight into the cabin into a large living room and behind that, his kitchen. The cabin was anchored in the front by a wrap-around porch. One side of the porch held a wooden swing draped in a red blanket. God, she hoped she was in the right place.

Leaning on her car door she strained to listen. A radio played soft country music. Romantic country music. *Crap.* Sam's low, smooth voice sang along, and she giggled. Finally, something he hadn't perfected. Through the window she saw him moving around and making dinner. Even being domestic he commanded respect. The muscles in his back contracted as he bent over to put a pan in the oven. She raised up on her tiptoes like a prairie dog.

Lord get a grip, Kirin.

He stopped singing and strode through the living room, then pushed open the screen door and stood, legs wide, wiping his hands on a small towel. His worn blue jeans hung low and he'd traded his usual T-shirt for an untucked white button-down that hugged his chest. No shoes. He looked so relaxed. As her eyes swept up to his face, a sexy, heart-dropping smile spread across his lips.

She shook her head, opened her back door, and took her time grabbing the bottle of wine and movie. She took a deep breath, shut her car door and walked toward him.

"Hello, beautiful," he said as his eyes swept over her. "You look nice."

Sam had a slight redness to his face as if he'd sprinted around his house.

"Nice place," she responded lightly.

"Thanks. Did you have any trouble finding it?" His eyebrows raised, hopeful as if he took great pains to make it hard to find.

"Nah," she lied.

He rolled his eyes and propped open the screen door with his backside. She turned sideways to slink between Sam and the door but didn't judge the distance well enough. Her chest brushed up against his abs as she passed him. Electrical currents almost stopped her in her tracks. He placed his free hand on the small of her back as she passed. A chill ran up her spine.

Holy Jesus, this was not gonna be easy. His entire house smelled like him. That intoxicating spice and manly smell permeated every crack in the walls. How was she going to stay aloof with all this maleness everywhere?

"Want me to take your sweater?"

She knew he'd be able to tell exactly how much his touch had affected her if she took the sweater off.

"No thanks, I'm good."

The smell of dinner wafted in over the manly smell and her stomach growled.

"Something smells amazing. What is it?"

"Dinner," he answered, eyebrows up.

She shot him a glare and one side of his lips curved, showing the dimple. "Baked chicken, potatoes, and green beans from last year's garden."

She nodded, then Sam led her through the comfortable living room and into his kitchen.

"The chicken has about twenty-five minutes left, wanna open the wine and I'll give you a tour?"

"Sure, point me toward the glasses?" He pointed to an upper cabinet. She pulled down two tall wine glasses and poured them each a full glass of sweet Pinot Grigio. She hadn't meant to pour so much. Then again, some liquid courage couldn't hurt.

Without warning, Sam stood right behind her. He leaned in, brushing her back with his hand while picking up his glass and taking a generous swig.

Lord, her knees shook. Something about him—his clean smell, this place, standing close…she couldn't put her finger on it, but every few minutes, she couldn't breathe. Even after his hand was gone, electricity pooled in the spot where he'd touched her.

Kirin picked up her glass. Her fingers trembled. She turned, pretending to look at something interesting outside.

"Ready for the tour, madam?" Sam held out his hand.

"Sure, lead the way." Sipping her wine, she put her hand in his. He stilled for a second and took another gulp. Maybe he felt the zing too?

Kirin followed Sam through each room, one by one. The living room with its two comfortable couches, massive flat screen TV and an old roll-top desk in the corner facing the front porch. It looked perfect to watch a game or read a book. Warm lamps gave off a glow in every corner, which made the room feel spacious yet homey and inviting.

Next, they headed up a dark, back staircase. Light illuminated from a nightlight, but she still couldn't make out what kind of room it was. Sam pulled her to stand in front of him on the top step.

As her eyes adjusted, she realized it was a loft with a half wall overlooking the living room. Sam flipped the light switch to reveal a long room with two sets of bunk beds, a toy box shaped like a baseball and a TV mounted on the faraway wall. It was a boy's room.

"What do you think?" he said in her ear. His chest leaned against her back, leaving her trying to remember why she didn't want to be near him.

Her first thought was he'd had kids with someone. He said he'd never been married, so maybe out of wedlock? Unwelcome, jealous thoughts of an ex somewhere spiraled through her. She shook her head and recovered her senses.

"It's nice. I didn't know you had kids." She turned. He hadn't budged backward an inch, which left her standing inside his arms and staring at his mouth.

"I don't. I've got nephews…" his voice was husky as it trailed off and then he added, "and maybe the hope of kids someday." His eyes pierced hers.

She swallowed hard.

Poking him in the chest she said, "Well, you better get to it, Mister, you're no spring chicken."

Sam laughed and put his hand on her waist, with the tips of his fingers squeezing a few of her ribs to tickle her.

"Thanks for the tip, coming from a woman who is what…three months younger than me? And what does that make you?"

"Doesn't matter. I'm still younger," she declared.

They stood inches apart, eyes locked. His warm hand wasn't budging from her side. Part of her, charged with a few sips of wine, wanted to tiptoe up and kiss him, but her chicken-sensible-side hesitated.

He smiled as if he heard her inner struggle. He moved his hand from her waist, turned off the light and grabbed her free hand to lead them back down the steps. They ambled down a hallway, toward a guest bedroom, and two bathrooms and finally stopped at his bedroom door.

He cleared his throat.

"And last but not least, my room."

It looked like a typical men's bedroom. Bed, TV, nightstand with books piled up and several remote controls, no pictures on the wall, no frills. It was in this room the gloriously Sam smell was the strongest.

Kirin stood inside the doorway, leaned against the wall with her eyes closed inhaling the manly scent, while Sam talked of renovations. After a moment, he stopped talking.

When she opened her eyes he stood on the other side of the room, arms crossed, watching her. He looked both curious and amused.

"What're you doin'?" His lips were upturned with one eyebrow cocked.

She straightened and smoothed down the imaginary crinkles in her skirt, not wanting to look him in the eye and answered, "Nothing. Dinner smells good."

Busted.

"Uh-huh …" he answered into his wine and walked past her into the front room, grabbing her hand as he passed.

She followed him and sat down on one of the plush couches. She assumed he'd sit on the other couch, but he plopped down hard right next to her. She squealed and bobbled her wine glass, narrowly catching it before it ended up on the floor.

"Sorry," he said, not sounding one bit sorry.

"It's fine, you startled me, that's all."

Truth was, she wanted him closer. This whole damn cabin had the intoxicating smell of him. She was a fly in the spider's web, but somehow it was a web she craved to be in.

Her mind fuzzed, and the wine wasn't helping. She needed to focus. Answers, that's why she was here, answers. Kirin placed her wine glass on the coffee table to stop gulping it and turned to face him. Lord, he sat close. Too close. His woodsy smell was more intoxicating than the wine.

Sam stared into her eyes and into her soul for a beat, then gazed out to the front porch. From his scrunched-up expression, he wrestled with something. She crossed her arms to stop herself from putting a hand on his shoulder. She was in danger if she touched him.

"What is it?"

Sam took a deep breath. "I'm trying to figure out what to say."

"About what?"

"This …" he gestured at the tiny space between them, "… and your dad."

Answers. Kirin scooted to the edge of the couch, touching shoulders with him. "What about my dad?"

Sam sat back on the couch and rubbed his hands together. Glancing over at her, she noticed his eyes and the sad look they carried. "Your dad was … kind to me. Family, when I pretty much had none. He mentored a reckless kid, trying to convince me to get out of the business. I was young, broke and ignorant. The money was more than I'd ever seen. His message about money not being important and finding true meaning in life never hit home … until now."

It made her green with envy her father had taken the time to get to know Sam, gave him advice and even cared for him. Why couldn't he have done the same for her? She picked up her wine glass again and gulped.

He took a breath. "I have a clear picture of what I want." His eyes locked on hers, Kirin swallowed hard, again.

Sam rubbed his hands through his hair. It bounced right back into messy waves of blonde and brown before he continued. "I need you to know things about me and about your dad. But I'm afraid of how you'll take it."

He took a long sip of his wine. He was about to spill answers to some of her looming questions. Maybe the conversation would segue into his true feelings for her.

Shut. Up. Wine.

"Go ahead," she prodded, "What do you have to lose?"

He said, "Kirin, I —"

The timer on the potatoes screeched across the kitchen.

"Crap!" he jumped over the back of the couch, "I'm never gonna get this out. Stay put, I'll be right back."

"I'm not going anywhere," she called over her shoulder, sarcastically.

This would give her a moment to gather her strength and her thoughts. *Stay strong. Find out about her father, the book, and the men in the black suits. Nothing personal.*

Through the divided rooms, she watched as he pulled the potatoes out of the oven and covered them to keep them warm.

Kirin gulped the last of her wine and poured another half glass. He walked back around and sat on the couch next to her, staring out the window.

"Where was I?"

"You were going to tell me something and you were dragging your feet."

Kirin placed her wine back on the table as Sam narrowed his eyes, with a slight grin.

He exhaled deep, then started again. "I'm not proud of things I've done, and not everything was legal." Sam winced, looking at her for a reaction. She nodded for him to continue. "Your dad, well, he was the money guy, but pretty much kept his nose clean, at least in the public eye." Sam turned toward Kirin, "I want you to know, I never killed anyone. That wasn't my job."

"What was your job?"

Sam shook his head. "I wasn't a thug, and I didn't intimidate anybody if that's what you're asking. A lot of guys I knew were forced into that work, though. Young guys. Your dad wasn't either, it's one of the reasons we bonded."

She wanted to know more, but the heat in his eyes suddenly turned up a notch.

"You're the first woman I've ever brought here." Sam scooted closer and took her hand. "The first woman I've been remotely interested in … well *ever,* it feels like. I can't sleep, I can't eat, and I can't do anything but think about you."

He searched her face, then continued. "I'm sure this seems sudden to you, but like I said, I know you. I've been protecting you for two years."

He paused for a second, taking another sip of courage. "I've fallen in love with you, Kirin, which is something as your protector, I should never do. But I can't help it."

Involuntarily, she smiled. She tried not to, but it was as if her mouth had a mind of its own. She couldn't even think of anything to say, because it all sounded crazy. She wanted to say she loved him too. And that she'd follow him anywhere and her world felt so safe when he was around.

But even in her tipsy state, Kirin knew he'd changed the subject, abruptly. She needed answers and that was the most important item on the night's agenda.

He stared, waiting for a reply. Kirin took a deep breath and when she found courage, she spoke again. "So, as my protector, wouldn't it make more sense to tell me about these people that are after me? And why they want the book?"

His smile faded as he shook his head. "No, it wouldn't. The less you know about that world, the safer you are Kirin."

She protested, "Hear me out. If you prepare me, I wouldn't feel so helpless and who knows, maybe I could help."

He scooted back on the couch with a scowl on his face and growled. "Don't even think about it. The least helpful thing for you to do right now is go snooping around and try to be the hero. It's too dangerous. Let me handle it. I think I can get you out of this without harm."

"What danger would I be in, Sam? I've already found out some of the clues of the book and I'll damn sure find the rest."

He scooted to the edge of the couch, red faced and angry eyed.

"What danger? Are you serious? Up until now I've convinced them you don't give a shit about that book. They think you have no idea what it holds, nor do you care. That's why they've let you live. They believe you hated your dad so much, you've got no desire to find out the truth. And the last thing you'd want to do is try and stop The Club."

Her eyes perked up. The Club? Now they were getting somewhere. His eyes narrowed again at the excited look on her face. He rose quickly and yelled. "I just poured out my feelings for you! You didn't come here for me, you came here to weasel information out of me, didn't you? All dressed up, pretending … just to get answers. I've busted my ass endangering my life to protect yours."

Sam paced around the room flailing his arms as he continued. "You're gonna get us both killed searching for something you can't do anything about. This club is unstoppable and runs so much deeper than you know."

Sam picked up glasses, cleaning up as if the date was over.

"What an idiot. I convinced myself you felt something. That your offer for a real date stemmed from your feelings and not that stupid book."

He stopped moving and glared at her for a long moment, giving her time. Time to deny it, or time to admit it, but she couldn't make herself say a word.

"I think you should leave," he growled, his voice cracked as he turned toward the kitchen, his body rigid and angry.

Kirin shouted the only word she could— "Stop!"

Sam slammed down the wine glasses, crossed his arms defensively and froze. His face was red, and double pissed. Angrier even than when she'd accidentally pummeled him with tomatoes.

She swallowed hard then crept toward him as if she was trying to pet a wild deer. Kirin stared deep into his eyes, then whispered, "You haven't given me time to respond."

Her thoughts were so muddy. She loved this man, of that she was sure. She came here for answers, that part was true, but maybe she came to discover his true feelings about her, too. He'd told her was in love with her. So, why was she hesitating? Her knees trembled with each step.

Trusting and loving someone were two sides of the same coin. What if she surrendered and it was all a trap? Inside this house, with its aromas and the electricity she felt next to him, she wouldn't be able to stop herself. Kirin crept closer. He didn't flinch. He stood rigid, arms folded, and angry.

It was then, she decided.

She stopped directly in front of him. He glared down at her. She unfolded his tightly held arms, stepped in, raised her hands to his face, and kissed him.

Kirin kissed him with her entire body. A hungry kiss like she'd kissed no one before.

His arms, stiff and unyielding at first, wrapped around her as he let go, kissing her back. Deeply exploring. His mouth, warm and full of tenderness at first, switched on a dime to heated desire. Pressing her body hard into his, she wanted him as much as she could feel he wanted her. All the questions pushed aside, all she could wrap her head around was the love she felt for this man as his warm body pressed against hers.

She didn't care about breathing or crusty old books or danger or anything as Sam picked her up and wrapped her legs around his waist. She barely registered the sound of her shoes clunking onto the wood floor.

Sam carried her, trailing kisses down her throat and gently laying her on his down-filled comforter atop his bed. The last bits of fading sun glowed through the window, warming her hot skin, making it even hotter. Hovering over her, Sam placed warm, wet kisses behind her ear as she wriggled to pull her sweater off. Raising up, he smiled, pulled off his shirt and helped with her sweater. He didn't miss a beat as he unbuttoned her shirt kissing his way from her neck to her belly button.

Kirin gut-laughed when he got to her belly button. Sam glanced up at her, raising an eyebrow, smirking.

"Shut up."

A low chuckle rumbled up from him as he stood, pulled off his jeans and her skirt. He took his sweet time kissing her up from her toes back to her neck. She wanted him so badly, but alarms were going off in the back of her head. This wasn't her. She was a good girl and didn't do this on a first date. But, it all boiled down to trust. Did she trust him? Her body involuntarily tensed.

Sam stopped and stared deep into her eyes.

"We don't have to do this now."

She couldn't help herself. "I want you. All of you. But I need to know you're on my side … and not *theirs*." There, she finally said it.

He smiled down. "Yours. Always yours, until the end of time."

That was her undoing. The rest of their clothes seemed to fall on the floor by themselves. She'd never been with anyone besides her husband. But Sam made her feel so at ease. He'd brought her to the brink repeatedly and when they each finally broke, she lay there exhausted and happy.

This was right and perfect and exactly where she was supposed to be: in his arms, in his bed, and in his life. She was sure of it. He'd never stop protecting her. She'd known it the first time they met and ever since. Lying next to him on her side, she pushed up with her toes and kissed him on the cheek. She couldn't say it yet, but she knew she loved him. This man who'd risk his life to save hers.

"You awake?" she whispered in the dark.

"I am now," he teased.

She poked him in the side. "I want to tell you something serious."

"You have a belly button fetish?" he said, he wrapped his arms around her tight. His face was serious except a slight grin with one eyebrow raised.

"What? No … shut up."

"Admitting it is the first step, you know."

Kirin jabbed a finger in his ribs. "I'm serious!"

"Okay, serious. What?"

Kirin took a deep breath and closed her eyes. "I want you to know that I'm not…well, you're only the second person I've slept with ever. The first was my husband. I was kind of a late bloomer."

Her face flushed hot.

His chest rumbled low as a laugh escaped.

"What's so funny?"

"It's just you're pretty good at it to not have had practice in a while, that's all."

Kirin pushed up and kissed him. "I can't believe we did this on our first date. And I'm sorry."

Sam stilled and raised his head. "For what?"

"You were right."

"Can I get that in writing? And I'm always right, but about what specifically?" he kissed her forehead and tucked a stray strand of hair behind her ear.

"About coming over here to get answers … that was my intention. But only because I convinced myself that I was only a paycheck to you. I didn't understand how you could work for them and still protect me. And I guess I was scared. I needed to know where your loyalties lay."

With no hesitation Sam said, "My loyalty is to you. It's always been you, nobody else. I still play double agent, so I can find out when they're going to strike. And because it's not like quitting a job. People don't quit The Club. As they say, the only way out is in a casket."

"What are you going to do?"

"I've got an ace in the hole. I hope it'll work."

Sam stared out his window. Kirin decided not to push any harder. He'd opened up more than ever, but she didn't want him to close back down.

The smell of burnt chicken alongside the shrill scream of the smoke alarm startled them both into action. Throwing on sweats, Sam ran for the broom to get the smoke away from the detector, while Kirin dressed and grabbed potholders to pull the black chicken out of the oven.

Sam with no shirt and Kirin wearing only his white button-down, cleaned up and put a pizza in the oven. They sat in the kitchen holding hands across the table, surrounded by candlelight.

Sam looked around his kitchen shaking his head. "Sorry about dinner."

"You're lucky I like pizza," she said smiling.

"Kirin," he said, "promise me something?"

"Sure."

"Promise me you won't go anywhere this weekend while I'm gone, okay?"

Crap. She'd already made plans to meet Kidd in Atlanta. She answered his question with a question. "Why?"

"Because I don't want to worry about you."

She hated to start their relationship lying to him, but she had to meet Kidd.

"Sure," she replied quick and too high pitched, but he didn't seem to notice. "Now, can I ask you something?"

"Anything," he whispered.

"Can you please help me understand why this book is so important?"

His smile faded fast. He stood and walked to the sink to refill his water. Staring out the kitchen window he said, "Anything but that."

Kirin walked to him and wrapped her arms around him from behind.

"If I know what I'm up against, I can better defend myself."

He turned to face her. "This isn't a game of softball, Kirin. These men are killers. Once the boss gives them the greenlight, they will kill to get what he wants."

He let the silence scare her for a minute and then added, "Besides, I'm hoping this weekend will solve all of that."

"Where are you going?" Kirin said, stepping back away from him, "not to LA? Surely you're not that crazy?"

He leaned against the sink sipping his water. A sweet smile washed over his face.

"You, worried about me? Well, that's a switch." Sam pulled Kirin in and squeezed her tight.

Her mind raced. What if they discovered she knew more than he'd told them? And what if they discovered she wasn't only a job, but more? She couldn't think about that now. Another question burned in her mind.

"Can I ask one more?" she said, pulling back and looking up at him.

He narrowed his eyes and answered, "Depends."

"Can you tell me something *good* about my father? I feel as if I know so little about him and most of it's bad."

Sam pulled her chin up, so their eyes met and smiled.

"He was a good man, Kirin." Kirin shook her head. That was hard to imagine.

"He was," he pleaded. "Much better than any of the rest of us. God, could he talk." Sam laughed and rubbed his face. "He could talk the paint off walls. Used to bug the shit out of me when I was younger, but I miss it now."

She'd have given anything to be a part of it. Tears welled in her eyes. Sam noticed.

"I'm sorry. You sure you want to hear this?"

"Yes."

"I'd gotten trapped inside this organization so young. He preached all the time about me finding a life for myself outside it. I think," he said, pulling her back to him, "he took me in after my dad died to make up for not being there for you."

"What do you mean?"

"I think he thought he could somehow make up for the time he lost with you, by saving me. He saved my life. You were all he talked about when we were alone. When he asked me to keep you safe if anything happened to him, I gave him my word."

She stepped back. "He talked about me? That's not possible. He never called, never wanted me …" Kirin's voice cracked. Sam reached out and pulled her back and held her.

"I promise, it's true. He adored you and regretted his whole life that he had to leave you."

Tears pooled in her eyes. It infuriated her that her father's approval still held so much power.

Sam kissed her forehead.

After pizza and slow dancing to eighties music, Kirin decided it'd be best if she went home. Sam protested, but she couldn't stay. Her morning would start way too early to drive to Atlanta and meet Kidd.

He finally gave in stating he'd only get a few hours of sleep before heading to the airport anyway. As she gathered her purse and sweater, Sam scooped her into a desperate, goodbye-like hug. Kirin pulled away and eyed him. "You're coming back to me, right?"

"Sure."

"And this wasn't a dream, right?" Kirin closed the gap and laid her head on his chest.

"Yeah, it was a dream. Tell me when you wake up, okay?"

Kirin pinched him, and he growled.

"You sure you can't stay?" He leaned down to kiss her.

"No, I gotta go," she said, squeezing him one last time before he walked her to the car.

"Wait, are you gonna follow me home?" Guilt ran through her.

"I always do." Sam smiled.

"See you."

"Not if I see you first," He said, shutting her car door. She glanced up at her rearview mirror and found him gazing at her. It took all she had not to turn around and go back.

Chapter Twenty-Two

The first pitch was to be thrown at one o'clock. Kidd said they'd meet after the third inning. The plan was she'd buy food in the mezzanine, and he'd find her. They'd joked he'd be easy to spot since he'd be wearing his favorite Philly's hat, and she'd have on an orange University of Tennessee baseball T-shirt in a sea of Braves red and blue.

The drive wasn't bad, three hours from Knoxville to Atlanta if there wasn't any traffic. There were a host of things she was good at but having a natural ability for navigating interstates wasn't one of them. So, she gave herself four full hours to get to Atlanta, find the stadium, park, and run inside.

As she drove, her mind wandered to the night before. She couldn't believe how she'd fallen for Sam overnight. It was so natural being around him. Her face turned hot as she remembered making love to him. *What was she thinking?* Stacy would be proud, though. She probably wouldn't tell Laura even though Laura wouldn't judge. She never did.

At Turner Field, she lucked up and found a space in the Green lot. It was the closest parking to the entrance, but still several hundred feet away from the gate. She took a Braves bus to get to the front entrance to pay. Looking around, her idea to wear a UT shirt was not her brightest. People stared at her as if she was special, and not in a good way. Most everyone else was decked out in Braves attire except her. Oh, she'd be easy to spot all right.

Kirin walked through the giant wrought iron gate and bought her ticket. She navigated the sea of people and found her seat. A real MLB baseball game, but not her first.

Memories flooded back. She'd forgotten her dad took her to a Braves game once when she was six. As soon as they'd entered the gate, she'd thrown up. Too much junk food and excitement on the drive to Atlanta she guessed. She smiled reliving the memory. A partially good memory, for once. She remembered little about the stadium since she only saw the entrance, but the field was more vibrant than she'd imagined it would be.

The first pitch was thrown. The sun beamed down on the stadium, warming her skin. She squinted even with sunglasses on, trying to follow the game. It was the first inning and fans were still filling the empty chairs around her. When the second inning kicked off, Kirin's stomach rumbled. She trotted up the steps to grab a pretzel. She could always eat a hotdog in the third inning. Halfway to the top two recently-familiar faces caught her eye to the left of the stairs.

Shit. *You've got to be kidding me?* She kept her pace steady and glared as she ran up the steps. Fear flew out the window and only anger filled the space. Scar had his head down texting, but Babyface looked up. Their eyes locked.

Kirin scowled. "Morning," she muttered, loud enough for everyone to hear. Babyface looked stunned. And then it hit her. Oh, no. If they followed her to get a hotdog after the third inning, she'd never find Kidd. Kirin turned and sprinted into a store filled with Braves swag. Time to devise a plan.

She'd ditch her current seat, make sure she wasn't followed and find a new seat on the other side of the stadium. She hoped Scar was still texting and Baby Face hadn't followed her yet, but somehow sensed they were outside the shop. She bought a Braves T-shirt and hat, stuffing them and the receipt inside her purse, then sauntered as if she had nowhere to be, toward the bathroom as if it was an afterthought.

Like it was a race, she changed her shirt and pulled all her hair inside the cap. She crammed her sweater and UT shirt inside her purse and walked alongside a gaggle of drunk women giggling on their way out of the bathroom. Her two goons leaned against a wall and eyed the bathroom door she'd gone into, never noticing as she crept out the other door.

Now, to search for Kidd. He wouldn't be able to spot her without her UT gear. Feeling like an idiot, she stared at every older man with a hat on. When she'd reached what she thought must be the other side of the stadium, her stomach growled again. She spotted a hotdog stand. Thank God for food. Standing in line for a hotdog, her phone buzzed.

Sam.

Crap. He'd hear the roar of the crowd and know she wasn't home. She couldn't answer. She winced and hit ignore shoving the phone back in her pocket. It immediately buzzed again. She squinted, afraid to look, then clicked the message,

"Where the hell are you? I intercepted a text. Tell me you're not at a Braves game?"

Her phone dinged again. *"Woman. Answer."*

Shit. The two goons had ratted her out. She kept forgetting they believed Sam was on their side. Time to face the music. Kirin's phone rang again.

"Hello," She answered, trying to sound cheery and not like a teenager who got caught after curfew.

His voice was low and deceptively calm. Calmer than his texts had been. "What are you doing?"

"What?" Her voice was high and innocent, "I'm watching a Braves game, of course."

"Kirin Lane, you listen to me. I can't protect you if you lie and don't tell me where you're going. Shit. This was easier when you didn't know I followed you. Why are you there? I want the truth."

Kirin took a deep breath. She trusted him. Knew him. He wouldn't put her in harm's way, so she told him. "I'm meeting someone here, Sam. Someone who has a page in the book. He was a friend to my family."

The phone went silent, "You still there?"

He blew out a long breath, and when he yelled, his voice shook with anger.

"Damn it, Kirin! It's a trap. When I tell you to stay put, stay put!" His rapid breath told her he paced the floor. "Shit, Shit, Shit. How am I gonna get you out of this?"

"Sam," Kirin interrupted, "he has a page in the book."

"*Everybody* knew about that damn book. Vigilantes have even been paid handsomely to get it, no matter the cost."

"May I help you?" The lady behind the counter asked as Kirin moved up. Her hands shook as she looked over the menu sign.

"Can I get a hotdog with relish and mustard, and a medium Dr. Pepper, please."

No sooner had she spoken then the man behind her whispered in her ear, "I thought you'd order popcorn." Then he said to the cashier, "Double that order, please and I'm buying."

Kirin twisted around to find a kind-faced, white-headed senior citizen smiling at her. He wore a Philly's cap way back on his head and a Mr. Rodgers cardigan. Kirin shoved her phone, still connected to Sam, into her pocket. She hoped he could hear the conversation. Her purse was crossed tight over her body and she knew from his bent stance she could outrun him if she had to. She must have looked terrified, he stepped back and apologized.

"I've startled you, haven't I? I'm sorry. Good God, Kirin, you look *exactly* like your mama." He smiled and put his hand on her shoulder.

This wasn't a menacing man. And she didn't feel threatened. She had to believe he was on her side at least for now.

The lady behind the counter said, "Twenty-four dollars, please." Kidd reached around her and put twenty-five dollars on the counter. Kirin was grateful she didn't have to dig around for money and expose the book.

"Thank you," she said.

"Wanna go find a table?"

Tall tables without chairs lined the common area for fans to grab a bite during the game. They picked one near the exit. Kirin snuck her phone out face down next to her. She hoped Sam was listening to ease his worry. As soon as they were both settled, Kidd motioned for Kirin to take a bite. She picked up her hotdog and took a bite larger than she meant to, coughed a little, and peered at him through watery eyes. His smile reached up to kind pale blue eyes as he leaned forward and whispered fast.

"I'll get right to it. The book in your possession contains information that will shut down an organized crime ring to which your dad and I unwillingly belonged. Kirin…" He hesitated, then scrubbed a hand over his wrinkled face. "You have to believe me when I say, your dad and I had no idea what kind of business we were getting into. On the surface, the business helped young women with little fortune flee from poverty, slavery and war in other countries and brought them to the U.S. But underneath, it was much worse."

He sighed heavily, then his gaze darted around them. He lowered his head and continued, "There's more than one set of operatives here looking for you. Your dad and I had been friends since the Marines. And I want you to understand, we were both drafted into this club. We had no choice, nor did we know the truth.

"Your dad placed clues in that book that will shut down the entire existence of The Club. Good men, forced as we were, would love to get out but can't find the way without endangering their families. *You* are the way. You alone can crush it. Your dad loved you, Kirin, but Saul enacted the wives' and daughters' clause. And this was why he was forced to leave you."

Kidd looked around again, then nodded at her. Kirin closed her gaping mouth then took another bite, smaller this time.

"See," he continued, "if someone had attributes the boss wanted, but they were reluctant to join or didn't cooperate, he'd go after the females in that man's life. Wives, daughters, and in some cases, moms. Sometimes he ordered for them to be kidnapped and tortured and sometimes terminated. If the man had a son, he'd coerce him into service too.

"If someone ratted them out, disobeyed an order or disappointed Saul, their wives or daughters were dead. Nobody crosses Saul."

Kidd swallowed his last bite, took a deep breath and reached out for Kirin's hand. Without hesitation, she gave it to him. "That's how your mom died, Kirin. Your dad refused to move to California and be Saul's money man. Oh, Saul covered it up and said it was an accident, but we all knew the truth."

Tears pooled in Kirin's eyes at Kidd's touch. She squeezed them shut for a moment. Finally, the truth about her mom. A slow burn of hatred for Saul flamed low in her gut. When she opened them, he continued.

"Your dad knew the truth. He decided right then he'd protect you from all of it, even if it meant he couldn't be in your life. He couldn't take losing you, too.

"They know you felt abandoned. And they know you hate him. The Club is counting on those feelings to make you toss the book and the secrets it holds, aside. Saul thinks he's won because you don't know how your mama died and you don't care about going on some silly journey for the truth to defend a man you hated.

"So I'm here, risking my life, to tell you your dad loved you more than I can describe. I hope by finding the truth about The Club, you also rediscover your love for him."

Kidd let go of Kirin's hand and swooped up his drink. His eyes darted back and forth as he sucked down half his Dr. Pepper before speaking again.

"Your dad was my best friend. I owed him my life on more than one occasion. I couldn't have called myself his friend if I didn't come here today to speak to you. You'll find if you dig far enough, the corruption and crime go deep.

"Saul ordered several murders, Kirin, and your dad had proof. You gotta figure out whatever information he had and get it into the hands of the authorities. You'll need hard evidence and proof to bring Saul down."

He stopped for a minute and glanced behind her. Fear flashed in his eyes. When they locked eyes again, his softened. "I won't be returning home."

Kirin's jaw dropped and Kidd clearly noticed. He smiled. "I'll be fine young lady, don't you worry. Your dad talked me into buying a retirement place out of the country. I'm all packed. It'll be much harder for them to find me once you blow this story wide open, which Kirin, is what we all desperately hope you'll do."

With that, he walked around the table, kissed the top of her hat and pointed at her phone. "And that's the reason your protector hasn't ever gotten close to people. He didn't want to lose a wife or a daughter. I hope *together* you two can bring down the establishment and be happy. You both deserve it."

He never looked back as he ducked down the ramp and disappeared into the crowd.

Far off, as if in a dream, the crowd roared, and the announcer droned on about the 4th inning. She sat in frozen, stunned silence. Kidd was gone. She didn't get to ask a single question, but she knew way more than she had. Her father loved her. He didn't want her to suffer her mother's fate.

And Saul had her mother killed and forced her father to abandon her. He'd ripped her happy little family from her when she was eight.

She would destroy him.

Chapter Twenty-Three

"Kirin!" Sam's voice rang out on her upside-down phone. She picked it up and held it to her ear. "I'm here."

"My God. Was that Kidd? How in God's name did you find him? Nobody knows his real name."

"He found me," she answered, "and then I found his name in my Dad's book and contacted him." She closed her eyes. "Sam?" Her voice held remorse.

"Yeah?"

"I'm sorry I lied to you. I had to know the truth."

"You got lucky. He could've been someone sent to hurt you to prove a point." He exhaled. "We gotta stick together, Kirin. And you gotta trust me enough to tell me what's going on. I heard … he told you about your mama, didn't he?"

"Did you already know?" she asked, harsher than she'd meant.

"I knew the rumor. I didn't want you to know. I'd hoped we could give the book back, and he'd leave us alone. Kirin," Sam pleaded, "you've gotta get this outta your mind. I know how stubborn you are, but now is not the time to get even. Let's get all of us out of this mess and go on with life. We can't beat him."

Watch me.

"Listen to me. I've got a plan that might work, so we're all safe. But I need time and for you to trust me."

"Was Kidd right? Was that why you never got involved?"

"Mostly. And because I didn't have you. Seeing other men grieve, I made a vow never to be in that situation. They used my mother against me once …" Sam went silent, then continued. "I never planned to bring anyone into this mess. I tried hard *not* to fall for you. Convincing myself standing you up was the right thing to do. I knew then, I was in too deep."

"What changed?"

"The idea you'd find someone else. And knowing you were supposed to be mine." His voice was still tight and strained, but her heart did a little happy dance as the corners of her lips curved.

"I *am* sorry I worried you. I promise I'll never do it again." Her grin widened.

"Sure you will. Woman, it's part of your DNA to worry the shit out of me." His voice turned serious again. "My meeting didn't go to plan so I'm coming home. Think I could drop by the house tonight?"

"I'd like that."

"Be careful, please."

"Always."

He laughed as the phone disconnected. She glanced around at the sea of red and blue Braves fans, snatched up the rest of her hotdog and drink, and jogged back to her car.

~*~

Driving home, Kirin's mind kicked into gear like the cogs of a clock on steroids. She knew what she had to do. She had to put her all into solving this puzzle and defeating this man.

She had to do it for her mom, her dad, and all the people who'd been hurt or killed by him and his organization. But most of all, because she'd never have peace, or a relationship not based on fear with Sam until that shadow was gone from their heads.

Kirin dialed her Uncle Dean's cell about halfway from Atlanta to Knoxville, hopeful that he'd deciphered the code. "Hey, how's Dollywood?" Carnival music played in the background. They were still inside the park.

"Hey there, honey. Oh, it's a blast. How was the baseball game?" God love him, he sounded tired.

"The Braves played pretty well," she half lied, hoping he wouldn't ask the score. She hadn't witnessed but a handful of plays and had no idea who won. "So, did you figure out my puzzle for me?"

"Oh, yeah!" He perked up. "Once I figured out the sequence it was a breeze."

"Great! What does it mean?"

"Well, the numbers are an IP code that differentiates one computer from another. It's like a social security number for computers. I found a program online that could take an IP address and tell you where the computer was, right down to the street address. You'll never guess where this IP address leads you … right here in Knoxville! Somewhere downtown, I think." Uncle Dean cleared his throat. "Remind me again, why did you need this information?"

"It's in a book I'm reading," she lied.

"Mm-hmm." He was not convinced. "So, you want me to go with you downtown and find it?"

Kirin stammered, then laughed it off. "Don't be silly. It's only a story." Subject change. God, she hated lying to him. And she was terrible at it. "Thanks for figuring that out for me. I should be back home around three. I'll run by and get the boys whenever you guys get back."

"No problem, honey. By the way, I emailed you the address for your curiosity." He drew out the last word as if he knew something was up.

"Thanks, Uncle Dean. I'll see you guys in a few."

"Be careful driving back, honey."

"I will."

She drove for a while, then pulled off at an exit to get something to drink. Sitting in her car, she pulled up the address and saved it: 1101 Market Square Blvd. She could walk downtown easily on her lunch break and scope out the business. How hard would it be to sneak into their computer system? The thought both nauseated and excited her.

She copied the address into the search engine and found it was a new age astrology store called Galaxy 10. The website had pictures of a tiny little store with incense, crystals, books, and other knickknacks. Not her cup of tea, but who knew. Maybe they'd do a back-room palm reading for her and she could scope the place out. Her real quandary: how would she waltz into a shop and hack into a computer when she had absolutely no skill in doing this? She was determined to figure it out. Back on the interstate, she made a knee-jerk direction change. She'd run downtown to look around the store and get the layout.

Next item: call Stacy. Her brother was some big dog for the TBI. Or was it the FBI? She vaguely remembered a recent conversation with a jealous Stacy. Big brother might have been promoted. She wasn't sure what he did or even if she could trust him, but she had to figure out what type of conviction she must get to put Saul away for life. She might use the old, "I'm writing a novel" excuse to get technical advice. That might fly. She could pull that one off.

Kirin called Stacy's cell, but she didn't answer. She left her an intriguing message designed to entice her friend to call back faster.

"Hey Stace, it's Kirin. I need to know how to convict someone of murder. Call me when you can, love ya."

Five minutes later Kirin's phone rang.

"What the hell, chick?"

"Hey, girl," Kirin answered, smiling to herself.

"So, who're we gonna kill? Wait. First, how'd the date go with Sam?"

"Better than I ever imagined," Kirin whispered.

Stacy got quiet and then said, "On a first date? Kirin Lane, I'm shocked! And at the same time, I'm so proud of you!"

Stacy could always read her. "I think I'm in love, Stace," Kirin admitted.

Stacy laughed, then added, "Only you could be single for two years, without one date, and come out of it a few weeks later, in love. Shoot, girl, I already had four or five prospective men lined up and now you're off the market! What am I gonna do with you?"

"You're gonna love him," Kirin beamed.

"So, spill. Who're we gonna kill off and why?"

"Well hypothetically, I need to know what type of evidence I'd need in order to get a conviction if I knew someone was guilty of murder, but couldn't prove it?"

"Kirin, what do I look like to you? How the hell should I know that?"

"Don't you have a super important brother in the TBI, or did I dream that?"

"Actually," she said, "*Mr. Perfect* is in the FBI now, thank you."

Even better. "So, you could call the golden boy and ask him the question for me, right?"

"This seems awfully deep for a girl in love. Why do you need this, K?"

"Well, love brings on creativity," she stammered, feeling stupid. "I'm considering writing a novel and the plot includes a man who's ordered others to kill. And maybe he's killed people himself, but nobody can prove it. I'd hoped your brother could help me figure out how to tie in the plot, so he goes to prison for life."

"Sure, I can ask him but only if you'll do a huge favor for me."

"Sure, but wait, Stace, you have to promise to call him today because I need the information like yesterday, okay?"

Kirin knew how Stacy's brain worked. If she didn't make sure Stacy understood it was urgent, she'd forget to ask him.

"All right, Nancy Drew, I'll call him after I get off the phone with you, I promise."

"Good. Now shoot, what's the favor?"

"So, Todd wants me to meet his parents. Well, his father and stepmother. They're coming into town this weekend. He wants me to throw a dinner party." Stacy's voice quivered at the words. "Would you and your new love, Sam, be free next Saturday night to come to the party and help me?"

"Sure, I'd love to! Not sure if Sam can make it, but I'll ask. I'll have to line up a babysitter—"

She interrupted, "Oh, Savannah would love to hang out with the boys downstairs. They can even spend the night! I need you there for support, whether you have a date or not, k?"

"Okay. But why are you so frazzled? You've thrown parties before …"

"When?" Kirin could envision her friend with her hand on her hip.

"Okay well, Jell-O shooter parties," Kirin conceded, "but we did have snacks there."

"Exactly. Todd wants good china, catered food, and maybe a server or two. He wanted everyone wearing long gowns. I nixed the long gowns."

"Smart."

"It's the way he speaks about his father, Kirin. Like he's a god. He says his father is super picky and super wealthy. I don't want him thinking I'm not good enough for his son. I know Todd has his issues, but I love him. The fact he invited him here to meet me is big for him. I want everything to be perfect. Please, please, please help me?"

"Of course. I wouldn't let you hang alone with scary people. I'll be there, and we'll decide on a fabulous menu this week, okay?"

After they hung up, Kirin immediately dialed Sam. He probably hadn't landed yet, but she wanted to leave him a message about Saturday, so she didn't forget.

~*~

Driving into downtown Knoxville, she still hadn't called Galaxy 10 to find their Saturday hours, so she winged it. It was a few minutes before five. They'd probably already be closed but she parked in the free downtown parking garage, grabbed her purse, and trotted toward Market Square. The square was usually filled with all kinds of sounds: kids, music, urbanites walking their dogs through the park. Bikes were parked everywhere along the one-way streets that surrounded the square. Inside the square were quaint little stores selling handmade jewelry, trinkets, and candles. Hip new restaurants boasted handcrafted beers and organic burgers. There were a few small pubs, homemade ice cream and coffee shops. The square held outdoor festivals each year. A Shakespeare in the Park, Dogwood Art's festival, and an ice-skating rink in the winter run by a friend of hers.

Nestled in the middle was Galaxy 10, an astrology store selling self-help books, homeopathic remedies, incense, crystals, and instrumental meditation CDs. According to the window, for a fee you could set up an appointment to have your astrological chart done by giving your exact date and time of birth. The astrologist could then predict your personality, your strengths, and your weaknesses and even predict life events that would happen, all based upon your birth time.

She would have thought that being in the Bible Belt, most older people would shy away from such a store, believing it to be voodoo or something. And in all fairness, the store did look like a ghost town. Kirin checked her watch. One minute until five and the open sign was still out. She took a deep breath and pushed open the glass door. A chime rang out. It smelled like a health store and a church combined.

She walked toward the left where some crystals gleamed against the late afternoon sun shining in the window. Curious, she touched one making it move. Rays of purple and red danced on the walls around her. She smiled.

A heavy-set woman leaned over the counter reading a newspaper. The woman stilled when she spotted her, then tracked her every move from above the rim of her red reading glasses as if Kirin was about to steal something.

This flower child must have enjoyed the seventies. She wore long unkempt gray hair, a flowered skirt, and rings on every toe peeking out of her Birkenstocks. When they locked eyes, Kirin smiled, "Hello."

The woman grinned wide. "I wondered when you'd come in."

Kirin froze. "I'm sorry?"

"Darlin' you can't fool this old lady with your hair tucked inside that Braves hat."

Kirin pulled the hat off and shook her hair.

The woman grinned even wider but said nothing.

"I'm sorry, do we know each other?"

"I know you," the woman answered, smiling. *Creepy*. Maybe this was some astrological mind reading ploy to drum up business? The woman interrupted Kirin's thoughts and said, "You look way too much like your mama to be anyone else."

Kirin's hackles rose. The woman knew her, but how? Kirin crept toward her and demanded, harsher than she meant to, "What do you know of my mother?"

The woman strolled toward Kirin then stopped a foot away. She placed warm hands on either side of Kirin's face and whispered, "You have her eyes and her kind face, Kirin."

The woman turned, walking away from Kirin toward the back of the store. She motioned for Kirin to follow. Kirin looked around. Nobody else in the store. She hesitated at first, but something about the woman seemed familiar. She followed through the store and pushed her head through a beaded door frame, slipping into a chaotic backroom office.

She immediately spied a computer, but it was buried in dust and paperwork. It didn't look as if it'd been fired up in the last five years. This was where sticky notes came to die. Stacks of paper and notes lay like kudzu on every flat surface in the room.

The woman rummaged through the papers and talked to herself. She bent over the desk, her voice muffled.

"It was here the other day. Ugh. It arrived a few weeks ago just like he'd said it would… Not supposed to give it to anyone but you… hmmm. Bear with me dear, I'm a crazy old bat most days, but I know it's here somewhere. Aha, here it is!"

She whirled around and handed Kirin a small manila envelope with her name on it. Kirin stared from the envelope to the woman.

"I know dear, it's his handwriting. I miss him too. Now, go on with you. I'm sure you have lots to do. Come back when I have time to talk, okay?"

The woman whisked Kirin to the front, hugged and kissed her on the cheek, then turned her around, and shoved her out the door. She smiled through the window as she locked the door, turned her sign to closed, and switched off the lights.

Kirin stood there like an abandoned dog.

What the hell just happened? She looked around. The square was eerily quiet for a Saturday. Thunder boomed above her head and she knew she was about to be drenched. Kirin shoved the manila envelope in her purse and ran back to the parking garage, not making it to her car in time to not be soaked.

Sitting inside her locked car in the empty parking garage, Kirin shivered. Drops of chilly rain slid down her hair, landing on her back. Her hands shook. She told herself it was from the cold, but something inside knew better. She had to get home.

All she knew for sure was the envelope was addressed to her and it was in her dead father's handwriting.

Chapter Twenty-Four

Kirin pulled into her driveway. She still had a good two hours until the boys came home, so she ran upstairs to take a quick shower. When she got out, she pulled on her favorite Notre Dame sweatshirt and black pants then ran back downstairs checking the doors and the alarm. She snuck around her house, as if she'd get caught stealing her sister's new sweater.

Sitting at her computer, she tugged the envelope out of her purse. She took her time, opening it with careful fingers without ripping the handwriting. Inside she gingerly poured out a circus of items.

There was a card she'd made for her dad years ago, after he left. The front had a colorful hand-drawn picture of herself, her Mama and her father. The paper had yellowed and looked as if it'd been handled, a lot. She was nine when she'd made it and sent it to him in the hopes he wouldn't forget about her. She turned the paper over in her hands, examining it carefully for clues or writing. She found nothing unusual, so she set it aside.

Next was a flash drive, plain orange and small. Last, a picture of a bunch of random people holding a little baby in an all-white gown outside of a church. That was it. No note, no nothing. *What the crap? What does this mean?*

Kirin popped the flash drive into her computer and clicked to open the file. The pictures that emerged put a lump in her throat. The first was of her and her mom and dad. Pictures she'd never seen. He must've kept those when he left.

The next ones were downright disturbing. Body bags, car crashes, burned out buildings and more body bags. And then, pictures of young twenty-something girls wearing bathing suits. Kirin squinted at them. Each picture had a caption indicating what country they were from, a number and a price ranging from $20,000 to $100,000. "What the hell?" Kirin whispered aloud, horrified.

The next file she clicked on was an Excel spreadsheet of names, dates, and order numbers. The heading read, "Ordered terminated by Saul for the good of The Club." Placing her finger on the screen she counted over twenty names and dates of people he'd ordered to die. Her father's name wasn't on the list and neither was her mother's. She guessed cancer got her dad before Saul did.

The next two files she opened concerned money. One spreadsheet was money incoming along with each girl's number, and the other file was money going out to purchase guns, houses, contracts for girls and cars. The last file she came across was a spreadsheet with codes and account numbers for several banks overseas. After that were documents photocopied and scanned.

There was one more file to click on, and it was a video file. It took a strong cup of coffee and closed eyes to click on that file. Dread filled her as she pushed the button. Please say this wasn't a graphic video of Saul killing someone. Then again if it was, her job of bringing him down might be easier.

The video opened with Kirin's dance recital when she was seven. As the camera panned from the tiny dancers on stage down a line of smiling adults, she recognized her mom and dad first. They sat holding hands and smiling. Next to them were Aunt Kathy and Uncle Dean. All with the same goofy grin on their faces.

A strong knock at her front door made her jump up and scramble. She pulled all the items together and shoved them back in the envelope, stashing them inside her purse, under the desk.

Kirin bounded down the steps and walked to the front door. Looking through the peephole the full face of her handsome Sam emerged. Kirin opened the door and without a word, he walked in and embraced her. A long, I-missed-you-and-I'm-never-going-to-let-you-go-type of hug. When he finally released her, she looked into his eyes and frowned. Fear. That's what she saw.

Sam released her, closed and locked the door, then walked around her, grasping her hand and pulling her with him into the front room. He let go of her hand and sat in an armchair with his head in his hands.

"Umm…want something to drink?" She proceeded with caution. Anger and fear rolled off him, together.

"No." His voice was tight.

"I said I was sorry." She whispered as she sat across from him.

"It's not that." Sam ran his fingers through his hair. His eyes locked on to hers.

"How tied are you to this city?" Before she could even answer, he continued, "If we needed to leave and live somewhere new, could you do that? We could find a new home together and enroll the boys in school there …"

She stared at him as if he'd grown three heads. "This is my home. They're not runnin' me out of it."

He stared at the floor. "That's what I figured you'd say."

Kirin scooted farther out on her chair, so their knees touched. "What's goin' on? Tell me the truth."

He let out a long breath. "I took a red-eye to LA after you left last night. Thought I could speak with Saul. Moved my flight up a few hours, so I could catch him at breakfast."

This she already knew but didn't interrupt.

He continued," I asked him if he'd let me out. Told him I'd get the book for him if he'd leave you and your boys alone out of respect for the years Sonny worked for him. They were tight at one time. Like family.

"He read right through me. He's a smug bastard. He's got me by the balls, and he knows it." Sam walked to the window and peered out. "He *respectfully declined.* Said he 'owed it to my old man' to keep me around. My particular skillset was too valuable to him."

Sam sat back down, leaned forward and grabbed Kirin's hands.

"We have to leave. Even if he gets the book tomorrow, he'll still order the hit on you and anyone else who gets in the way, to teach me a lesson. We could change our names and get married. I'll adopt the boys as my own. I won't stand by and watch them take you. We gotta leave now." His voice broke at the end.

Kirin stared at him as if he was insane. She stood, shaking, then paced the floor raising her voice.

"So, you're telling me he'd kill an innocent woman and children over *a book*? He had my mother killed! And he enslaved you and my father pretty much your whole lives. And I'm supposed to sit by while he tears my family apart? That's insane! I've got enough guns and ammo downstairs to defend myself. I've been trained how to use a gun since I was six! He'd be wise not to underestimate me."

Angry didn't even describe it. *Hell no.* This man would not run her out or harm one hair on her boys' heads. Kirin spun around and faced Sam.

"You're welcome to go, but I'm not going anywhere."

She turned and stomped to the kitchen. She needed a drink and a damn plan.

Kirin snagged a beer out of the fridge. Without closing the fridge door, she popped it open and chugged some of it. When she pulled the bottle away and slammed it down on the counter, Sam stood on the other side of the fridge door, leaning and grinning at her.

"What?" she said, harsh.

"You truly believe I'm gonna leave you, Kirin Lane? I've saved your scrawny butt too many times to let them get you now."

He reached around, tugging at her shirttail and pushed the fridge door closed. He pulled her in for a kiss. It startled her how a small kiss and the pressure of his body could stir up a lightning flash of longing.

His hands fisted into her hair as his tongue desperately searched for understanding. Sam pushed her up against the fridge. Her limbs wrapped instinctively around him.

The crunching of gravel from Uncle Dean's truck echoed through the house as he pulled in and two doors creaked open. Kirin pushed away from Sam, stopping them both. She had to catch her breath before the boys walked in. Although she suspected Uncle Dean would've found it hilarious to find her in a compromising position.

The chatter and laughing of Little Jack and Will echoed from the garage into the kitchen. She looked over at Sam. His mischievous grin had turned grim, and he looked pale.

Never mind surviving Saul and his imminent arrival, *this* was even more terrifying for the bachelor. The real test. Meeting her boys and Uncle Dean. The door swung open and in ran Little Jack and Will.

"Mommy!" They said together. Kirin bent down and grabbed them both. Will opened his eyes first, noticing Sam. He let go of his mom, walked over to Sam, stuck out his hand like he was twenty-five and said, "Hi, I'm Will."

Sam's eyebrows lifted. Impressed, he extended his hand and shook Will's saying, "My name is Sam, Will, and it's nice to finally meet you."

Will smiled up at Kirin. She couldn't have been prouder. Little Jack followed suit, stuck his hand out like his big brother and said, "I Jack." Sam shook his small hand and said, "Why hello, Jack, it's nice to meet you as well." Jack giggled and ran upstairs after Will.

Kirin spun around to introduce her Aunt Kathy and Uncle Dean but stopped in her tracks. Her aunt's face was splotched as tears ran down one cheek. "What's wrong?" She reached out and touched her aunt's arm.

"I don't know!" Kathy swiped at her eyes, laughing.

Kathy walked over to Sam and before Kirin could get the introductions out, she grabbed Sam and hugged him. He looked so shocked at first, but then tough Sam melted into her, embracing her tightly. Kathy approved. Dang, that was easy.

Uncle Dean stepped forward with a friendly grin and stuck out his hand. "I'm Dean and the basket case there is my wife, Kathy. We raised Kirin after her mom passed away. And if you hurt her, I'll kill you."

Sam swallowed hard with wide eyes and a half smile on his lips as the larger man shook his hand vigorously. Uncle Dean's massive bellowing chuckle rumbled out of him, laughing at himself. Sam visibly relaxed.

Jeez, talk about awkward first meetings. Aunt Kathy and Uncle Dean stayed for dinner and after they played a few rounds of cards: guys against girls. The women, of course, stomped the men. Sam had never been so talkative or laughed so much around her. Uncle Dean was downright giddy to have another man around. They seemed to have bonded instantly.

Kirin pulled the pie out of the oven while Aunt Kathy gathered plates, forks, and napkins to set the table. Kirin hesitated as she walked toward the open dining room with the pie. Uncle Dean and Sam were engrossed in a deep conversation in the front room. She sucked at eavesdropping but pretended to clean up spilled crumbs off the table straining to hear. As she cleaned up the last ghost crumb, the two men stood and hugged. Kathy walked into the dining room with a coffee pot and cups.

"What's up with the love in?" she asked loud enough for everyone to hear.

"Nothing," Uncle Dean said, slapping Sam on the back, "we just speak the same language." Kirin narrowed her eyebrows at Sam, who shrugged as if he was completely innocent.

They laughed over pie and coffee until Uncle Dean's yawns drowned out their giggles. Kirin thanked them for keeping Will and Little Jack and walked them out to their truck while Sam went upstairs to check on the boys. Uncle Dean spoke before they reached the driveway.

"I like him, Kirin. A lot."

"Good." She said, smiling, "That makes two of us."

"He's handsome, and he's got a great personality, K. Your mama would've loved him." Aunt Kathy smiled and touched Kirin's face. As they backed down the driveway Kirin bounded back into the house.

Laughter, along with what sounded like a large bookshelf crashing to the ground, set Kirin on a dead run upstairs. As she got closer to the door, Sam's cries for help sounded muffled.

Great. The boys were snuffing him out.

Kirin opened the door. Sam called out again for help. He was buried under two little boys tickling and karate chopping him. He looked at her, fake fear lacing his voice. "Please?!"

The boys laughed with delight when she answered, "Nope. You got yourself into it, you can get yourself out." Sam lips turned up as he narrowed his eyes at her. She grinned back as she closed the door.

She headed downstairs to clean up. She knew Sam made an impression on them when their evening prayers took longer than normal because both asked God to bless Sam twice. She couldn't be sure, but it looked as if Sam wiped his eyes in the dark.

After the boys were fast asleep, Kirin and Sam trudged into the den and melted into the couch together. Dog tired, they curled up on the couch talking until both fell asleep. When she woke in the morning, Sam was gone. He probably didn't want the boys to know he'd stayed. A note in the kitchen said he'd stop by late in the afternoon after they got home from church.

She dreamed at least part of her plan to stop Saul, that night in his arms.

Somehow, in her dream, she'd lured Saul into a long, dark room. He was gagged and bound to a chair. She stalked around him, spinning a gun on her finger like an old gunslinger in the Westerns her dad used to watch. She flashed the USB drive at him, bragging it had all the evidence the FBI needed to put him away for life. Off in the distance stood Stacy's brother. Saul was led away, kicking and yelling. And he never bothered them again.

A ridiculous fairy tale, yes, but it showed her something. What if she could pull a confession out of him and record it? From what she'd gathered, he was power-hungry and cocky. What if he was the type that didn't think he needed to hide or apologize for what he'd done? She knew it was a long shot, but it was the only plan she had so far.

After church, they drove to an electronics store. She needed a gadget to record sound and video and a device that would hang invisibly in her house. Kirin found everything from tiny little button cameras to crystal-clear recorders that worked from inside a pocket. They were expensive and had to be shipped overnight if she was to receive it by the weekend. She ordered two: one recorded every sound and the other was a camera, but it looked like a pen.

Pulling into the driveway after church, Kirin's hackles rose. Rosa's car and Sam's truck were both parked in the driveway, way too early.

Kirin and the boys walked up the steps to the front door. Rosa had been so jumpy lately, she hoped her nanny hadn't clobbered Sam when he knocked at the door. The boys ran into the kitchen, hugging Rosa, then Sam.

Two sets of thunderous feet ran upstairs as Kirin stopped in the kitchen doorway. Her mouth gaped open. Sam was in pressed khakis and a baby blue button-down with a blue striped tie. His normally sexy tousled hair had been meticulously combed. He'd shaved the stubble and in its place were the smoothest looking cheeks set atop his strong jaw. God, he was beautiful. His eyes locked on her, fiercely. His half smile and the way he shifted his weight from one foot to the other, told her he was nervous.

Kirin glanced at Rosa, thinking she'd forced on him the *Rosa Inquisition*. One look and she knew that wasn't it. Rosa's eyes showed signs she'd been crying, but now she smiled like the cat that ate the canary.

Creeping closer as if she snuck up on a dragon, Kirin placed her purse down on the bar and waited expectantly, "So … you two have met?" She hoped she could draw out whatever was going on, but neither gave her any clues.

Rosa spoke first, "Sam and I have been talking about the future."

Kirin looked from Sam to Rosa. She knew. Sam must have told Rosa they should leave and make a run for it to survive. Anger crawled up her spine.

"What future?"

Sam pulled his hands out of his pockets and swiped them on his pants, strolled over and slowly knelt in front of Kirin. He had a ring box in his hand.

"The future where you marry me?" He smiled and opened the box revealing a giant, gleaming, diamond ring. "I asked permission from Kathy and Dean, then from Rosa," he glanced back at her smiling, "but I also need Jack and Will's permission."

Her world moved in slow motion as Sam yelled to the boys. They bounded back down the stairs. Little Jack walked over and stood next to Sam, with his hand on Sam's bent knee, peering into his face. Will stopped at the doorway, probably as stunned as Kirin was.

"Boys, I know it seems sudden, but I'd like to marry your mom."

Little Jack nodded and flung both arms around Sam knocking him back. Will eyed Sam, then turned to his mom. Sam's huge grin faded when he caught sight of Kirin's face.

Lost in her own thoughts, she wasn't smiling. *He couldn't be serious.* Yes, she loved him she was sure of it, but Lord, they hadn't known each other a full month yet. Well. He'd known her for years.

Was she getting swept away by hormones or was this the man for her? He was perfect for her and her gut told her so. She loved him and had since that first night at the store. He'd taken her heart then.

Or was he asking her to marry him merely because he thought they would die by the end of the week? Then it hit her. He was rushing into marriage because he couldn't see a way out. As he looked into her eyes, she knew. Knew she loved him. Kirin bent down and placed her hands around both sides of his face. She whispered so only he could hear.

"I love you. Yes, I'll marry you *someday*, but we're not going to rush this because you think we're gonna die. We're not."

Sam looked down, but she pulled his face back to hers. "We're gonna be fine." Kirin smiled at him and slowly he grinned.

Kirin glanced up and caught eyes with Will. Slowly she nodded yes and smiled. Will bit back a smile and nodded when Sam glanced back at him.

Kirin announced to the kitchen a loud, "Yes!"

Sam rose and kissed her as her family cheered.

Chapter Twenty-Five

Sam and Kirin ran to the store for their normal Sunday grocery run. There were no tomato avalanches or crackheads to contend with. After Sam helped her put her groceries away, while Rosa couldn't stop grinning at him. Kirin was amazed Rosa could keep her sarcastic side at bay for this length of time.

She already couldn't remember her life before Sam.

He left to run errands at four. Perfect. She needed to get working on her plan. Rosa went home, and the boys played outside on the backyard swings. Kirin sat on the back porch and scribbled down her to-do list.

~Plan food for Stacy's dinner.

~Take the family picture to Aunt Kathy to identify.

~Call Stacy again about Steve.

~Bring down Saul and save her family.

As she finished her list, the sun caught the glistening diamond on her left hand, blinding her. How the hell was she gonna explain this whirlwind romance to everyone at work, without telling them he'd followed her for two years? It sounded insane even to her.

Her cell buzzed on the table. She turned it over and read the text from a blocked number.

"Hearing rumors. He's headed your way. If you've not found anything substantial in your artifact yet, you and the boys need to leave. Now. ~Your favorite Philly's fan."

She texted back, *"Staying to fight. What does he look like?"*

"Your dad would've wanted you to run."

"Not running," she typed, tearing up. *"Need details."*

She waited. No return texts. She wrote again. *"I need to know."*

The buzz came back. *"I'm old—I type slow. Bastard is short, tan, always travels with at least two bodyguards. Wears a yellow power tie everywhere. Likes to play with his food before he eats it. Doesn't like to lose. Ever. He will track you."*

Kirin bit off a hangnail.

Another text.

"He likes to watch, if you didn't get that foody reference." She had to smile. Kidd wrote again. *"Still with Pat?"*

"Yes." She typed. *"Why?"*

She waited and waited with no response. Her boys ran the length of her property playing tag. She looked out over her land and her small garden, and especially the forest where she watched the does in the morning. This was her land, her house. She wouldn't be torn from it and she wouldn't spend the rest of her life running each time Saul got close. She'd have to take a stand. For her dad and her mom, but especially for her boys and … Sam.

"Hello?" She texted after a minute.

"He carries guilt over what he was forced to do. Don't let him. We all did things we're not proud of, but he was never a killer, know that. Gotta go. Consider your escape route. ~Kidd"

She wrote back a weak, *"Thank you."* But her phone indicated the text didn't go through.

She stared at her phone. What job had Sam had in the organization? She'd never asked. Kidd said he wasn't a killer, but should she fear him? Everything in her arsenal of intuition told her no. Kidd was right though, he carried guilt.

The crackhead in the parking lot sure feared him and left when Sam ordered him to. Was she engaged to someone capable of killing?

Anxious after Kidd's text, Kirin ran inside and brought out her laptop. What if she couldn't get Saul talking first? Or she was tied up and couldn't engage the pocket sound device? She needed something to record him that wasn't on her body. Something she could engage remotely. Why hadn't she thought of this before? Kirin found cameras online that she could mount inside her house and at the front door. Best Buy had small, invisible ones that would interface with her phone and computer to record audio and video.

She ordered two high definition video surveillance cameras. Both recorded for at least an hour and up to thirty feet away with the top of the line clarity and sound. She'd ordered them for rush delivery. They could be wired into her cell and home computer, but she'd have to call an electrician to install them. Kirin added to her list:

~Call electrician to wire the house on Tuesday, Laura's hubby?

She struggled with telling Sam any of it. Not that she didn't trust him. But she knew he wouldn't approve. He already had some plan brewing, which she was sure wasn't as crazy as confronting Saul in her living room with cameras.

Kirin glanced up. One boy swung upside down on the playground while the other pretended to sword fight with a stick.

Her first call was to Laura. Her husband, Adam, was an electrician. She spoke to him for all of three minutes. As they spoke he googled the tiny cameras for the installation specs. They set it up for Adam to add wire in the walls for the cameras on Tuesday, then come back Wednesday night to install them.

Laura being her normal unassuming self, never questioned why Kirin would need the tiny cameras, but the excitement in her voice was evident. She loved mystery novels, and anything spy related. But Laura was a steel trap. She wouldn't tell a soul.

Next, she called Stacy again. Surely, her brother had returned her call by now. Stacy reported she'd left him a message on his cell, but Mr. Perfect hadn't returned it yet. According to her parents, he could be anywhere. He sometimes had to travel on a moment's notice because of his job. He was always showing up at her parent's house unannounced, but only for a few hours then he'd be off again.

Stacy promised to keep trying and Kirin promised to go through her cookbooks and find a southern recipe to wow her dinner guests Saturday night.

Sam called after she put the boys to bed. They talked for two hours while she cleaned the house until she couldn't hold her eyes open any longer. Sam spent most of the time asking her questions about Jack of all people. Like, what sort of husband had he been? It was odd and made her uncomfortable, but she knew he was taking notes to be the perfect husband.

He'd taken the news of not getting married immediately, well. She was relieved he'd understood and wasn't hurt by her less than enthusiastic answer. For a guy with a mysterious past and a "desirable skill set" who admittedly had never been in love, she didn't want him to rush into marriage. Especially for any other reason except he was completely in love.

He might change his mind about her if he discovered her plans. And the sacrifice she would go through to save her family and put an end to the monster who'd stolen her parents.

Chapter Twenty-Six

Monday morning. The day she'd been dreading. *Accidentally forgot.* That's what she wanted to do with the giant diamond on her left hand. Explaining her whirlwind engagement to the girls at work made her stomach churn. At the last moment, she decided she'd wear it. Maybe they wouldn't notice.

From the squeals echoing down the hall when she got to work and took her sweater off, they must've noticed.

When their patient load thinned, Laura, Stacy, and Kirin met in the break room and Kirin explained everything except his real reason for popping the question so quick. She told them she loved him. They'd get married in about a year but hadn't settled on a time or a place. Stacy looked shocked and Laura was so excited she bounced up and down. She wanted to help plan it.

"Absolutely," Kirin said with a smile. Laura squealed and hugged her. "I'm so happy for you! He sounds amazing."

Laura's chipper attitude always gave her confidence as if she'd made the right decision. Stacy grabbed both their hands and squeezed. "Leave it to Kirin to find Mr. Perfect in a flash and live happily ever after."

Not quite.

On their next break, Stacy called her brother. She left him another message with Kirin's cell, so he could call her back directly.

~*~

Aunt Kathy and Uncle Dean sat together on the deck, drinking cold beers and laughing at Little Jack. His rendition of the Teenage Mutant Ninja Turtles' theme song was his go-to for a crowd these days. The sun sank over the top of the trees as Kirin handed a plate of patted burgers to Sam who manned the grill.

She'd hoped to get her Aunt Kathy alone and show her the picture her father had included in the envelope.

After dinner, Uncle Dean, Sam, and the boys went out back for flashlight tag. Kirin and Aunt Kathy retreated with their dessert coffees to the front room. As soon as they sat, Kirin pulled out the picture and handed it to her aunt.

"Who are these people in this picture?" Aunt Kathy grabbed her glasses out of her purse and sat back down, slow. Her eyes scanned the faces.

"Oh my," she whispered, "where on earth did you get this, Kirin?"

"An old box of my dad's junk the attorney brought to me," she lied.

Aunt Kathy stared at the picture for a long time. Probably deciding what to tell Kirin and what not to.

When she couldn't take the silence any longer, Kirin said, "Well?"

"Well, dear, this was your baptism. We are in front of the steps at Sacred Heart Cathedral right after the service. Of course, holding you in the front is your mom and dad."

"I know *those* people!" Kirin blurted out like an impatient twelve-year-old. She silently chided herself. Clearing her throat, she added, "I was more interested in the *other* people. That's you and Uncle Dean to the left of my parents, right?"

"Uh huh," Kathy muttered still staring at the picture.

Kirin bit back a smile, "Nice bell bottoms. And holy cow, what happened to your hair?" She giggled, elbowing her aunt.

"I was stylish!" Kathy laughed and elbowed back.

"So, who are the other four people? That looks like Uncle Shane, but who is that next to him?"

Kathy sighed, "That was the girl we hoped he'd end up marrying. She was so sweet and smart. But no, he ended up as a playboy. Marrying a drunk girl in Vegas, then getting an annulment." Now she sounded like Kirin's mom.

"All right, what about the last two people?" Kirin pointed. Those were the two she couldn't place.

"Ah. That's your dad's sister Margaret, or Maggie as we called her back then. Don't you remember her, Kirin? No? Well, you probably wouldn't. She passed away when you were little. She was … different. We thought she had mental issues. She dated the toad next to her."

Aunt Kathy's nose crinkled up. "None of us could stand him, especially your dad. Never knew what she saw in him. But, your dad

181

tolerated him because Maggie was so in love. He was okay, I guess, just *possessive*. And money hungry. He carried a chip on his shoulder—little man syndrome. His only redeeming quality was that he adored Maggie and worshipped the ground she walked on."

She turned. "They were your godparents, Kirin. Maggie and her boyfriend. Oh, what was his name? It'll come to me. Give me a minute."

She closed her eyes to think and Kirin pulled the picture from her hands to stare at the couple. The more she stared at the woman, the more she looked familiar. The woman was thin with long beautiful brown hair and a flowy sundress on and wait… Kirin put her face right next to the picture.

She had rings on her toes.

Kirin jumped straight up and off the couch as if she'd been shot out of a gun. *Holy Crap*—this was the lady in the Galaxy 10 store downtown. She was sure of it.

Because of her sudden revelation, her aunt toppled head-first off the couch.

"Kirin! What's wrong?" She yelped, picking herself up off the floor.

"Oh, sorry… I remembered the pie, that's all!"

"Dear Jesus, girl!" she held her heart, "You should maybe consider a warning to others before you set your mind to doing something!"

"Sorry." Kirin took her aunt by the elbow. "You okay?"

"Fine dear, just startled." She chuckled and stared at the picture again, trying to remember the man's name.

Kirin trotted into the kitchen to put the pie in the oven as the boys came running in. Two laughing, grass-stained, and sweaty adults trailed behind them, playfully arguing.

"Kirin, Little Jack is as fast as lightning! You should consider putting him on a track team." Sam laughed.

Dean ribbed him, "Sam's only mad because Jack smoked him every time he tried to catch him!"

"I wouldn't be talking, old man," Sam said to Dean, "you couldn't catch Will and he walked!"

Lord, they were at it again. Those two had bonded like brothers in such a short time.

Sam walked over and hoisted Kirin up, kissing her. His eyes danced. She remembered how he'd described his nonexistent family

182

growing up. The more time he spent with hers, the more he opened his heart and let them inside.

Later, as they dove into their pie, Kirin cleared her throat, "What happened to my Aunt Margaret—er Maggie?" She caught the twitch in Uncle Dean's eye at the mention of her name.

"Well," Aunt Kathy began slow, "it's not a pleasant story, Kirin. Maggie was a wonderful girl, passionate, creative and always talking to herself. She was an avid photographer who went nowhere without her camera. Boy she had an eye for a good picture.

"Toward the end of her young life, we all thought she might have been schizophrenic. She became paranoid that someone was out to hurt her. She wasn't dangerous, mind you, just looney. It was odd, she was normal one day and then she changed." Aunt Kathy stared off into the distance as if she remembered Maggie, then shook her head.

"We never figured out what happened to her. But for all her drama and craziness, her overbearing boyfriend never left her side. He did everything for her. He ignored his family and friends. He wouldn't leave Maggie. Lord, he was crazy for her.

"There came a time where she needed to be hospitalized, but her doctor wanted her to travel to Ohio to seek out a specialist. She'd stayed a month for treatment and nobody, not even the boyfriend, had access to her.

"While there, she fell from a second story window. She was pronounced dead on the spot. We were all devastated, especially your dad. The boyfriend moved away. He was heart-broken. But your dad was happy to see him go.

"Maggie was cremated soon after, and they had a small service for her here in town. Her urn was sent to your Uncle Shane."

They all sat in silence eating their pie.

"I'm sorry dear. Somehow, I assumed you knew about her, but, how could you?"

The pie was put away and the laughter died down. Little Jack yawned and rubbed his eyes. After kisses and hugs from everyone, Sam jogged up the steps carrying Little Jack on his back with Will at his heels. Aunt Kathy and Uncle Dean headed out the door toward their car while Kirin walked toward the kitchen to start the dishwasher.

The front door swung back open. Kathy ran back inside panting. "Kirin!"

Kirin ran into the hallway, "What? What's wrong?"

"Saul." She said out of breath, "That was Maggie's boyfriend's name, it was Saul. Dean reminded me. He'd be your Godfather, wherever he is now."

She kissed Kirin's cheek beaming, proud of herself for remembering, then turned to run back to the car, shutting the front door behind her.

A stunned silence hung in the air. She was thankful Sam was upstairs. Or did he already know this? She wasn't sure, but it was all clicking into place. Saul had dated her Aunt Maggie, and she'd bet her last dollar her father helped fake her death to get him to leave.

Then Saul must have come back trying to convince her dad to join his club. When he refused, Saul had her mother killed. What a heartless son of a bitch. Now, she better understood the character of her opponent.

New plan.

Wednesday, when she got out of work at noon, she'd head downtown for a quick visit to her Aunt Maggie. Maybe even take the boys with her. If she truly was Kirin's aunt, she'd be able to coax more information out of her about Saul and how to defeat him.

After prayers with the boys, Sam sat on Kirin's bed talking, while Kirin folded a warm load of laundry.

"You know," he said as he stretched out on her bed propping his head with his elbow, "the night I brought you home from the bar, I had to stop myself from sleeping next to you after you passed out."

Kirin froze. She'd have flipped out if she'd woken up with a man she barely knew next to her.

Sam pointed at her. "Yep. See, that's the reaction I was afraid of."

Kirin folded again, smiling. "You know, in the drunken state I was in and as handsome as you looked and smelled, I'm surprised I didn't try to kiss you. I told you, I'm a terrible drunk. I wouldn't have had the brain power to follow through, though."

"I would've taken the kiss," he whispered. "I did give you a peck on the forehead while I covered you up. That was the first time you told me you loved me."

"What? I did not!" Kirin's lips turned up automatically as her mouth gaped open.

"Yes, you did. Afterward, I convinced myself you were probably dreaming about Jack, instead of me."

Kirin stopped folding again and stared at him.

"Sam." She took a long breath. "I loved my husband with all of his quirks. But I think, at that point, I knew. I knew you'd left a mark on my heart." She got quiet for a moment, then added, "And as hard as it was to let anyone in, I knew you'd walk over fire for me. I felt it."

Sam stared at her as she put the last of the folded clothes back in the basket, "Plus remember, I'd been *stood up*, so I was feeling a little sorry for myself, too." Kirin narrowed her eyes pointedly.

"You know," Sam rolled to the edge of the bed, sat up and pulled her close, "the only reason I left you alone was fear. I figured if I loved you, they'd find out and take you from me."

Too late now, they already know.

"I watched you sit in that restaurant and I decided it didn't matter. I'd trade the rest of my life for a few weeks with you."

Kirin cupped his face with her hands and gently kissed him. He stood slowly from the bed, took her hand and walked her into the bathroom. Leaning past her, Sam started a bubble bath for her and lit a few candles around the room. He kissed her. A long, deep stirring kiss.

"Goodnight," he whispered, then shut the bathroom door.

Kirin undressed and stepped gingerly into the steaming hot bath. Normally, she'd take her time, maybe even fall asleep, but something in his kiss made her hurry. She washed wondering if he'd still be there when she was finished. She listened for his truck engine to start outside.

Kirin dried off and put on an oversized white V-neck T-shirt and shorts. She tiptoed out of the bathroom and scanned the room. He'd turned off the light, turned down the covers on her side and put the laundry basket on the floor. She stood for a moment, allowing her eyes to adjust to the darkness. He wasn't there.

She snuck downstairs and strolled to the front window to check if he was gone, but his red truck glistened in the moonlight. Sam crept up behind her and hugged her. It took all she had not to scream. She smacked him when she turned around and noticed a pillow-and-blanket bed made on the couch. She pointed at it.

"What's this?"

"I didn't want to drive home. I'm gonna sack out here on your couch. I'll be gone before Rosa gets here. Is that okay?"

"Absolutely not!" Kirin stepped back, hands squarely on her hips. Sam stammered, rubbing his hand on the back of his neck.

"Oh. Okay. No problem. Let me clean this up and I'll go."

He bent over, grabbed the blanket and folded it. Kirin snatched it from him and put it back in the closet while he tugged his jacket on. She couldn't help but smile. He'd believed her.

Before he could make it to the door, she turned him, grabbing both sides of his jacket and kissed him gently.

"You're not allowed to sleep on the couch, ever," she said, smiling. "I've got plans to fall asleep in your arms." Kirin took his hand and led him toward the stairs.

"Woman," he growled, a low chuckle rattling in his throat. Without warning, he picked her up and carried her up the steps and into her room, flinging her onto the bed.

He strolled into the bathroom and got ready for bed. Kirin was already tucked under the covers waiting for him. It wasn't human how warm he could be. He climbed in and she snuggled up next to him nestling her face into his neck. She'd be asleep in seconds. He made her feel so safe and so warm.

But soon the memory of that last kiss hit her. She leaned up and kissed him. Within minutes, their bodies intertwined, and their clothes were scattered. This time was much easier. She didn't know if it was the ring on her finger or the fact that she trusted him.

In the morning, as promised, he was gone. Not sure how he did it, but she woke to six red roses on the pillow next to her. She smiled all morning.

Driving to work, her phone rang with an unknown number. *Not again.*

"Hello?"

"Kirin?" The low voice on the other end bellowed, "Steve Withrow, Stacy's brother."

"Steve! How are you?" Without giving him time to answer, she added, "Thank you so much for calling me back!"

"No problem," he said. "So, what's this I hear about you needing some advice on how to trap someone?" His voice was serious.

She'd met Steve years ago when Stacy and Kirin were in nursing school. He was a house of a man, intimidating, with an inability to fail. The overachiever of the family, while Stacy was the divorced, single mom who barely made it out of nursing school without a rap sheet for her partying.

Steve was the straight-A student, valedictorian of his class, college class president, with a master's degree in criminal law. He was a former police officer turned TBI agent and now FBI agent. They used to joke he'd be president someday, but only to make Stacy look bad.

Kirin nervously laughed, then carefully replied, "Well not exactly to *trap* someone, but I need to know what type of evidence could convict someone and put them away for life if, let's say, they ordered others to be killed?"

"And this is for a novel you're writing, correct?"

"Yes," she answered cheerfully.

"Hypothetically, of course," he cleared his throat, "you'd need concrete proof he ordered the killings. You'd also want credible witnesses, ones who saw the events firsthand or a heard a confession. Hearsay or someone telling you the story doesn't work. You need something tangible to convict."

This was what she needed. So, if she could push Saul to admit he'd ordered people killed, she could help convict him, then pray the justice system didn't let her down. Still too many unknowns, but it was all she had.

"So, if my main character recorded a conversation, could I ... I mean could *she* send it to the local police department, or would it be better to take it to the FBI?"

He paused then responded, "I'd say both. That way all her bases were covered. But there's a caveat to it in Tennessee law. It's illegal to record someone unless at least one of the parties speaking knows he or she is being recorded. For instance, if you and I were having a conversation, I could record it because I'm part of the conversation. But if you and Stacy were having a conversation, I couldn't record it and use it against you two because neither of you knew you were being recorded. Does that make sense?"

"Sure," she said, "Cool. Hey, thanks so much for taking the time to talk with me, I appreciate your help."

"Not at all, Kirin, my pleasure. Oh, and Kirin?"

"Yes?"

"I was sorry to learn of your father's death."

"Oh, thanks."

"Save this number in your phone, it's my cell. Call if I can help with *anything*, okay?"

"Sure. Thanks again, Steve."

Kirin hung up and stared into the distance. She got her answer. She'd need to converse with Saul *herself* for the evidence to become admissible. Something inside of her knew he was exactly the type of man who'd come after her children. She'd have to anger and push him hard enough to get a confession on camera.

She had no choice but to end this. Even if it meant the murder she recorded was her own.

Chapter Twenty-Seven

When Kirin arrived home from work Tuesday, Laura's husband Adam had run the wire for the two new indoor/outdoor cameras. Kirin checked, and they were on schedule to arrive on Wednesday. He'd wired one in the corner of the living room where it would be partially hidden next to a picture. The other one would be placed up high on the front porch.

Both cameras would connect to her cell, the family computer and the one in the panic room. She'd be able to remotely hit record even if she wasn't home. These panoramic cameras would capture both video and audio and send the file to all her devices.

Since Kidd texted her that Saul was headed her way, Kirin asked Aunt Kathy and Uncle Dean to babysit the boys for the weekend. She wouldn't allow herself to think that she wouldn't be coming to get them.

That night Kirin and Stacy went over the menu for her dinner party with Todd's parents. It was a welcome change from planning the takedown of a mob giant. Kirin would prepare bacon wrapped organic chicken breasts, with garlic mashed potatoes, asparagus with white sauce, tossed salads, wine, and red velvet cake for dessert. While Stacy focused on everything else.

Stacy hired a decorator, a cleaning service, and a few servers for the evening. Between the three, her house would be cleaned, decluttered, and freshened. She was more nervous than when she and Kirin had taken their clinicals in nursing school.

Wednesday was Kirin's half day at work. She came home at noon to Rosa and Little Jack discussing how at four, he was too old for a nap. He used his words and made a pretty good case for himself. Maybe he'd be an attorney. Will's school had early dismissal for parent-teacher conferences, so he was home too.

Rosa left to spend time with her sister. As Will played math games on the computer and Little Jack stared at the TV, Kirin paced back and forth in front of the window. Come on FedEx. Her mind listed the questions she'd ask her Aunt Margaret.

What was Saul like as a young man? What type of man would sell women or kill them for that matter? What were his weaknesses?

Maggie would help. She'd have to, wouldn't she? She'd see the boys, her great-nephews, and help Kirin bring Saul down. She wondered what their relationship had been like and what attracted her to him? From the old picture, she was much better looking than he was. Maybe back then he'd been charming, or a slick talker. All she knew was her Aunt Maggie needed to give her some ammunition to help her survive.

Around 2 p.m. the slim FedEx woman dropped off two boxes. One box housed the cameras and the other had the pen and wiretap. Kirin texted Adam who ran over between jobs and had everything installed in minutes.

Right at 3 p.m. she woke Little Jack up from the nap he hadn't meant to take. She grabbed a bag of snacks to go and everyone jumped in the car. Kirin told the boys they were visiting a friend, and she wanted them to be on their best behavior.

They drove downtown and parked in the main parking garage. It was filled with cars from the elite who worked downtown in suits or heels. She'd made sure both boys looked clean and gave them a talk about politeness. She'd even grabbed the old baptismal photo, in case she needed to jog Maggie's memory.

Two other patrons perused the tiny store making it appear crowded. Behind the counter was a young girl with a pierced lip and a mostly shaved head. She spoke as they entered.

"Hi, can I help you find something?"

"Yes, we were looking for the owner of the store, please?"

"Oh," she said. "Mary?" she yelled behind her through the curtains. The young woman said under her breath, "Where is that crazy woman? She was just here."

The girl walked through the curtains and after a moment reappeared, looking apologetic.

"I'm sorry, but she's not here. Can I help you with something? She must've gone out to grab a bite to eat."

"Thanks, but we can wait for her." Kirin smiled.

The store clerk twisted one of several hooks in her ear nervously. "She may not be back for a while. Can I take your number and have her call you?"

Something in the way the clerk changed her tone after going into the backroom made Kirin think her Aunt Maggie was there and avoided her. She'd try a different tactic.

"That's okay," Kirin replied. "Do you know if she works tomorrow? We might come back around noon?"

"Oh, yes." The clerk said, clearly relieved. "Mary works tomorrow."

"Thank you," Kirin sang and ushered the boys out the glass door. Will looked up at her, confused. Kirin ducked into the candle store next door and waited. After a quick minute or two, the two customers in Galaxy 10 left the store. Her Aunt Maggie peeked out the glass door. She walked across Market Square and glided up to the ice cream vendor on the sidewalk. They crept in behind her.

"A double mint fudge please," Maggie ordered in a cheery voice.

Kirin smiled. Her father's favorite. She snuck right up behind Maggie and whispered loudly, "That was his favorite too, wasn't it?"

Maggie whipped around and almost spilled her open wallet on Will's head.

Wide-eyed and white as a ghost, she trembled. "What do you want?" her tone was harsh, and she was visibly frightened until she cut her eyes down to Will and Little Jack. Maggie searched Kirin's eyes and exhaled loudly, "Oh dear…child, for some reason, I didn't recognize you. I'm sorry."

Maggie squeezed Kirin's arm and looking around said, "How about we get these boys an ice cream and go back into my shop?" The boys cheered. They liked her already.

On the short walk back to her store, Little Jack reached up with his free hand and grabbed Maggie's hand as he licked the drips running down his ice cream cone. Maggie's eyes glistened as she dropped his hand and opened the door. Kirin couldn't have choreographed it better.

As soon as they entered the shop, Maggie told the young clerk to take the rest of the day off. Kirin had never seen anyone move so fast to leave work. The girl moved like a hungry cheetah.

Maggie sat down at the glass counter and pulled up a stool on the opposite side for Kirin. The boys sat on the carpet near the front of the store, entertained as the sun danced on the hanging crystals making rainbow shapes come alive along the inside walls. The store was quiet as they ate their ice cream. Maggie spoke first.

"They're so perfect. What handsome little boys you have, dear."

"Thank you," Kirin said, "I think they look like their dad."

Maggie searched Kirin's eyes for recollection. "He died, didn't he?" she whispered innocently.

"Yes. Not long after Little Jack was born. Cancer."

Maggie nodded understanding. "I'm sorry."

Kirin fished the picture out of her purse as she finished her ice cream. With one finger, she slid it across the glass counter to Maggie. Pulling the glasses from around her neck up to her eyes, Maggie squinted at the picture. Her face briefly turned white. She looked from the picture to Kirin's face, and back again. Methodically, she licked her ice cream and said, "Nice picture. Who are they?"

Kirin glanced up and whispered, "You know every person in this photo, and I know who you are."

Maggie glared for several seconds, then shook her head. "Dear, I'm not who you think I am."

Maggie pointed to herself in the picture. "That was your Aunt Maggie. She died, God rest her soul." Kirin stared into Maggie's eyes searching for the truth. Maggie's half-smile never faded. She was practiced and confident in her statement.

Kirin leaned forward. "I think you're her, and I need to know more about him," she said, pointing to Saul. The corners of Maggie's mouth turned down. Will interrupted, politely asking for a napkin for himself and his little chocolate-faced brother.

"Mary" jumped up and tended to them both, getting wet wipes and laughing as she helped Little Jack clean his face. Kirin rested her chin on her fist and observed. Maggie was enamored by her boys. She'd use whatever it took to keep them safe. Maggie walked back over, studying Kirin's face. Kirin picked up the picture and pretended to study it even though she'd looked at it so often, it was ingrained into her brain. Maggie sat slow and cautious.

"Kirin dear, please understand. I'm not your Aunt Maggie. My name is Mary. But I was close to your father's family. I knew your parents and I knew Maggie, but I am not her."

Kirin wasn't buying it. She looked like an older version of the woman in the picture. It had to be her. Kirin raised her voice, slightly.

"So, did you know him? My Godfather?" A tiny cringe crept across Mary's eyes at the terminology.

"I'd met him a few times, but I didn't know him well."

Maggie stared out the front window, not focusing on the people walking by, but lost in her own thoughts. Kirin got the feeling Maggie's last statement was true. She probably didn't know what he was capable of when she dated him so young.

"Kirin, I only remember a few things. His name was Saul. He had a witty sense of humor and he loved Maggie. I believe she loved him too, but he had a terrible temper and a mean streak."

She stood as she finished and snapped, "And that is all I know!" She turned and faced the boys.

Kirin stared after her. She wasn't going to break. She was strong. She wasn't about to admit to her identity. The woman's attitude was self-preservation, learned over many years. She'd have to force her hand.

Kirin rose quick, making the stool squeal behind her.

"Don't you get it?" Kirin whispered, loud. Maggie spun around, mouth gaping.

"He's coming for me ... and them." Kirin pointed to Will and Little Jack who listened to a sample of meditative music with headphones squeezed on their heads. Maggie stared from Kirin to the boys.

"He will kill them! Do you understand that?" Kirin stepped around the counter and stood toe to toe with Maggie, shaking. "This isn't only about you staying hidden anymore. He killed my mother, and he's coming here this weekend to do the same to me. Do you want that? Your brother's only child, dead? His grandsons murdered?"

Maggie shook her head, hard. Eyes closed tight as a tear hung in one corner. Kirin lowered her voice.

"You can't fool me. And I know there's something you can do to help me stop him before he hurts them."

The tear in Maggie's eye let loose. Kirin grasped both Maggie's hands.

"I know you're scared. God knows, I'm scared too. But you can help us. You must be brave and tell me anything you can remember that'll help me defeat this monster before he destroys my family. I promise. I'll never tell a soul I found you alive. You have my word. But I need some insight to bring him down. Can you do that? Can you help me?"

The Galaxy 10 phone rang with a shrill cry. Both women startled, then Kirin released Maggie and stepped back. Maggie waddled to the back of the store, swiping at her tears.

Kirin's whole body quaked. She was glad her intuitive boy, Will, had his back to her. She slowed her breathing, but her heartrate drummed loud, as it had the day she ran from the mob. She didn't know what got into her. She'd never yelled at anyone that way, let alone someone she'd just met. She prayed she hadn't scared her off. God, she hoped she got through to the woman.

Through the beads in the back room, she couldn't help but overhear bits of Maggie's conversation.

"Yes, I'm fine ... No, now is not a good time, I have customers. Yes, I will call you back. Yes, I have your number from the last three times you called. Good day, sir."

She hung up with force, then took a minute to return. Kirin assumed Maggie took a breath to compose herself. She was wrong.

Maggie glided through the beads toward Kirin carrying a small set of papers. She placed them on the glass as if they'd break, folded the papers up and put them into a bright white envelope. She licked the envelope never looking at Kirin. In beautiful script handwriting, Maggie took her time and wrote on the front of the envelope then handed it to Kirin.

As Kirin grasped it, Maggie held it tight. Her eyes held a warning. "Do *not* open this. I don't know if this can save you, It might help, but only if you don't open it. Hand this to him as a last resort, in your moment of need. He'll figure out where it came from and I'll have to leave, but if it helps you and them ..." Her voice trailed off as she glanced over at the boys. Tears pooled again in her eyes.

Little Jack and Will came over to show them a soy candle that smelled like rain. Kirin took a whiff and encouraged them to let their new friend "Mary" smell it too.

Maggie knelt, wiping her face before they could see her tears. She breathed deeply and smiled at them. Will hugged her, and Little Jack followed.

Kirin gathered up her keys, then sadness hit her like a wall. What if Maggie fled? What if they never saw her again. It was her turn to wipe away tears. Maggie looked so much like her father. The man who she was slowly developing a pocket of forgiveness for. They had the same skin tone and kind eyes.

She ambled slowly toward the door with her boys in hand. Stopping, she turned around and ran back and hugged Maggie tight.

She whispered, "Thank you," then walked out the door, swiping tears, before holding two little hands.

Chapter Twenty-Eight

Before Kirin knew it, Thursday and Friday had come and gone. Sam had been entangled in some scheme of his own, because the only time they spoke was over the phone late at night. He'd carefully tiptoed around his whereabouts and it took every ounce of discipline to trust him and not to allow her mind to run wild. He'd promised to see her Saturday evening.

Every minute had been filled with prep work for Stacy's party anyway. At least when she wasn't second-guessing her own flaw-filled plan. She'd knelt in prayer several times over the past few days for Sam and her boys. Her last will and testament had been prepared years ago, when Jack died, giving her aunt and uncle full custody of the boys. She knew they'd keep Sam inside their circle too.

Uncle Dean and Aunt Kathy called to let her know they'd taken the boys camping for the weekend. She was thrilled with the offer to get them as far away from the house as she could. She didn't want to think what would happen if Saul got a hold of her boys. She shuddered at the thought.

Kirin woke early on Saturday and made coffee. Curled up in a blanket, she sat on her porch to watch the sunrise. Not sure if it was the caffeine in her morning brew, God answering her prayers, or witnessing the sunrise over the trees, but she was filled with hope. Everything was gonna be okay.

Kirin made a huge breakfast and woke the boys. They ate together while Saturday morning cartoons played on TV. Bags packed and ready, Aunt Kathy walked in first with Uncle Dean trailing behind. He looked at the floor when he spoke. Kirin wondered how much Sam had told him.

He bear-hugged Kirin tight as if she was ten again. Like he didn't want to let go.

She grabbed Little Jack and Will with that same fierceness. Kissing them both, she choked back tears as she pretended to be happy. She jogged back toward the house as they left, never looking back.

After checking the cameras for the hundredth time, she moved the pen to the outside pocket of her purse, then made a copy of everything her father sent to her on a flash drive and put it in an envelope in the panic room. She addressed it to Stacy's brother Steve. The original, she placed in a hidden zipper inside her purse. That way if something happened to one copy, there'd still be another copy to survive. Kirin packed her bag and dress clothes and set off for Stacy's house.

Driving away, she was glad to get out of that quiet space. Every time her old walls creaked, she wondered if someone was outside.

She needed to put her focus into Stacy's party and yet she couldn't get her mind off Saul. Was Saul as personable as her aunt described him? She'd called him witty. And she'd said even back then, he had a mean streak.

He seemed like the type to play with his prey before killing it, that was for sure.

Chapter Twenty-Nine

Stopping Stacy from drinking the entire bottle of wine Kirin brought, proved to be a full-time job. When her friend insisted on re-setting the tables, re-folding the napkins for the third time, and rearranging the flowers repeatedly, Kirin wanted to clobber her.

Two silver serving spoons clanged to the floor at Stacy's feet.

"You've got to calm down," Kirin said, stooping to pick them up.

"I can't remember my own damn name." Stacy said, checking her watch for the fifth time.

"It's soon-to-be-gorgeous. Now, go upstairs and get ready. I'll go check on the food, deal?" Kirin swiped the bottle from under Stacy's arm as Stacy passed her to climb the steps.

"Fun sucker," Stacy whined. Kirin shot her a look before she stuck her tongue out and took the stairs two at a time.

Kirin headed for the kitchen. She hoped Todd's parents would be gracious and grateful for all the work Stacy put into making this dinner special for them.

Todd had come over to help set up but ended up disappearing into the backyard to smoke away his nerves. He was an odd duck most of the time, but Stacy adored him. His parents were set to arrive at 5:30 for drinks before dinner. The sound of rushing water above her meant that Stacy was quickly showering.

The doorbell rang.

Kirin swiped a nearby towel for her hands and strolled to the door. When she opened it, Stacy's perfect older brother, Steve, stood beaming at the door.

"Hey, Kirin," he said without a trace of surprise, as if Kirin always opened Stacy's door. She was shocked.

"Steve!" Kirin hugged him. "Stacy didn't mention you were coming for dinner."

"That's because she doesn't know," he leaned in and whispered, winking.

Oh great. A drop-in from Mr. Perfect on an important day like today, Stacy would be thrilled.

Seconds later Stacy bounded down the stairs with wet hair in rumpled sweats to see who'd arrived.

"Steve!" she squealed, half-surprised and half-irritated. "What are you doing here?" she grumbled. "Don't you ever listen to your voicemails? I told you this weekend wasn't good for a visit since Todd's parents were coming to town."

The only thing Steve could say for himself was an insincere "whoops." Grinning widely, he picked Stacy up and swung her around as if they were kids. By the look on her face, she didn't find it funny.

"Well, sister dear," he said, mouth full of an apple supposed to be a decoration, "I'm here, and there's nothing you can do about it. I warned you it was time for a visit. And here I am." He laughed then added, "Don't worry, I won't embarrass you." Steve winked at Kirin.

Stacy huffed loud like a teenager, socked him in the arm and ran back upstairs to finish her hair and makeup. Steve followed Kirin into the kitchen, grabbed a coke from the fridge and leaned against the sink.

"So," Kirin said, a little unnerved, "what's new?" He took a swig and ignored her question.

"How's the book coming?"

His tone held something...anger maybe? Or sarcasm. Kirin stopped chopping and turned toward him. "Pretty well, why?"

Never taking his eyes off her, he answered her question with another question. "What do you know about Todd's parents?"

"Oh," Kirin said, "Not much. Only that Todd worships his dad, calls him 'Father.'" Kirin made a funny face. Steve's expression didn't waver, so she continued, "His stepmom isn't much older than us, and I guess the trophy wife. That's pretty much all Stacy's said about them."

Kirin turned back to cutting the veggies, but Steve's stare never faltered. She could feel his eyes looking at the back of her head. Kirin picked up the veggies and headed straight for him at the sink to rinse them off.

"Move it, mister," Kirin said, smiling to lighten his mood. Steve scooted over about a foot, looking at her as if he was in the middle of solving a puzzle and never cracked a smile.

Steve took another sip of his coke, still watching her every move, "So, that's *all* you know about them?"

"Oh wait, I do know they're from out West somewhere, and your sister is absolutely crazy-nervous, so you'd better not mess this up for her!" Kirin poked him in the arm playfully.

"Trust me," he said, "I won't be messing this up for *her*." He threw his drink in the trash and walked outside to talk with Todd.

Kirin shook her head. Cryptic dude. The whole FBI thing had made him weird.

Kirin checked the time. She needed to change for the party, text Sam to make sure he was on his way and check her cameras. She stopped to take a deep breath. She'd rehearsed everything she'd say to Saul enough times in her head but the idea of being face to face with the man sent hatred through her veins.

Kirin picked up her phone. With three swipes she moved the camera outside to the left and right. Nothing looked out of place. A carpenter bee darted in front of the camera making her squeal, knocking a few veggies off the counter. She looked around Stacy's kitchen holding her chest, then picked them up and washed them off. *Get a grip, Kirin.*

Her playfully abusive text to Sam, chiding him about being late, went through but no reply. Kirin trotted into the guest bath off the kitchen. She changed into a nice sleeveless brown silk blouse with dress khakis and copper wedge heels. She fixed her hair and makeup and sprayed a touch of Sam's favorite perfume. She came out of the bathroom at the exact same time as Stacy walked down the main stairs.

Kirin had to stop and pick her jaw up off the floor. Stacy wore a beautiful spring royal blue dress that hugged every curve and set off her dark skin and hair.

"Wow." Kirin let out a whistle and smiled. Stacy had always been pretty, but today, today she looked stunning.

Stacy grinned wide and appreciative. "Thanks, friend. I needed that, and I'm so glad you're here with me."

"I wouldn't be anywhere else."

~*~

In one corner of Stacy's formal living room, they'd set up a small bar complete with sparkly crystal glasses, top-shelf liquors, wine, and beer. Her house looked like a page from *Southern Living* magazine. Huge bouquets of purple and yellow flowers were placed strategically on tables and in corners. Freshly laundered linens and all her good china, crystal and silver were lying about in complete harmony. It was 5:20 and Stacy's guests would be there any minute. Kirin went back into the kitchen to check her phone. No text from Sam.

Odd. He didn't like to be picked on without replying some sarcastic remark, and he hated to be late. She put her phone on vibrate and dropped it in her pocket. She looked out through the kitchen into the foyer. Stacy fanned her face with one hand and rearranged flowers on the table with the other. Kirin poured two small glasses of wine and handed one to her friend. She'd fretted over this day for two weeks.

"They're going to love you," Kirin told her.

Todd walked over and for once, sounded generous adding, "Of course they will!" Todd wrapped his arm around Stacy and hugged her. Her tight shoulders loosened until the sound of a car pulling in wafted into the living room.

"They're here," Stacy whispered, exhaling. Todd grabbed her hand and said, "It'll be fine, relax."

Todd and Stacy walked hand in hand to the door. Kirin jogged into the kitchen where Steve had taken up residence. She placed the pan of chicken and veggies into the oven, setting the timer. The front door opened, and voices carried into the kitchen.

"Stacy, this is my father. Father, this is Stacy."

Stacy said, "Nice to meet you," to Todd's father, but Kirin noticed either he spoke softly, or he said nothing in reply. Todd then introduced Stacy to his stepmother, Jennifer.

"Nice to meet you," Stacy said in her singsong voice. Knowing Stacy's judgmental side, Kirin knew that voice meant she'd sized up the new stepmom.

Kirin peeked through the kitchen doorway and into the formal dining room to catch a glance of Todd's parents. They stood in the entryway talking with their backs to her. From her vantage point, she couldn't see much.

The back of the man's silver head and the thin, straight line of his stepmom's tanned jaw. She was taller than him with long blonde hair falling effortlessly down the back of her short red dress. When she turned to walk into the main room with Stacy, she was relieved the woman had a kind face. She'd be grateful for Stacy's hard work.

Todd and his father hadn't turned yet, but his father's booming voice carried. So much for thinking he was soft spoken. He was balding, and the back of his neck looked tan and leathery.

His gray fitted suit, Kirin noticed, looked tight as if it'd been made for him, yet he'd gained a pound or two. As he and Todd turned toward the room Kirin's breath caught in her throat.

She couldn't rip her eyes from the sight of his bright yellow tie.

Chapter Thirty

All at once, the air around Kirin's face became stagnant. Too thick and too hot. She couldn't force air into her lungs. Recognition of this man hit her like a wall of heat in August. As she stumbled back toward the sink in the kitchen, her vomit reflexes kicked in and she ran through the kitchen to the half-bath next to it. Kirin shut and locked the door and threw up her entire day's food. She slumped to the cold tile floor making a small thud. A soft knock at the door made her body freeze and her mind alert all at once.

"Hey?" Steve whispered. "You okay?"

"Fine," she whispered back, voice shaking. "I'll be fine."

It was him. Todd's father was Saul. Dear God. What was she going to do? *Please God, don't let Sam come here,* she thought. With shaky hands, Kirin pulled her phone out of her pocket and checked for a message from Sam.

Nothing.

An email silently popped through from her video monitoring system telling her that her cameras had initialized due to movement in her house. Kirin searched her brain for a minute. Rosa was headed out of town with her sister, so she knew it wasn't her. Might be Sam. But why would he be there when he was supposed to be with her? Kirin texted Sam telling him not to come to Stacy's because she wasn't feeling well, and she'd be home later. Still no answer.

Something was wrong. She could feel it. Voices close by in the kitchen sounded as if they were right outside the bathroom door. Kirin laid still, holding her breath and trying to get her head to stop spinning. She prayed her stomach would settle and not heave again. Stacy spoke eloquently, giving Jennifer and Saul a quick tour.

"...and here's the kitchen, and my brother Steve. Steve, this is Saul and Jennifer Calamia, Todd's father and stepmother."

"Hello," Steve said, using his authoritative voice, "pleasure to meet you both." His voice and footsteps trailed off. He walked away from her door. Jennifer commented on the great smelling dinner.

Oh God, Stacy, please don't say my name. Kirin tried telepathically sending her a message.

Stacy said, "Well, I can't find my cook, otherwise known as my best friend. I don't know where she's run off to, but she's mainly responsible for that wonderful smell."

Steve was quick to speak up.

"Stacy, I think your cook's not feeling well and went home." Steve's voice shifted as he continued, "Saul, why don't you let me buy you a drink over here in the living room?"

The muffled voices sounded fainter as they dispersed from the kitchen.

Kirin stood, trying like hell not to throw up again despite her pounding head. She braced herself on the sink as her options fled through her mind.

If Saul found out she was Stacy's friend, he could use it against her and possibly hurt Stacy. How in the hell was she going to sneak out of Stacy's house unseen? And where was Sam? Did he know Todd was Saul's son? He had to. And if he did, why didn't he warn her before now?

Kirin checked her phone again. The pictures had uploaded to her phone, but they were fuzzy. Shadows of three humans were all that was visible. She nor Laura's husband had thought about how the sun would affect the lighting. The men looked like Transformers with the sun at their backs and their faces dark.

She had a live feed from inside coming through, but it hadn't loaded yet. Part of her hoped it was a mistake and they weren't inside yet. This was disastrous. The main player in her equation was inside Stacy's house with no cameras and standing in front of someone she cared about. Her phone buzzed. The video finally loaded.

They hadn't turned on the lights in the house, so she couldn't make out anything except shadows. No noise came through except the ticking of the clock on the wall closest to the camera. She hadn't thought that through either, dammit.

Something gnawed at the back of her mind. The kitchen timer. The timer for the chicken would ring soon to remind her to take the chicken out of the oven. She had to make a run for it now or she'd be discovered.

Kirin pressed her ear to the bathroom door. No noise in the kitchen. The laundry room and back door were a few feet from the bathroom and they too were quiet. Lucky for her, she'd left her keys and purse in the car with the keypad engaged.

She could release her car door in a matter of seconds by entering the code.

Switching off the light, she pulled the door open a crack. Holding her breath, she peeked out into the hallway.

Nobody.

From her vantage point, she saw the kitchen timer. Fourteen seconds remained. *Oh God.* Faint footsteps and muffled laughter upstairs reached her ears. Stacy was showing them the workout room upstairs.

Good. Kirin took off her wedges, sucked in a quick breath and ran out the back door. She'd parked her car in the grass on the right back corner of Stacy's wide driveway. As she caught sight of her car, she couldn't have been happier, nobody parked behind her.

With shaking fingers, she entered her code. Red light. Crap. Once again, pressed in the numbers, slower this time. Thank God, it opened. Kirin slipped into the driver's seat, grabbed out her car key and prayed while she started the car. Her hand shook as she backed down the driveway too fast with her head down as if she stole it.

The entire drive back to her house she prayed, *"Lord, help me. Please keep the boys and Sam safe."*

Kirin rang Sam's number several more times, but he never picked up. She couldn't help but think Saul's men had him. She wondered what they'd do to him. She hoped he was one of the shadows she saw on her phone. Kirin tried calling Rosa to make sure it wasn't her at the house, but she didn't answer either.

Why aren't they answering their phones?

Slow down. She hadn't even thought through what she would do when she got there. What was her plan, to waltz in the front door? Sneak in the back? They'd be ready for that. Then it came to her. What if she parked in the trees between Arthur's driveway and her own? She could rush to the old trap door in the yard beyond the swing set and enter the safe room. Where Jack had stashed his guns. Yes! Why hadn't she thought of that before?

Turning off the main road she cut her lights. Twilight had settled in, but it wasn't yet dark enough to need them. She pulled into the mouth of Arthur's paved driveway and parked her car inside the small dense patch of trees that separated his property from hers.

She prayed Arthur wouldn't notice. This would shield her from their view as she ran toward her backyard. One final time, she checked her phone and found nothing from Sam. She touched the icon to initialize the cameras to record and prayed it worked.

The sound of her car door shutting was drowned out by the songs of the cicadas in the trees. Kirin crouched and pulled her purse across her body. Then stood and jogged through the dense trees toward her backyard. She stopped and crouched again, low at the base of the forest and held her breath. Her eyes darted from left to right searching for movement but found none. If she could get the outside hidden door of the panic room to open, she could sneak down, grab a gun or two and quietly enter the house through the pantry.

Not a foolproof idea, but the best she had. Finding the grass-covered door would be as impossible as opening it, plus there were no trees to hide her, but it was getting darker by the minute and she had to try. She'd be exposed in the backyard with only the swing set as cover.

She hoped they were all occupied trying to find the book. Kirin snuck down the property line a little farther where the trees thinned out on the left side of the house. Her eyes adjusted to the fading light. Taking a deep breath, she ran from the woods to the side of her house. Her heartbeat thumped in her chest. She must have looked around the corner thirty times. She had to move before someone saw her.

The unwelcome inhabitants she knew were inside, still hadn't turned the lights on and weren't moving around from what she could tell. Kirin crouched low, ten feet from where the painted rock marking the hidden door laid in the yard. The door was heavy, creaky and covered with grass. In theory, if she could make it to the handle, she could yank on it and scurry down before anyone caught her.

A stick snapped behind her. Kirin spun, ready to fight. A rabbit spooked by her sudden movement bolted away toward the small forest. Shaking her head, she shook out her shaking hands and cinched her cross-body purse tighter. After a beat, she crawled, head down and fast toward the rock.

Halfway there, she glanced down and saw the flaw in her plan. Her dark shirt might have been a good idea in the fading sunlight, but her khaki pants stood out like a rose in the snow. She was exposed. Crawling past the rock, her hands searched frantically around the grass for the handle. Her left hand skimmed across something hard and metal. Praise God, there it was.

Kirin squatted over the top, yanking upward as hard as she could. The door had been closed tight since before Jack died, but she hoped the reason it wouldn't budge was only a rusted seal and not that the door was locked. As long as it was only rust, she could yank hard enough to open it. Besides, she had no plan B.

Two more times she pulled as hard as she could, looking around between times. The third try, the door moved, making a sound and giving her hope. Kirin summoned up all her strength, sucked in a deep breath and pulled.

The grass crunched behind her.

The thud of wood hitting her skull rattled inside her head. Then pain and darkness. As she fell to the ground, the last thing she remembered was a faint shadow of a tall man holding what looked like Will's old wooden T-Ball bat.

Chapter Thirty-One

Kirin was inside her house. Her face smushed against the cold, wooden floor. She smelled the familiar floor cleaner she used every week.

Her head ached from the inside out, and she faintly remembered being carried in and dropped on the floor like a bag of dog food.

The next sense that slowly came back was her hearing. Voices. Male voices stood above her, but she couldn't figure out who was doing the talking. She knew enough to stay still with her eyes closed and listen. But she had to focus her mind and concentrate to determine what was going on.

"Stupid son of a bitch!" One man yelled. "We're not supposed to kill her yet. "

She knew that voice.

It was Sam, only different, harder somehow.

"Sorry, boss," came another voice. Younger. She assumed this was the one who'd hit her on the head.

"Boss, she dug for something. You think she buried that book out there?"

"No, dumb ass, it's in her purse. Pick her up, carefully this time, so I can get it off her."

The 2nd man lifted her up and Sam yanked off the purse, angry and harsh. Her body was lowered back to the floor.

Quick footsteps and a third man came into the room. He stopped right in front of Kirin's face. She could smell the leather in his shoes and the smoke on his clothes.

"You ready to do some real work and stop *whoring* around lover boy?" The second man sneered. She knew that voice too. Scar. So, the one that hit her over the head had to be Babyface.

"Right. Trade getting laid and paid for breaking thumbs? Nah. I got the better deal. All you get is to go home alone or sleep next to this goon every night."

The room fell silent and she imagined Scar seething. Sam's voice had sounded smug yet angry. Kirin fought hard to hold back her fury, so she wouldn't move. She wanted to jump up and punch Sam in the face. How could she have been so stupid? He didn't love her. His promise and her father's money weren't nearly enough to keep him honest. This was all part of his plan. Sam was one of Saul's leaders. She knew that now. She'd been a fool to trust him.

But wait. She knew better, didn't she? This was part of his game. He had to play both sides to keep them alive. Her head injury clouded her ability to reason. But it didn't stop her sudden urge to sweep his legs out from under him.

Not only was her head pounding, but by the warm, wet trickle running into her hair, her scalp bled profusely. Even with her eyes closed, the darkness spun making her dizzy. This wouldn't be easy when it was time to stand and fight.

Sam barked out two sets of orders. "Check all the doors and make sure the house is clear, I'll text Saul and let him know the package is here. And you, *slugger*, go turn on a few lights and don't hit anybody. It's getting dark."

As soon as the footsteps of both men were gone, Sam strolled toward her kitchen as if he owned the place. She opened one eye, but the island in the middle blocked her view. The creak of her lower cabinet and the sound of rushing water told her he'd pulled a hand towel out and wet it.

She closed her eye once he walked back over. Sam knelt holding two fingers to her neck to feel her pulse and the towel to her head. His words still floated in her memory. It took every ounce of restraint not to reach up and choke him.

Sam leaned over and whispered, his voice a low growl, "Lay there. Don't move. Hear me? I can still get you out of this."

Sam touched Kirin's cheek and rose, tossing the towel on the floor and kicking it under a chair with his foot. Heavy footsteps fell closer toward the kitchen.

Kirin laid still. Systematically flexing each muscle in both legs, then her feet. Making sure not to make any sudden movements. She had to stand up at the right time. Her mind battled back and forth. Were they still on the same team? She searched her heart. She loved Sam, that she knew.

And he loved her. He'd told her. She knew it too every time he'd kissed her. And at his cabin and inside her house, he'd been real. Even with the boys he'd shown the real Sam. Surely her faulty heart hadn't picked the wrong man to trust.

The sound of gravel shooting out from tires startled her back to reality. She twitched then froze, hoping the men standing over her didn't notice. The car stopped. The sound of four car doors shutting echoed through the front entryway.

This was it.

This was the meeting she'd dreaded since she discovered Saul had killed her mama. At the thought of that, her anger mingled with her confidence. One way or another, this would end today.

One man inside ran to the front door to stand.

The air changed as soon as Saul walked in with his entourage. Even on the floor, she could feel it. The men standing near her froze. Kirin's body tensed up as a cold breeze from outside rushed past her.

Now or never. Kirin opened her eyes and stood. She misjudged the extent of her head injury. The room spun. She fell backward crashing into a dining room chair. Much to her delight, it put her into a sitting position. Not her most graceful move, but at least she wasn't on the floor. She blinked hard forcing her eyes to focus.

Startled by her sudden movement, two of the men who walked in with Saul immediately drew their guns and pointed them at her face. Saul only smiled and waved their guns away.

A third man, who she instantly recognized as Scar, stood closest to Saul and anticipated his needs by grabbing another chair from the dining room and placing it directly in front of Kirin, but out of arms reach. Saul grunted as he sat, never breaking eye contact with her.

"Well, Kirin," came his loud, deep voice, "What did you do to your head?" He oozed with fake concern.

She glared at him then found her voice, "Nothing that can't be fixed, *Godfather.*"

It worked. It stunned him. For a second, he lost his creepy smile. A smirk of caution immediately took its place. Saul shook his head as if he warned a four-year-old not to touch a hot stove.

"Someone's done their homework." He drew closer to Kirin and reaching out he touched her chin with one stubby finger. "My, my. You do look like your mother, God rest her soul."

Kirin came unglued. She lunged, scratching his face and neck as rage bolted through her like lightning, only to be restrained and forced back into the chair hard, by Sam and one of the other suits.

Saul chuckled turning to the suits, "Guess I hit a nerve with that one."

All his suits, including Sam, laughed.

Kirin gathered her thoughts, leaned forward and replied, "Actually, I've always been told I look more like my Aunt Maggie looked before she died. Don't you think?"

If he could have shot her right there, she was sure he would've. His icy glare sent ripples of fear down her spine. She'd hit a nerve and knocked him off balance. Perfect.

Sam, dressed in a dark suit like the others, slammed Kirin back into her chair again, extra hard. Apparently, he was not at all pleased with her tactics in taunting this dangerous man, but she didn't care. She knew she had to get him emotional to get any confession out of him on camera. She had to end this. To ensure her family's safety, and in a perfect world, hers, and Sam's too. She pressed on.

"She never truly loved you, did she?"

"This isn't about her," he said, teeth gritted and clearly riled. "It's about returning the fucking book like you should've done weeks ago. It's about your crooked father hiding my money from me, but he'll get his in the end. He never could do anything right. The deal he made to protect you backfired. How do you like your protector, Kirin?" he said, pointing to Sam.

"You think he's in love with you? Come on. It's a game. And he's quite exceptional at it. He's my whore. You aren't the first woman he's screwed to get something I need, and I'm sure you won't be the last. He's an excellent actor, isn't he? Too bad I own him. He does whatever I say. And as I understand it, he's tired of playing house with you."

Kirin didn't even blink. "No harm done," she fired back, "I got everything I wanted out of him."

The other men in the room nervously laughed. Everyone except Sam. He and Babyface held a tight grip on her arms after the last outburst. Kirin felt a pinch. Sam's grip suddenly got much tighter than Babyface's.

Saul yelled, "Enough!" and the men instantly obeyed.

"The book. Now."

Kirin asked for her purse and Scar threw it at her feet. Sam and Babyface released her arms. She reached into her purse and pulled out the picture from her baptism. She handed it to Saul as if they were old friends, then stole a glance up at Sam. His jaw was banjo-string tight and his perfect face was blotchy-red and angry. He glared at Saul with a hatred she recognized.

Saul's expression was smug, then changed to sadness, then anger and finally rage. He shot up from his chair shaking the picture and yelling in her face.

"Do you think this old picture changes anything? That this is going to help you live? Is this what you've pinned your hopes on? Yes, I loved your Aunt Maggie, she was the only person who truly understood me, and she died."

Saul flicked the picture like a playing card toward Kirin's face. "But I have no loyalty to keep you alive. Your father hid my money and I want it back. The codes to get into my foreign accounts are inside the pages, and I want the fucking book now!"

Crimson faced with murderous eyes his hot breath covered her face. She felt for sure, her death might be the one captured on camera that puts him away.

Kirin reached into her purse to grab the book, never taking her eyes off Saul. The envelope from Maggie touched her fingers. Kirin closed her eyes briefly, hoping whatever was in the envelope wouldn't enrage him enough to kill her, but would help get a confession. Kirin pulled out the envelope and placed it in his outstretched hand.

"What now?" he turned the envelope over and rubbed a chubby finger over the handwriting, slow and deliberate.

Saul sat gingerly in the chair across from her as if he sat on eggshells. A blank expression crossed his face. Confusion covered his eyes as he stared at the envelope. Saul opened it, careful as if he'd rip a million-dollar check inside. His sausage fingers shook as he pulled out three pieces of folded paper and inspected them. From the back of the pages, it looked like pictures of people, but Kirin couldn't tell from her angle.

Saul stared from the papers to Kirin, repeatedly.

Shaking his head, he rose slowly. Without warning, he drew a gun from the back of his belt and pointed it at Kirin's head.

"Saul, stop!" Sam yelled, quick and loud. "You don't want to do this. Listen to me, it's me … it's Pat, put the gun down, Saul, you don't want to do this."

Saul turned toward Sam, a crazed and puzzled look of disbelief washed over his face, then he turned back to Kirin.

"Where did you …" his voice trailed off, lost in his own thoughts. His gun still absentmindedly pointed at Kirin's head. One slip and she'd be gone.

Saul spoke again, louder, pronouncing each word distinctly.

"Where did you get this?"

Kirin swallowed hard. "A family friend."

Saul looked stunned. He mumbled a monologue she could barely understand. He paced back and forth waving his gun toward Kirin every few sentences. Sam jerked each time he swung it past her forehead.

"I … I don't understand … didn't mean to kill. I was an immature young man. Jealous. I was so jealous of anyone who might want to take my Maggie from me. Never deserved her. She was so beautiful. We'd only stopped for gas. Heading to hike in the mountains. Nasty old trucker had the nerve to speak to her while I paid. It wasn't her fault, she was only being polite. I could see him for what he was. A pervert who *wanted* her. Wanted to touch her. I didn't mean to kill him. …didn't know…but she took pictures of it. Why'd she take pictures?"

Saul stopped pacing. He stared down at the papers in his hand. Through the back of the paper, she could make out the faint red of blood and the shadow of a young man holding what appeared to be a stick or maybe a tire iron.

Written on the outside of the envelope were the words:

Dearest Saul,
I have sent these to the FBI. I am so sorry. ~Maggie

Saul paced again, mumbling this time only to himself. Every few steps he'd turn and stare at Kirin, then continue pacing.

The room was dead silent, but Kirin's heartbeat thudded in her ears. This was it. He was on the verge of breaking. Kirin locked eyes with Sam. There was a mixture of terror, anger, and sadness in his eyes.

Kirin gazed up toward the camera mounted and hidden on the wall behind them. She hoped it'd recorded Saul's confession. The other two pictures he held must have been the aftermath of the trucker's death. She wondered what possessed Maggie to take the pictures. But maybe even back then, Maggie must've known he was dangerous. Maybe she'd wanted a way out someday too.

Kirin had gotten her confession, but now they had to survive this heartbroken, crazed, and unpredictable man waving a gun and mumbling to himself.

Again, he stopped moving and spun slow toward Kirin. With one fluid motion, he bolted across the room and placed the cold barrel of the gun against her forehead and cocked it.

Faster than she'd thought possible, Sam drew his gun and aimed it at Saul's head, which caused the other operatives to draw their guns on Sam.

Kirin closed her eyes. Her mind drifted to the face of each of her loved ones as she said goodbye to them, then prayed the Our Father. Her neighbor Arthur's papery-skinned smile flashed across her mind. *"New beginnings, Ms. Lane, that's what spring is all about, but you got to watch out for the danger. That doe can sense it. Sometimes we have to use our instincts to sense the danger."* Her time had come.

Saul had no reason to spare her now. His pain was too great, and he had nothing to lose. Why hadn't she held tighter to her boys when she'd left them? No, they'd be fine. Sam would make it out of this and make sure Saul was put away.

His question that followed shocked her. Saul bent down and whispered only to Kirin, "Is my Maggie still alive?"

With her eyes still closed and keeping to her word, she lied. "No, she is not."

He didn't need Kirin's answer. He already knew the truth. He let out a whimper she was sure would be followed by a loud gunshot and darkness.

What happened next flew in slow motion. Kirin's front door busted open and ten armed FBI agents with guns drawn descended upon her living room like ants on a marshmallow. Their deafening yells for everyone to get down and drop their weapons surrounded the room like a blanket of snow.

Saul's gun scraped across her forehead as Sam used the distraction to jump him, knocking them both to the floor. Both their guns slid into the dining room. Several agents wrestled both men to the ground. Saul, Sam and all Saul's men lay face down on her floor, hands behind their backs with guns pointed at their heads.

Three agents grabbed up Saul to walk him into the backyard. Sobbing loudly, he rattled on mindlessly that Maggie had been alive all these years and didn't want to be with him.

Kirin swayed in her chair, arms up instinctively. She was afraid to stand up feeling so fuzzy headed. Her mind tried desperately to catch up.

She was alive. And her family was safe. Kirin's head throbbed so hard that part of her wished she'd been knocked out. Putting one hand over the wound on her head, she began to shake. One of the armored officers knelt in front of her and held out a towel. When he lifted the shield over his face, her eyes focused on Stacy's brother's angry face.

She smiled.

Steve's voice cracked as he scolded her like a child. "What were you thinking going up against the leader of a well-known mob group? And why didn't you tell me? I could've helped." His tone was angry, but she was just happy to be alive.

"He confessed." It was all she could say. Kirin held the towel to her head and pointed with her free hand to the hidden camera behind her.

Steve's face lit up as he spotted the cameras. "Where does it record?"

"My phone and both computers," she said, shaking.

He squeezed her arm then instructed another agent to confiscate her phone and computer. Steve bent to pick the pictures off the floor. He crouched again in front of her, shaking the papers. "We received another set of these yesterday in the mail along with the article out of the paper about this unsolved mystery. The woman who sent it was brave."

Kirin grinned. Maggie had sent them into the FBI to save them. She was the hero.

"Hey, Steve?" Kirin's voice sounded small. "Thank you."

Steve smiled back as he walked over and ordered his men to release Sam.

As soon as they took the cuffs off, Sam ran to Kirin, scooped her out of the chair and sat her on the floor. Her body, always picking the worst possible moment, shook even harder.

Sam held Kirin tight. Between kisses to her forehead, he whispered, "Part of me wants to hold you and part of me wants to kick your ass for taking such a chance with your life. I knew he'd kill you, and my life would be over." His voice cracked at the last word.

"I like the kissing idea instead of the other," Kirin whispered, hoarse.

When her shaking slowed, the close-range bang of a gun rang out from the backyard. Everyone in the room dove. Four armed agents ran through her back door and into the night. Sam released Kirin and followed them, unarmed.

A scream barely escaped her throat, "Sam, no!" she begged, but he was gone. Two more quick gunshots and Kirin buried her face. She couldn't even look. They'd made it unscathed right to the end, but she was sure Sam was the victim this time.

An agent yelled inside for another to call an ambulance, but then after a beat said it wouldn't be needed. Inside her home, the noise level had risen dramatically, but now was as quiet as a whisper. Two agents walked back inside, visibly shaken and relayed the events outside to the other officers.

Her mind sputtered and garbled their words, but she'd comprehended that Saul had wriggled loose, grabbed an agent's gun, and they'd all wrestled him to the ground. After the two shots, all movement outside ceased.

Another officer walked in from her backyard, dialed a number, then after a beat said, "Mr. Calamia took his own life."

She crawled from her spot on the floor to look outside into the floodlight-soaked backyard. She had to get eyes on Sam. Had to see for herself he was okay.

Kneeling with his head in his hands, Sam rocked back and forth while another agent talked to him. One of Steve's men walked inside and homed in on Kirin.

"He's okay." He knelt and touched her shoulder. "One of our guys is talking him through it right now. He'll be fine."

A rattling noise inside the pantry set all the agents into motion. Guns pointed, they crept single file into Kirin's kitchen like a line of ants. They held their guns at the ready. From her vantage point on the ground, Kirin recognized the tuft of black hair when it emerged from the panic room under the floor of the pantry. Rosa's eyes snapped up and she screamed. Her hands shot up. Kirin held her head and ran toward the pantry.

"Stop! Stop! She's family."

Steve gave the signal and they lowered their guns as Kirin pushed past them.

Kirin grabbed and hugged Rosa. "What were you doing down there?"

"Somebody had to make sure the computers were recording." Rosa reached up and put a hand on Kirin's cheek and smiled, then she pulled a yellowed piece of paper out of her pocket and handed it to Kirin.

It was page 288 from her father's book.

Epilogue

Time passed, and wounds healed.

Well, most of them.

Nightmares haunted Kirin. Vivid images of Saul shooting Sam in the head right before taking his own life plagued her. Sometimes the images would vary. He'd target Will or Little Jack instead of Sam, but Sam was the prevalent nightmare. Would she ever sleep well again?

As the long days of summer got underway, she pushed the pictures out of her mind. Barbeques, hiking and lazy weekends were now her focus. Spending time with her family was a top priority. But hard as she tried, Saul and The Club were never far from her mind.

Sam was distant right after Saul's suicide. Something ate at him. Guilt maybe? She didn't know. He wouldn't talk about it. Truth be told she still wasn't sure what his job had been in Saul's army. When summer hit though, he was himself again. He laughed more. Maybe he forgave himself for whatever he'd done while enslaved in The Club. Either way, for once they were happy and at least on the outside, nobody chased them.

Yet.

She'd overheard Sam and Steve talking one night. Some die hard members of The Club were talking retribution. It made sense they'd come after Sam and Kirin for Saul's death.

She'd heard Saul's son, Todd, took over the business. But with their leader gone, most operatives fled. A few of the decent ones kept up with Sam, who was expunged from all wrongdoing by the government since he was trapped into service at sixteen.

Stacy transferred from day-shift with Kirin and moved to nights. Abruptly, she shut down all contact not only with Kirin, but with her brother Steve. Through the nurse grape-vine she discovered Stacy and

Todd had flown out to Vegas and gotten married. Stacy still spoke to Laura, who encouraged Kirin to keep trying, hinting that maybe Stacy didn't know who Saul was or how he'd died.

She missed her. Missed Stacy's infectious laugh and her mischief. Missed their long talks and calling up at any hour and meeting for coffee to bounce things off one another. Kirin prayed her friend knew what she was doing. She worried about Stacy more and more. But all her attempts to reconnect were ignored.

Kirin busied herself with other things, not wanting to focus on it. She'd spent the last months being a paranoid wreck and she refused to go down that wormhole again. All she could do was pray Stacy would come to her senses and the organization would disband since their ruthless leader was dead.

One evening during their weekly Sunday cookout, Sam got an odd call. He'd developed a bond with a few guys on Steve's team and they offered him a civilian desk job within the FBI. Sam howled. The irony of offering a member of a well-known organized crime outfit, a job where they'd seek justice. He smiled as he told them although he was flattered, but he couldn't accept. He and Uncle Dean stood by the grill and pondered all the implications of it over a beer.

Aunt Kathy pulled an apple pie from the oven and it made Kirin smile at the thought of Kidd. She hoped he was safe and living somewhere tropical. She'd hadn't thanked him for his help, but she was sure with his connections, he knew Saul was gone by now. The boys grabbed Arthur, Rosa and her sister and set up board games in the living room for after dinner.

As Sam walked into the kitchen carrying the burgers, his face fell. He set the burgers down and walked toward the front door. Kirin followed his line of sight. An old four door sedan had pulled down the long driveway. It sat running with the lights on just a few feet away from the porch. The driver hadn't turned off the car and the headlights prevented them from determining who was inside.

Sam adjusted the pistol he carried on his hip. Kirin followed him to the front door, holding her breath. Sam pulled Kirin around behind him, protective as usual, and opened the front door a crack.

The engine cut. A long moment passed. When the creaky old door opened, a woman stepped out wearing a flowered dress, rings on her toes and holding a camera. Kirin squeezed Sam's shoulder and pushed past him. Sam opened the door wide, with an even wider grin.

No matter what name she went by, Kirin's Aunt Maggie had finally pushed past her fear and answered the dozens of invitations to come and be part of a family again. They welcomed her with open arms.

Maggie had saved them all with her pictures, and finally, they could give her lonely existence some life. As she walked through the front door, two little boys ran from the living room and hugged the woman they recognized from the store. Her face changed in an instant from anxious to full on joy.

Kirin glanced around at her life as loved ones bustled toward the dining room, food-filled plates in hand. She stood at the threshold of the door and smiled. Sam joined her and kissed the top of her head wrapping a warm arm around her. Like taking off a winter coat two sizes too small, she felt a release.

Kirin had turned over all the evidence to the FBI except for the smelly old Marine Corps Manual. She let them keep it for a few weeks to inspect it but demanded it back.

It had a special place on the mantle next to a picture of both of her parents.

Her family was intact, together, safe and happy.

Kirin knew her parents were proud.

~*~

Turn the page for a sneak peek of Book Two in the Kirin Lane series titled, *Unraveling.*

EXCERPT from Unraveling~

For a woman who lived the first thirty-nine years of her uneventful life wishing for more excitement, Kirin Lane now begged for ordinary. It was the second time in less than a year, she thought she was dead.

Obviously, she wasn't livin' right.

The first time, Saul Calamia—the leader of the crime group who enslaved her father and killed her mother—pressed a desperate gun to her forehead. She'd prayed then for a quick end.

As if that hadn't jolted her enough, this time...she *felt* dead. Noise had ceased to exist. She lay face down on the cold, cafeteria floor of her employer, St. Mary's hospital. Shards of glass rested comfortably next to her face like someone had sprinkled a sack of rock candy all around her. Vibrant rays of purples, reds and yellows reflected and bounced off the glass from sunlight filtering through the demolished wall next to her. It was terrifying and beautiful at the same time.

Black smoke hung in what was left of the hospital cafeteria, choking her like a dark cloud that refused to rise. She felt the pressure of a second blast, and closed her eyes, but still—no noise.

Nothing made sense. Her mind flashed images of the crisp fall day, her short drive to work and the smart, yellow scrubs she'd worn to instruct a fresh crop of incoming nurses. She remembered her jittering nerves dancing in her stomach in anticipation of today's lunch date. Today was the day she was to see Stacy, her BFF who'd abruptly ended their friendship the night Saul died in her back yard.

Their mutual friend, Laura had been the one to hatch a plan to put them in the same room to air things out. She'd invited Stacy to lunch in the cafeteria where they'd all once worked.

In the few short months since Saul's death, Stacy had become a recluse. She'd quit her nursing job, moved in with Todd—her fiancé nobody particularly liked who was also Saul's son—and cut all ties with some friends and family. And most especially Kirin. Gone was the audacious, southern, spitfire she'd loved since nursing school. Now, she was skittish, pimped out with Saul's money, and closed off.

The plan was for Kirin to grab food, waltz over and sit with them. Laura was positive they'd laugh and talk, like old times and pull Stacy out of her trance. The perfect plan. Except for one person who shouldn't have been there—Scar. He was Saul's brother and right-hand man. The undertaker of "The Club." The same man who'd chased her in the airport and ransacked her house.

Kirin had snagged a chicken salad sandwich and an unsweet tea. As she'd waited to pay, she caught sight of a familiar face with a scar running down one cheek. She'd frozen in place. His head snapped up at that exact second. Their eyes met. A smirk trickled across his lips. She'd been so nervous to see Stacy, she hadn't thought to check her surroundings first, like Sam and Stacy's estranged FBI brother Steve, had cautioned her to do, always.

Now, her hearing came back. Every noise sounded like loud whispers directly in her ears. Muffled screams, glass breaking, thuds that sounded like blocks falling on tile, car alarms—or maybe hospital alarms, she couldn't tell, all were jumbled inside her ears.

She was a nurse for Pete's sake. She'd been trained to help in an emergency. She should get to her feet and help the others. But in that moment, she only wanted to close her eyes and let the dark overtake her. The scraped fingers on her left hand however, had other plans. They walked curiously toward one large piece of the blown-out window to touch it.

Squinting, she pulled her eyes into focus. Through the broken glass, a distorted wave of sandy brown hair covering a face, came into view. The person's neck was coated in dust and blood.

Focus. Kirin pushed off her toes and balanced her weight on her left elbow. Then she dug her elbow in like an oar, barely registering the sharp glass cutting it. She used the momentum to shift her body forward. A few more inches and she could move the hair covering the person's face. Her right arm must've been broken or gone because it wasn't responding. And she couldn't turn her head to the right without unbearable pain shooting through her right shoulder.

She pushed off once more to align her good arm within reach of the hair. As her brain and eyes focused better, she realized this was a woman. With her fingers outstretched, she gently lifted the blood-soaked hair off the woman's face. Kirin's hand recoiled as if she'd touched a snake. A sob bubbled up in her throat right before everything went dark. One thought screamed in her subconscious as tears fell and she let the dark pull her under...

Laura. They got Laura.

Please visit www.kelleygriffinauthor.com to sign up for her newsletter for the latest information on the second installment in the Kirin Lane series, **Unraveling** *available soon at all major outlets.*

Made in USA - Kendallville, IN
1171555_9781706341314
09.29.2020 0900